confessions of a
terrorist

confessions of a
terrorist

RICHARD JACKSON

Zed Books

LONDON | NEW YORK

Confessions of a Terrorist was first published in 2014 by
Zed Books Ltd, 7 Cynthia Street, London N1 9JF, UK
and Room 400, 175 Fifth Avenue, New York, NY 10010, USA

www.zedbooks.co.uk

Typeset in American Typewriter by seagulls.net
Cover design: www.stevenmarsden.com
Printed and bound by TJ International Ltd. Padstow, UK.

Distributed in the USA exclusively by Palgrave Macmillan,
a division of St Martin's Press, LLC,
175 Fifth Avenue, New York, NY 10010, USA

A catalogue record for this book is available from the British Library
Library of Congress Cataloging in Publication Data available

ISBN 978-1-78360-002-1

contents

introduction

The premise of this novel is quite simple: if you sat down face-to-face with a terrorist, what questions would you ask him or her? What would you like to know about their life, their upbringing, their reasons for taking up armed struggle, their aims and goals, their sense of morality, their feelings about what they do? This question is important, not least because terrorism seems to be everywhere these days, and yet, paradoxically, we appear to know almost nothing about the people who perpetrate it. It is on our television screens and in our newspapers virtually every day, and everywhere we go there are reminders of how much efforts to prevent terrorism have changed our way of life. In fact, it is true to say that there has never been so much public discussion and information about terrorism at any time in history. And yet, whenever a terrorist incident occurs, the first question on everyone's lips is: Why did they do it? What turned this person into a murderer? What is really going on in the mind of a terrorist?

There's another reason why this question is important: if we don't understand what really goes on in the minds of terrorists, we will be forced to simply try to imagine it. We'll have to just guess at what they're thinking. I suggest that this is actually what we have been doing for many years now: guessing, imagining, fantasising about what goes on in their minds. And thus far, if novels, movies, television shows and media portrayals are anything to go by, we imagine that terrorists are insane, fanatical, psychologically damaged, cruel, immoral, essentially 'evil' and, most importantly, quite inhuman. In part, this is because we look at what they do and extrapolate from there: they commit inhuman acts, therefore they must be inhuman. Certainly, looking at their horrific deeds, we cannot imagine them to be normal human beings like you or me.

The problem with viewing terrorists through this veil of ignorance, with trying to understand them through the lens of our usually frightened imagination, is that ultimately we cannot help but turn them into monsters and bogeymen. They cease to be real people, human beings with a history, a childhood, feelings, life experiences, aspirations, values. They are instead reduced to what they've done or what they perhaps intended to do. And when this happens, they inevitably become a 'cancer' and a 'scourge', a 'savage', an 'animal', an 'extremist', an 'evildoer'. At this point, we not only compound our original ignorance – there is no reason, and no way, to understand the mind of a cancer cell or an animal – but we also give permission for them to be treated as less than human. Cancer is to be eradicated, after all; scourges are to be quarantined; animals are to be tamed.

In other words, it is precisely because we have failed to see the humanity of the terrorist, because we have imagined them as something other than a fellow human being, that we have tortured, rendered, imprisoned without trial and summarily killed thousands of people we suspect or imagine to be terrorists in the past few years. Apart from compounding the original wrong of terrorism with even greater wrongs, I would argue that this is a counter-productive and ultimately self-defeating approach. It cannot work to end or prevent further acts of terrorism; its only certain result is to create more terrorists and engender more violent retaliation. There are, therefore, both moral and practical imperatives which drive the quest to better understand the mind of a terrorist.

Apart from my ethical concern over our ignorant response to terrorism, one of the main reasons for writing this novel was because after studying terrorism for more than a decade, and after meeting individuals who had been imprisoned for terrorist offences or who had joined militant groups that were widely considered to be terrorist organisations, I have rarely found artistic or media depictions of terrorists that seemed authentic or which corresponded to the completely normal, often intelligent, complex and committed people I had personally spoken to. The fact is that in all the thousands of popular and literary novels, all the newspaper columns and news reports, all the movies and television shows and even in many academic books and articles, terrorists are virtually always depicted in stereotypical terms and as caricatures of what we imagine terrorists to be – fanatical, extremist, aggressive, hateful, dysfunctional, damaged.

It seems that artists, novelists, film-makers and others who write about terrorism have embraced the veil of ignorance which currently characterises our collective understanding, and have chosen instead to rely solely on imagination and fantasy in their depictions of terrorists. This is surprising, given that there are hundreds, if not thousands, of former terrorists and militants one could quite easily talk to, and hundreds of published interviews, autobiographies and in-depth studies of them. Even a cursory glance at any of these widely available sources immediately destroys our ignorant imaginings: they are simply not the inhuman monsters we most commonly imagine them to be.

So what's going on? Why do we stutter and stumble about in trying to explain their actions and motives when they are perfectly willing to explain it all, and when there is plenty of information available to understand them? I believe it is because, as anthropologists tell us, there is a kind of taboo against 'talking to terrorists' or trying to understand them at a human level. According to this taboo, condemning terrorists and trying to eradicate them are the only socially acceptable actions to take. A taboo is an unspoken prohibition that functions to maintain the limits of social behaviour and which is designed to protect society from certain culturally determined dangers. In this case, much like the taboo surrounding paedophiles, the terrorism taboo is designed to segregate them, and to protect society from their perceived malign influence. Talking to them, listening to their voices, hearing their arguments, trying to understand their point of view is, therefore, prohibited. It is prohibited because it might lead to sympathy, understanding or even justification for their heinous behaviour. The fear is that getting too close to a terrorist may lead to some kind of infection or contamination, and thus will the cancerous evil of terrorism spread. This taboo is so powerful and so prevalent that you will almost never hear the real voice of a terrorist in a public forum such as the media. They are not allowed to speak for themselves, lest their words prove too tempting or seductive to the audience.

Novelists, artists, journalists, scholars, politicians, ordinary people – we have all, almost without exception, succumbed to the dictates of the powerful terrorism taboo and sought to uphold its prohibition on obtaining direct knowledge of the terrorist. This is why few novelists, and few scholars of terrorism surprisingly, have ever spoken directly to a terrorist, and why their descriptions and depictions so rarely ring true. And this is how the veil of wilful ignorance is maintained. In the end, we are left wanting to know and understand what they really think, but also *not* wanting to really know at the same time. Perhaps we only want to know what's in the mind of a terrorist if it confirms our initial stereotype of evil, damaged fanatics. Anything else, such as that they were perfectly understandable fellow human beings, would be a destabilising contradiction.

The purpose of this novel is to try to break through the taboo on 'talking to terrorists' and on understanding their points of view, their motivations, their thoughts, their feelings. As such, it treats the terrorist as a fully human being, not a stereotypical monster or an inhuman, incomprehensible fanatic. Most importantly, the novel allows the terrorist to speak and have a real voice, uncensored and unrestricted, honest and intimate. Many of the arguments made by Youssef in the following pages are the same arguments I have heard and read made by former terrorists and militants. Moreover, I have tried to allow my imagined reader to ask all the questions that are normally avoided in the typical engagement with a terrorist: How did you come to choose a life of violence? Why do you attack us? What do you hope to achieve with your violence? What do you really want? What are you really like? Although the real answers to these questions may not be what we want to hear, they are nonetheless what we need to hear.

Of course, the danger of taking this approach, as warned by the taboo, is that in listening to the voice of the terrorist, we will begin to understand their point of view. Their reasons may become comprehensible to us. We may even find that we share their grievances, their perspective and their aims. The key point is that understanding – or even sympathising – with the goals of the terrorist is not the same as condoning and legitimising their violent actions. I can understand the necessity of resisting oppression without accepting the need to strap on a suicide vest or leave a bomb in a train station to kill commuters. However, without understanding the mind of the terrorist in the first place, we are left with nothing but our terrified imagination as the foundation on which to construct a counter-terrorism policy. More importantly, we have no foundation from which to hold our leaders to account for the counter-terrorism policies they enact.

In the final analysis, I believe that it is only through such direct, sustained dialogue of the kind I have tried to write here that we can begin to exorcise our tabooed imagination, begin to see the human behind the terrorist label, and start to think about how we might deal a little more constructively with the threat of political violence and the grievances that drive it. A novel like this is a small step, but a necessary one, towards tearing down the veil of ignorance which currently lies over most of what we currently say and do about terrorism. And if it leads to a reconsideration of some of the destructive and self-defeating counter-terrorism approaches our leaders seem determined to persist with, then it will have achieved even more than I had hoped for.

Richard Jackson
October 2013
Dunedin, New Zealand

confessions of a
terrorist

TOP SECRET

MI5 RECONNAISSANCE UNIT

* Annotated by GH for JM 22/7/11.

Broad assessment: I know the spooks have blacked out anything related to national security, but we have a different responsibility now. How much of the following is really in the public interest, in your view, or will substantially help the LS inquiry? Apart from the legal issues highlighted below, I fear that parts of the text could provide grist for the anti-Western radical fringe, the RO, protestors, jihadists, etc. Given that our prime responsibility is to protect the reputation of HMG and shape the public narrative of what happened to its most important elements, I suggest a few more 'recording interruptions' – as annotated. As my previous correspondence noted, accompanying documentation will need to make clear that 'recording interruptions' were technical problems in the field (I assume the techies can provide explanations of electrical disturbances) – and not authorised record alterations. The PR kids will also need to brief the Home Sec to answer numerous criticisms of foreign and domestic policy when the transcript is released. And we have to keep every digit crossed that the original video never surfaces, otherwise there'll be egg on everyone's faces.

PS: Do NOT forget to shred this annotated copy.
It doesn't bear thinking about what would happen if it leaked.

File Number: MI5/200311.2256-0613.

File Type: Digital Audio File, MP3.

Source: Audio-surveillance, MI5 Counter-
                        terrorism Field Unit.

Date and Operation: 19–20 March, 2011; 'Operation Moriarty'.

Location: Disused storeroom, former Royal
                        Transport Warehouse, Stockton
                        Industrial Estate, 18–20 Khyber Road,
                        Leeds, UK.

Subjects: Professor Youssef Said, aka, Samir
                        Hamoodi, aka, 'The Professor'; Captain
                        Michael ██████████, MI5 officer;
                        Members of SO19 Armed Response Unit
                        (names and ranks in Appendix 1.1 –
                        NOT FOR PUBLIC RELEASE).

Document Status: In final preparation for submission to
                        the Public Hearings Section, Lord Savage
                        Inquiry into the Leeds Terrorist Plot,
                        20 March, 2011.

Draft Number: Edited Draft #4, to be confirmed and
                        authorised prior to submission and
                        public release by the Home Office.

Transcription Date: 21 March, 2011, 8:47am.

Transcribed by: ██████████

Translation by: ████████████████

Transcription Notes:

P: Professor Youssef Said, 'The Professor'

M: Captain Michael ████████

I'm sure you agree that there's nothing in this initial exchange we need to be concerned with. Could we just send this first section and call it quits?   Say the rest of the recording was ruined?? GH

[TRANSCRIPTION BEGINS]

[5.1 seconds silence, occasional scraping sounds]

P: Ahem... so... here we are. Can I assist you with something?

[1.8]

This is very nice, is it not? [laughter] Very salubrious accommodations! Ha! [...] The bare walls... this, ah... concrete floor... that horrible fluorescent light... lack of windows... it has a certain, ah... charm. It is like a scene from a very bad Hollywood film. And these rusty chairs are making my... ah... well, I am already starting to feel sore, I can tell you.

[2.3]

Do you have any questions for me, or, or... or are you just going to keep staring at me? [...] Put it another way... is there something specific you would like to know... something I can tell you now that you have me here? This is your big chance. I can promise you... right here and now... I will answer <u>any</u> questions you care to ask... within reason, of course. I am <u>not</u> going to tell you what our operational plan is, or name any names... nothing like that...

Actually, in a way... I can honestly say that I have been looking forward to this moment for a very long time. I have imagined it in my mind a thousand times... rehearsed it in my head... meeting you face to face... explaining everything... telling you my reasons. I am ready to, ah... make my confession, if you like.

[1.9]

Come on now, please do not hold back. You must be at least a little bit curious. It cannot be every day you are able to talk to the, the... the, ah... <u>terrorist</u> that you have been looking for, for so long... and he promises to tell you everything you want to know. Of course, we must get this out of the way right now... I do not for one second accept your description of me as a terrorist. It is not how I see myself at all. I am not that crazy, evil... caricature in your television shows who, who, who... threatens to randomly murder innocent people and blow up everything... and, I must say, you are not the muscular hero... even if you look the part! You ████████████ ████████████████████████████ ████████████ colleagues.

[2.9]

You know... some might even argue, given the fear your government rains down on millions of innocent people in, in, in... Iraq, and, and... Afghanistan... Pakistan, Libya, Yemen, Somalia... and all those other countries where you drop five-hundred-pound laser-guided bombs or send guided missiles down the chimneys of people's houses like Christmas presents... where you, ah, shoot people from helicopters while they walk down the street... maybe I should call you the terrorist.

No! Please do not make such a look, sir! The fact is your heavily armed soldiers in dark sunglasses shooting people at roadblocks... ah, smashing their doors down in the middle of the night... cause a lot more, ah, terror among a lot more people than

someone like me ever will. [...] Not to mention the
fear that every young Muslim man, innocent or
not, constantly has of being tortured in Abu Ghraib,
Guantanamo... or, or, or being picked up and beheaded
by one of those death squads your people trained in
Iraq... kidnapped off the street... ah, never to be seen
again... or when you ███████████████ and that

village elders ████████████████████████████████

The point is... it makes you wonder, does it not? Who is
the _real_ terrorist here?

[3.9]

M: You—

P: —I am—

[1.8]

M: Oh, I'm sorry—

P: —No, no, I am being quite rude... talking too much, as
      usual. Please, please... go ahead...

M: OK... Samir Hamoodi, Iraqi, born 7 December 1965,
      in Kirkuk... or, should I say, that's what it says on the

passport you used when you entered this country.
You arrived here ███████████ on the train from
███████████... before effectively disappearing. We
decided to let you in unmolested, as it were, in order to
see what you might be up to. But then you evaded our
surveillance, Mr Hamoodi... and vanished for a time.
How did you do that, by the way? Did you know we
were watching you? Did you deliberately try to lose us,
or was it just luck?

We need to prepare a credible story for why we let a known terrorist come into the country without arresting him at the station – and then promptly lost him. I suspect we will get raked over the coals if we claim the Firm had the situation under control. I suggest we claim lack of resources, as well as strategic necessity.
This way we might get something out of the upcoming budgetary hearings [1.9] – a small silver lining in a pile of shit! What do you think? GH

OK... in any case... we both know that your real name is
Youssef Said, formerly Professor of Economics at Cairo
University. Actually, you were born in 1963, in Suez.
But then your father moved the family to Cairo. You
lived in Shobra. You studied at a private international
school in Cairo after your father secured you a special
scholarship from the school authorities. He was a
maths teacher to all those expats at the school, and
they liked him. Next, with no little intercession from
your school principal, you went to University College,
London to study for your honours degree, before
taking a doctorate at the University of Chicago. You
were appointed to the Faculty of Economics in Cairo in

1994. Not long afterwards, you started an investment consultancy for the multinationals scouring the Middle East for new opportunities... as a side business. Lecturing doesn't pay all that well in Egypt, does it? But then you resigned from both your posts suddenly in April 2003. [...] That's when you travelled to Iraq.

In Iraq, you joined the insurgents and led a terrorist group which gained quite a reputation among British and American intelligence... as well as the other jihadi groups. As I recall, you acquired your nom de plume, The Professor, at this time. At least, that's what your associates called you. We ███████████████████████████████████ ████████████████████████ London.

[1.2]

What are you doing in Britain, Professor? [...] What exactly is your, ah, <u>confession</u>? Are you here to recruit... resupply... what? Or are you planning an operation? Where've you been these past months? Who've you been meeting with, exactly... in ████████████, for example? Who's been looking after you? Those two men I saw you with earlier, or ████████████████████████████████████ █████████████████████████████████ ██████████████?

P: Ohhf... well! You <u>are</u> very well informed. Of course, this is not completely surprising to me. I know for a fact that you have been following my, ah... how shall we say... <u>activities</u>... for some time now... almost nine years... since early 2003?

I confess it sounds strange to my ears. I have not had anyone call me the, the, the... <u>Professor</u> for such a long time... that name comes from a different time... a different place. I used to be called that all the time by my students when I actually worked at a university...

Can I tell you something? I miss those days when I worked at the university, I really do... when I was just a scholar with my, my, my books... and my, ah, chalk. We used to have chalk in those days. We would write our formulas and equations on a blackboard. My hands would be covered in dust at the end of the day. It dries the skin... makes it crack. Can you imagine that now? [inaudible]...

Back then, I would sit quietly in my office... looking over the university courtyard where the students would take time out to smoke and the boys would try and flirt with the girls. I think I was quite at peace with myself back then. I was a real person. I had a real life... not like now. I had my books, my, ah, research... all

Why do so many terrorists come from university? If they haven't got a degree, they're the bloody professor! What the hell are they learning? I hope we have someone in Research looking into this. At least we ought to be watching universities a bit more closely – instead of the mosques. What's your view on this?

GH

those adoring students who looked up to me. Respect from my colleagues. I had a loving wife and family, a community to which I belonged. And I could sit and just think, or read a book... and in those days, I could be still... really still... like a rock, or an old tree. I had a measure of peace... calm...

But look at me now, sir. I cannot control my nerves. I am so full of nervous energy... always moving... twitching all the time... I no longer have a quiet place in my soul. That place has been trampled down by all the noise and violent fury of war. The sound of, of... ah... battle and blood is lodged permanently in my head now...

This must be why I have to be moving every minute of every day... like one of those Energizer rabbits... you know, the ones on the television? Have you seen it? Ha! [...] I know it must be so irritating to those around me. Let me tell you... in Iraq, my comrades would always complain. 'Sit still!' they would say. 'Stop twitching and scratching all the time!' They worried that we would be hiding from the soldiers and I would make too much noise and get us caught!

But really, I do not believe I will ever be still again. There are too many thoughts swirling around inside me, I suppose... not like you, sir! You are like one of those... one of those, ah... street performers. Do you know who I mean? Those people... buskers... who stand in the street... the ones who dress up like a man blown in the wind and stand perfectly still for hour upon hour. Yes? I can see you know what I am talking about... You need real discipline for that...

So, you know a lot about me... including my name. What should I call you, sir?

[1.8]

M: Please call me Michael.

P: Michael? OK... yes... Michael. You can call me Youssef... or Samir... whichever you prefer. I do not mind... really. No one has called me Professor Said for such a long time now. Phew! That was literally a lifetime ago. No one calls me that any more... seriously... even ███████████

████████████████████████

I am really not sure I even know who Youssef Said is now, if I am honest. He is another person entirely. If you, ah, look at the old photos you no doubt have in my file, you will see that I do not even look like the same man any more... I was quite a smart dresser once upon a time, when I worked in Cairo. Nice clothes... proper shoes... like you. Is that a designer suit? [Are] those silver cufflinks? [...] You look very nice. Very smart...

like a million dollars. Savile Row? No, no, no... you do not have to answer that...

Mmmm... yes... you know I also used to exercise quite a lot... I was a lot trimmer then than I am now. When I was a young man... closer to your age... you look like you are still a man in his thirties... at least a decade younger than me. Anyway... back then I was a pretty good sportsman... even if I say so myself!

Do you play a sport, Michael? You look very fit... very athletic.

M: I used to play rugby—

P: —Ah, rugby! It is a very violent sport. You need great strength for this—

M: — but I don't really play any more. It's been years, actually. These days I mainly swim. It's less bruising.

P: Swim? Yes, yes, yes. [...] Well, in my youth I played football... basketball... cricket... hockey... anything, really. All those games loved by the expatriate students at my school. But not rugby! I think I am too weak for this game... too fat by far, now. But back then, when I was young, I loved all sport... and I used to run... like a gazelle. But now... ohhf... I can tell you, having to live my life underground, as a hunted fugitive... well... it just means bad food... no exercise... very little sunlight... lying around all day. This belly... [slapping sound]... my bad skin... it is the price for my chosen... ah, occupation...

M: So, if I might ask, why do it? Why not go back to the university then, the life of the mind? [...] Why are you here... now... in this room?

P: Why not, indeed? Well, I guess that is why we are here. [tapping sound]

[3.8]

I know I am a mess. You do not have to tell me! I really feel I must, ah... apologise for my, ah... slovenly appearance. I seem to be quite underdressed... especially as we are going to be on video. [...] The camera over there makes me self-conscious, I can tell you. I cannot conceive where they got these terrible clothes for me... one of those charity shops, no doubt... or maybe from the market stalls. Who wears track pants and a dress shirt together... and these trainers... oh my God! They are so, so... so loud! You could light the street walking in these! [...] Ha! Yes, I got a small smile from you...

M: You look perfectly respectable, Professor.

P: You are too kind, for sure. Anyway, I expect you must
be rather, ah, disappointed to be here with me in
person... to see that, ah, your elusive prey... the great
terrorist you have been hunting for so long, is so, so,
so unimpressive in person. Not quite Che Guevara, am
I... or Carlos the Jackal? In truth, my, ah... occupation,
as it were, means I no longer have much concern for
outward appearances... except inasmuch as it allows
me to do what I have to do. I do not really care what
I look like... not at all... it actually helps to look a bit
ordinary. I find no one gives me a second glance, which
is a real asset in my line.

M: May I call you Professor? It's your formal title after all,
even if you no longer work at the university. It's also
what we've been calling you for years. I'm used to it,
even if you aren't—

P: —Joseph Conrad...

M: What?

P: Joseph Conrad... The Secret Agent... that anarchist in
Conrad's book? He was the Professor... I am not like
that, I can assure you.

M: Oh, yes, I see. No, no, we didn't think of that at all. I'd
completely forgotten Conrad. Ha! No, I can assure you
it's just a... ah, you know, a coincidence. [...]

In any case, can I just say, you speak very good English, Professor. I knew that you studied in the West, and I don't mean to appear, ah... what I mean is, I don't intend to stereotype you or anything... but your English is pretty much perfect, as good as anyone.

P: Thank you, but it is not so hard to understand. My mother would read to me in English when I was a child. She was a strong believer that learning English was the key to success. Sometimes she would say 'What's the point of learning Arabic?' Then she would tell me all those fairy stories... Kipling... The Jungle Book, it was my favourite! These days, I can see that this belief by my parents... that fluency in English was a path to be successful... well, it was the colonial legacy... believing that the language of the Europeans was superior. So in a way, English was my first language. I think if you learn it young enough, you can speak any language perfectly. Also, my father sent me to an English school... an international school... right from elementary. And then after that I went to university in London and America... as you already know.

M: Yes, I see... In any case, I'm impressed. Now, can I just ask you again... why are you here? What exactly have you been doing during your visit to our country? Who've you met with? ███████████████ ██████████████████████ What is the aim of your operation, exactly?

P: Dear, dear, dear... ohhf [inaudible]... Michael, why are you asking me this? I think you already know why I am here. You know exactly what I am doing! You know everything, it is clear! ███ Why do you need me to, to, to... confirm what you already know? Besides, I have already told you I will not answer questions of this nature... no matter how you try to sweet-talk it out of me. It is beyond the limits of what I am prepared to say. I will not reveal anything that will put my, ah, comrades... my friends... in danger... nothing about any ongoing operations. You are clearly a former soldier... I can recognise it. You must understand.

[2.3]

You are very good at holding your silence, I must say. [...] I can tell how good you are at interrogating suspects... making them talk by keeping silent for so long... until the silence becomes tense. [...] Either that or you have something to hide. Is that it, Michael? Is there a dark secret you do not want the world to know... something you do not wish to be forever recorded on that camera over there? ██

[2.9]

Oh, do not look so serious, Michael. It is still early.
There is plenty of time for serious talking. [...] At times
such as this you cannot help thinking about your life...
at least for me... what you have lost... those days you
have left behind...

I was just remembering a story about my daughter.
I do not know if you have this story in your files.
Anyway, one time [laughter] my daughter...
███████████... she once brought a, a, a... huge rat...
and not just any old rat, but one of those massive, ah,
cane rats, whose body is the size of a large rabbit...
into my wife's dinner party? Can you imagine?
[laughter] Pure chaos, Michael! Our dearest friend...
she is quite a large, old lady... well, she fell off her
chair! She landed on top of my cousin. He told me
later he thought she was lungeing at him because she
could not control her amorous feelings... which he did
not return! When he was pinned under her, he felt
he was going to suffocate! [laughter] Another guest,
my neighbour's wife, actually threw up on the table!
[laughter]... I don't know why I was thinking about
that...

M: That's very funny, Professor. Why on earth did she
       bring a rat into your party?

P: ███████████ went out after a rainstorm and saw
it drowned in a puddle. I think she had never seen a
rat that huge and she just really wanted to show it
to her mama. It was like some kind of, ah... fantasy
monster to her. So she got some of her little friends...
kids from the neighbourhood... they put it on a plank
and carried it into the dinner party we were having.
[laughter]...

I have to say, my wife took it so well. She did not get
angry. She saw what her daughter was trying to do...
that she was just expressing her sense of wonder...
and she made sure not to upset her... make her feel
bad for what she had done. This is a story we used
to laugh about as a family all the time... in the days
before...

[2.3]

OK... now, I have told you something personal... to
break the ice, as it were. What about you? Are you
married, Michael? Do you have children? [...] What do
you like to do?

M: You know I can't tell you that—

P: —Come on, you can tell me something. Where is the
harm?

[4.1]

Nothing to worry about here, in my opinion. The press will eat this stuff up, I expect – personal details of the terrorist and the 'secret agent' – parties, fishing, etc. Keeping them distracted

M: OK. Let me see... I guess I like to fish.   *from all the nasty political stuff can only be to our advantage.*

                                                                                 GH

P: Fish... as in a line on a pole... in the water?

M: Yes.

P: So what kind of fishing do you do? On a boat?

M: No, no, no... fly-fishing, actually.

P: Fly-fishing! That is the upper class of fishing, is it not? I have seen it. It looks amazing... and hard. As you know, there is not so much fishing where I come from... the Nile is very polluted. No one fishes there. I have not much experience myself... but I can see it must be very nice. What do you like specifically about fly-fishing, Michael? What is its appeal to you, would you say?

M: Well, there's always the beautiful scenery, out by a lake or a river—

P: —Ah, yes, I can see that—

M: —and then there's the... the total absorption. The way you concentrate totally on what you're doing. You can really get away from everything, you know. And of course, there is the poetry of fly-casting... the way the

line loops through the air, gliding over the surface of
the water. It's a real skill. It took me years to learn.
I also like the thrill of stalking a wild trout, a superb
and cunning hunter itself. You have to find it first,
wherever it is hiding, and then outsmart it. And you
have to be so patient. You can't strike too soon or you
will frighten him away. And that moment when you
trick the trout into taking your imitation, when it
opens its mouth and leaps from the water to grab your
perfectly presented fly... it's... well, I, ah, I mean... you
just can't beat it. I would say it's sublime.

P: I have to say, you make it sound so wonderful, Michael.
I fished a few times... when I was a little boy in Suez.
Me and my cousins would go to a, a... a *kobry*... a
bridge, and fish off it. We would use bamboo poles with
a line tied to the end. My father would cut up the soles
of old flip-flops and tie a little piece on the line, for
the float. For bait, we would put on worms dug from
the garden, or maggots. I used to love to see the float
bobbing up and down in the water... I would flick the
rod quickly to try and catch the fish... small bream. Do
you know this fish? Yes? [...]

One time... this is funny [laughter]... my cousin
██████████ tried to flick his line out. He did not know
his small brother was standing behind him and the
hook went right into his chin.

M: Ouch!

P: Yes, the barb of the hook went right through his skin
and out the other side. He was screaming so loud!
Everyone came over. I was laughing so hard. I do not
know why, but it was very funny to me. We took him
to the clinic, but they could not do anything. We had to
go to the repair man for some pliers to cut the barb off
and then carefully ease the hook out. Ha! [...] That is
my only fishing story. It is not like fly-fishing, I believe.

Anyway, I can see where your patience and
cunning comes from. Me and my comrades,
we used to comment on that in Iraq... how
you would bait the trap... wait for someone to
walk into it. You snared many insurgents that
way... including some of my, ah... associates.

[2.9]

But to the business at hand... why not ask me what you
do not know? Why not ask me the real why? Why am
I doing this? Why would a man like me... an educated,
professional, middle-class man with money... a, a... a
professor of economics... a well-respected man with a
wife... a family... a man with status... standing in the
community... a man with seemingly everything to live

for, you might say... a bright future... why would <u>he</u> be risking his life and liberty to live the life of a criminal? Why would <u>he</u> give up everything he has to become a fugitive? I mean, what would make him willing to become a, a... a killer... a despised <u>terrorist</u>?

[2.3]

Can I tell you something? I have actually read a lot of books about <u>terrorists</u> written by Western scholars, those so-called experts you see so often on television... the ones who write learned comments in the Financial Times. I have not completely forgotten how to be a scholar, Michael... even when I was fighting in Iraq! When you are waiting in a basement or a tiny room somewhere, and you have to hide for forty-eight hours, you can get quite a lot of reading done, I can tell you. I must have read... oh, phew... it must be a thousand books these last few years. It is a kind of total absorption... living underground like that... very much like your fly-fishing, I expect.

M: But how did you get books like that in the middle of an insurgency?

P: Oh, Michael. Were you in the war? Don't you know? The fact is that a man can get anything he wants in a war... books, magazines, DVDs, video games, single-malt Scotch, Coca-Cola, cigars, chocolates... whatever your imagination can think of. You just need to know the right people. I knew them, those kind of people. I asked for books. Anyway, as I was saying, it was so enlightening to read all those books written about people like me... to see what they thought... how they described me. [laughter]

Well, after reading these books, I can tell you for a fact that most of your experts do not know anything at all about why someone like me would do something like this. They lack... ah... insight... understanding. It is amazing, but it is patently clear to anyone with even half a brain that they have never, ah, corresponded with, let alone actually met, someone like me. They have no intimate knowledge of their subject. To them, a terrorist is an abstraction... not a person with a history, a will of his own. It is as if they get their knowledge from newspapers. Or maybe they just watch those terrible Hollywood films. Ha!

I can see from your nodding that you agree. It is a scandal actually, pretending to be an expert when you know nothing about the people you are talking about... although, in a way, it should not really bother me. It is an advantage, really. Such ignorance on the part of your advisers, your experts, it means you will always be one step behind me. It is impossible to stop an enemy you have no real clue about, don't you think?

I hate to admit it, but P is right. We don't really have a clue. We always seem to be scrambling after something like this – and the so-called experts are no use at all. Why do we keep listening to them, I say? GH

[1.8]

At [inaudible] they have never [inaudible]

M: Pardon?

P: I was just saying that these scholars... these experts in
       the mind of others, it is clear... well, they have never
       struggled with the question of violence... personally,
       I mean. They have never faced a choice about how to
       respond... looking directly into the face of inhuman
       oppression... blood flowing in the streets... in their
       own neighbourhoods! I mean, they don't know! They
       don't know what it's like... the, the... the struggle, the
       contradictions... how should a man respond to protect
       his family... his community. [...] If they had, they would
       not write those things.

[2.3]

M: Mmm.

P: What is the source of a man's will, in your opinion?
       What drives him to particular actions? What makes
       him choose one path and not another one... revolution
       over protest... resistance over submission... activity
       over passivity? How does a man wake up one day...
       only later to discover himself in a bare concrete room
       without any windows being questioned by a counter-

terrorism officer from MI5? By what twists of fate did this come to pass? That is the real question you want to ask me, Michael.

M: All right, Professor, why <u>are</u> you doing this? Can you explain what has led you to this room tonight? Why are you so, ah… angry? What was it, would you say, that turned you into someone willing to murder other human beings for an ideology… for a belief system? Why would someone like you do this, because frankly, from your background, as you say, you just don't seem the type? What do you think made you into a terrorist?

P: I think you mean to say… what <u>radicalised</u> me? Is that not the term your people prefer these days… the process by which someone is transformed into a terrorist?

M: OK. Yes, how were you radicalised? How does an intelligent man come to embrace violent extremism?

P: Yes, yes… OK, OK. Let us take your word for the process that supposedly led me here… <u>radicalisation</u>… although, I have to say I find it to be a, a, a horrible term… practically useless… and not just intellectually. I cannot fathom what it is supposed to entail. It seems entirely tautological to me. A person has been radicalised if they engage in radical activity and hold

radical views. So you, you... you look for evidence
of radicalism to prove a process of radicalisation?
This is nonsense! [...] Not only this, but who decides
what makes a certain viewpoint... or a certain action,
radical, anyway? Is that not a subjective value
judgement?

M: You're being a bit obtuse, Professor—

P: —No, no, no. Not at all... Listen, I, I... you know the
word extremist is no better. That is a value judgement
too! Where is the line between moderate and extreme,
precisely? Surely, it is completely relative to where
one begins... what perspective one thinks is normal to
start with? Were, were... were the slavery abolitionists
not radical in their time? Were they not extremists
in terms of their society and its values? And the, ah...
Levellers... the suffragettes... the anti-colonialists? Was
not Socrates a radical? Was not Jesus an extremist?
Galileo? Einstein? Mother Teresa? Did these
individuals not all challenge the established values
and dominant ideas of their societies? Did Jesus Christ
himself not advocate justice for the poor and turning
the other cheek to the violence of your enemy? Did
he not preach for the cancellation of all debts so the
poor could escape from their poverty? That sounds
like an extreme ideology, even to our modern ears.
Are environmentalists and animal rights campaigners
not radical... the Occupy protestors? Do pacifists not

radically challenge all societies with their renunciation of military violence?

M: There's a big diff—

P: —I find it quite ironic... in their time, these <u>extremists</u> were denounced for, for, for wanting to destroy society... for being too radical, too extreme. They were viewed so negatively at the time, hated by their own group, as radicals always are. Many of them were martyred for what they stood for. They were murdered... burned alive... hanged... imprisoned for trying to change their societies. They were complete outcasts! But today, we honour them with statues... even churches... whole religions which are now respectable, part of the Establishment.

But do you know, I think that if Jesus was alive today and he attacked those money changers in the temple with a whip, he would probably be charged with terrorism, according to your laws. What do you think about that, Michael? Jesus Christ... the terrorist! [laughter]—

M: —You're surely not comparing yourself to Jesus Christ, Professor... or the suffragettes? None of those people planted IEDs or blew up synagogues, did they? Not like you lot. Anyway, I thought you people were against women's rights... the right to wear make-up, whatever clothes they like, going to work, voting in elections? Your lot seem to think they should all stay at home and cover up when they leave the house.

P: *Afahemmo ezay dah?*[1] [...] I am not... ah... hmm... I am not going to dignify your ignorance with a response, Michael. You must know a lot better than that... if, as you say, you have been tracking me for so long... if ███████████████████████████████████ [inaudible]... I am merely trying to make the point that you and I probably have very different perceptions about what might be radical, or, or, or extreme... or not. This is to be completely expected, as a radical idea is completely relative to the individual or society within which it arises. It is simply an idea which falls outside of your own worldview and way of living... one which goes against your own established view of how the world should be. What is radical or extreme to one person is completely normal to another... like the question of Sharia, a topic so hotly discussed by your Western media these days. For the vast majority of the world's Muslims... a billion people... wanting to live under Sharia is a normal, totally acceptable viewpoint. It is not a, a, a... radical proposition at all. It is equivalent to wanting to live in a liberal democracy for Westerners.

---

[1]   Trans. 'How would I make him comprehend?' Note: Arabic Egyptian colloquialism.

But because such an idea falls outside of the Western norm it seems extreme to you.

M: I'm not sure—

P: —No, no, listen! It is, ah... it is... I mean, environmentalism is the same. The idea of living in a society in which oil and waste are no longer a part... in which profits and consumption are balanced with sustainability... it still seems so radical because it cannot be imagined... because it is not part of accepted, normal everyday life. I believe the term radical... in this sense... simply means, ah... disruptive. It is an idea which disrupts and challenges the status quo. It disrupts a society's commonsense...

[1.2]

M: Mmm...

P: Do you know why you fear us, Michael?

M: Fear who, exactly?

P: I mean people like me... activists... militants.

M: Because you're terrorists who blow up innocent civilians?

P: No, these are just flea bites on an elephant. The reason
      you fear us is because our minds are free... because
      we question the status quo you want to maintain...
      because we see you for who you really are.

M: Is that so?

[2.3]

P: In my own humble opinion, bombing a country to,
      to, to... try and establish democracy is a pretty
      extreme idea... or, or, or building a massive reinforced
      concrete wall around an entire nation to try and
      feel more secure... like the Israelis. But for you, this
      probably does not seem extreme at all. You have been
      conditioned to accept it as reasonable behaviour. It fits
      within the current status quo. You would not call it an
      expression of <u>radicalisation</u>.

M: Oh, I think you're twisting things ag—

P: —And I also happen to think that advocating a form of
      social and economic organisation based on the virtual
      destruction of any notion of society and all bonds of,
      of... of social obligation... which seeks to replace it with
      the completely mythical idea of market forces driven
      by individual material pursuit... is also an extremely
      radical idea. After all, this market-driven ideology,
      enacted by successive right-wing governments, and

enforced on dozens of poor countries across the global South, was truly, ah, revolutionary. It destroyed, or at least changed, entire societies... mostly for the worst. Hundreds of millions of people suffered greatly. We will never know the number of people who died from these policies... or were harmed... but it could be in the millions... while a tiny number of others made unimaginable fortunes. I know what I am talking about! I was an economist, for God's sake!

Do you understand what I am saying, Michael? Were Thatcher and Reagan not radicals... according to your own definition? Were they not ideological extremists? Did they not advocate totally radical ideas, based on a, a... a blindly accepted ideology... and then commit a vast social and economic violence against their own people to realise their extreme agenda?

I saw what they did with my own eyes when I studied the economies of developing countries... and when I lived in Britain and America. The generational poverty... the hopeless generation... the breakdown of communities... the unimaginable levels of inequality, which seemed to increase every year. The urban decay... the sink estates... the gangs, drugs, drink, crime...

M: If you let me—

P: —And what about your Tony Blair? Could you not call him a religious extremist? He blindly followed his, ah... faith... declared war in the name of it... destroyed hundreds of thousands of lives... devastated a whole region. For what? A complete mess! It achieved nothing, as all the experts predicted. Bush was the same... God spoke to him directly, did you know that? Told him to run for President... to attack Iraq? But, as you know, extremists do not listen to evidence or respond to logic.

M: That's an interesting perspective—

P: —Those are very nice cufflinks, by the way, Michael. Did I say that already?

The clues were all there from the start, weren't they? It's so bloody obvious now. I assume the instructors at the Farm have taken the appropriate lessons. You might want to get ST to double-check. GH

M: What? Oh, these. You like them? A birthday present from my wife... I wear them every day, normally. ███████████████████████

P: They are very smart. They really finish off your image. What is your wife like? How did you meet?

M: You know I can't talk about that—

P: —Oh come on! Surely this is an exception? This is not the usual interrogation where you are required to remain all, ah... professional... detached. Can you not tell me anything at all about her... even in general terms? I really would like to—

M: —OK, OK. I, ah... what I can tell you is that she is the one who keeps me sane. She grounds me in reality. I come home after dealing all day with the, ah, violent side of life... all the truly evil and debased things that people do to each other... She reminds me that there is an ordinary world where people laugh, and get along... And ████████████████████

P: She sounds like a wonderful person, Michael.

M: She is... she really is.

P: How did you meet?

M: I was her patient. Would you believe it? She was my physiotherapist. I'd rolled my ankle in a rugby match. I was sent to see the local physio... her. I must have seemed like a big, lumpy rugby oaf to her! But when I met her, I knew she was the one. [laughter] I actually started faking injuries so I could see her! [...]

██
██ The rest is
history, as they say.[...] And what about you? How did
you meet your wife... ████████████ ?

P: Oh, I am sure you already know... we met at university.
     I saw her in the corridor... she was so beautiful, so
     elegant. I thought she looked like an angel. I know it
     is corny, but it is actually true! She looked amazing...
     honey-coloured eyes... raven hair... perfect skin. I knew
     I had to meet her. It was not hard to arrange, as we
     were both from the Middle East. It was a small circle
     in those days... soon, I started seeing her regularly.
     Like you, the rest is history... although we did break up
     several times before she agreed to marry me. She, ah,
     took a great deal of convincing to take a, a, a chance
     on me... which is ironic, considering how things turned
     out...

[2.3]

     I am sorry for the, ah... diversion. Shall we go back to
     what we were talking about?

M: Yes, of course. Please continue. You were telling me
     how you became a... ah...

P: Terrorist?

M: Yes... a terrorist.

P: Mmm, yes... the, ah, point I was trying to make
is simply that if we can call people like Thatcher,
Reagan, Bush, Blair... if we can call them violent
radicals... did they not therefore go through a process
of radicalisation? What were the main factors, do you
think, that radicalised Margaret Thatcher or Tony
Blair? The churches they attended? The, ah... sermons
they heard? The books they read? Were they groomed
by some right-wing extremists, do you think? Or,
actually, is this question completely nonsensical to
you? Does it disrupt your way of thinking—

M: —think you're using the term too broadly, Professor.
It doesn't really apply to your examples. Thatcher,
Reagan, Blair, Bush, that's just politics. They didn't try
and enforce their policies with extreme violence—

P: —apart from Thatcher with the miners. That was
pretty violent, was it not? And Iraq? Afghanistan?
Libya? Sierra Leone? [...] All their other wars?

M: Professor, we know what radicalisation is. I can give
you chapter and verse. It's when individuals advocate
the use of extreme violence to realise a political goal
or to enforce an extremist ideology. It's when a young
lad from Shepherd's Bush or Bradford goes from
wanting to play football in the park with his friends to

wanting to kill as many innocent civilians as he can on a commuter train... and blow himself up in the process, all because he wants to turn Britain into an Islamic state, or bring about some medieval version of the Caliphate in Europe.

P: So you are defining radicalisation as using extreme violence as a means of achieving a political goal, or as an expression of an ideology?

M: I suppose you could put it like that.

P: Then, when a person advocates a massive bombing campaign... which is a pretty extreme form of violence, you must agree? No, do not shake your head! That <u>is</u> violence! It is! A, a... a single fighter plane can drop a lot of bombs. They can fire a lot of missiles and can kill thousands of people in one go. [...] What you said was that someone who advocates this is a violent radical? Or, or... or that someone who believes that invading a country to bring about democracy is a violent extremist, because, after all, they are advocating the use of an extreme form of violence to enforce an ideology?

M: No, I'm not saying that at all. You're twisting my words, Professor. There's a clear difference between someone who supports internationally sanctioned intervention to try and <u>save</u> innocent lives... to help people... and someone who illegally and deliberately targets innocent civilians.

P: Oh, I see now! If the international community sanctions it... or, or, or if a government legally goes to war... this is not really violence! If a farmer gets his legs blown off by the UN in Sierra Leone, it is not really violence? But if an invading trooper from Manchester gets his leg blown off by a Taliban fighter in Afghanistan, this is extreme violence? This is absurd! But apart from this absurdity, it appears to be a question of who can legitimately use extreme violence... some people can use as much violence as they like, and some cannot—

M: —That's not what most people mean by violence—

P: —No, no, listen! I'm saying that is what people like me are disputing... whether Western governments can claim the sole right to use violence to achieve their political aims and enforce their ideology. Besides, I think this is a, a... a different question. For me, I just find it problematic... from an analytical viewpoint, you understand... wearing my professorial cap... that the radicalisation term is reserved only for some groups or individuals, but not others. It is applied to an, ah, individual who decides to travel to the Middle East to fight for the freedom of oppressed Palestinians... but not to a respected scholar, or a politician who recommends invading an entire country to overthrow the regime and put in a puppet democracy... even though an invasion will undoubtedly lead to many thousands of innocent deaths!

M: Oh, OK...

P: All I am saying is... one rarely hears it used to describe all those extreme nationalists or Christian fundamentalists in your country... the ones who think that all foreigners should be deported or forced to convert to Christianity... those individuals who think they should be allowed to rip off the veils of Muslim women in public. Frankly, ah... if you are looking for violent radicals, you should just go to a, a... a BNP rally... or one of those Christian fundamentalist churches in America! And what about Timothy McVeigh or Anders Breivik... were they not radical Christians? Were they radicalised in a church, do you think?

What I mean is, I, ah, well... is it not strange that the term is never used to describe Irish terrorism? You never hear politicians or scholars talking about how IRA or UVF terrorists were radicalised, do you? I never heard it. They are never referred to as violent radicals... or ideological extremists. Why is that?

Ironically, I have, ah, I mean... I have also met a few radical pacifists in my time. Apart from trying to convert me to their cause... unsuccessfully, I must say... they were willing to go to some fairly extreme lengths to promote their cause... including imprisonment and death. Their own, I mean. You have come across people like that? They would try and break into military bases and damage the weapons stored there... smash bombers with hammers and suchlike. Should they not also be included in your category? Is it, ah... I mean, this is not <u>extreme</u> enough for you? [...]

It seems this word is reserved for Muslims these days. This is why it is such a pointless term... in my humble opinion. Nothing more than a term of abuse.

[3.8]

I am sorry. I can see I am boring you. It is in your eyes... and I can understand it. This must seem rather pedantic to you... debating the meaning of words. But it is important... the way we speak... the language we use. It shapes the way people think... the way society thinks—

M: —No, no, please don't apologise, Professor. I'm sorry if I appeared uninterested. We've had a very long day already, haven't we? Ever since ████████████

███████████████████████████ I'm very
interested to hear what you think. It's a very
interesting perspective. Please don't feel inhibited...
it's your show, really.

P: OK, I, ah... these chairs are very uncomfortable, aren't
they? They are designed for discomfort. [...] Do you
mind if I stand up for a moment? Stretch my legs?

M: No, no, please... Stretch your legs, by all means.

[scraping sound]

P: I find I think better if I keep moving. [...] Back when
I was a lecturer, I would pace up and down in front
of the class. [...] Anyway, you want to know what
made me into a, a... a terrorist? Well, let me tell you a
story. I think you already know that I was born into a
very poor family. We were always hungry when I was
growing up. I think this is also why I cannot completely
control my eating today, why I always keep going
even when I am sated. [...] Subconsciously, I think I
must worry that the food will run out and I will have
nothing later. [...] But then, looking out from our little
house, we could see the political elite driving past
in their Mercedes-Benzes... with their chauffeurs...
their golden children... on their way to some foreign
shopping spree—

M: —You didn't come from a poor family, Professor.
Your family was middle class. Your father was a
schoolteacher at a prestigious private school.

[tapping sound]

[1.8]

P: Are you going to let me speak?

[2.1]

Anyway, as you also know... later, when I was a young
student protesting against Mubarak and his cronies...
we were demanding free democratic elections... I was
arrested by the Amn ed-Dawlah. You know them? The
Egyptian secret police? This is why my father got me
a scholarship... later, to get me away from trouble... to
start a new life. [...] Anyway, they took me to a cold,
dingy room with no furniture and plain walls... very
much like this one, actually. I could hear the screams
of my fellow students and other poor souls during
the night. In the morning, they beat me on my feet
continuously for six hours, until I could not walk.
They had to drag me back to my cell. It was a level of
pain... I, ah...

Again, they tortured me with electricity. You know,
when they attach electrodes to your hands and feet...

it feels like the flesh is being literally torn off your bones. And when they attach them to your private parts... well, my God... I just kept fainting... I, ah, well... I can hardly speak about it...

M: Prof—

P: —it still surprises me I was later able to have children. [...] Then, after they have brought you to the edge of madness, they tell you that you have been sentenced to death and will hang in the morning... it is not just the pain which seems to go on, and on, and on... it is the way they use pain to break you down into nothing. You lose all, ah... all sense of yourself. You become empty... like a blank page on which they can write whatever they wish... I seriously thought I would go mad. Sometimes... lying alone in the cell... I thought I <u>was</u> mad. I still do not know how I survived... how I came out of that filthy, dark cell and got my life back again.

It was more than six months before they released me. Six months! I was so thin my mother did not even recognise me. I could not walk properly... I could barely speak. But then, after a while, my anger, it began to grow. I wanted to, to... to hurt them for what they had done to me... what they had done to all those others I could hear screaming in the darkness. And you know what upset me the most?

It was that they did not appear to care what they were doing... as if they knew they were untouchable... they were subject to no law... they faced no accountability. And your government supported them! The Americans gave them weapons, billions of dollars' worth. I expect that some of the equipment used to torture me was made in Western factories by Western companies, probably subsidised by Western taxpayers...

[1.2]

The real breaking point for me though, was the moment I decided I had to take revenge on my enemies... make them suffer the same way. When I realised I had to <u>act</u>. [...] It was the day my little daughter was blown apart, killed by an American bomb. [...] Ah... I can see you know nothing about this. Am I right? Ha! I have managed to surprise you... and so soon!

M: Professor, I, ah... when did you—

P: —Wait, wait, I will tell you... I had sent my daughter, ██████████, to Baghdad to visit her auntie. She was six years old... so beautiful. You have never seen such a beautiful girl... so full of life... always laughing. She was staying with my wife's relatives. [She] was there when the Americans tried to kill Saddam with their shock and awe bombing campaign. A misplaced smart-bomb... not so smart, hey... landed in the street where she was. You know, her body was blown into so many pieces. They could not find enough flesh to fill even a child's coffin. We buried her in a tiny box. It was so small... this big... like a shoebox! Can you imagine what this does to a man... to see nothing but pieces of his daughter?

M: It's not really true, is it... about your daughter? I thought your daughter was a student at secondary school in Cairo? If your daughter was killed in Iraq, then who is the girl studying right now at ██████ ██████████

P: —OF COURSE IT'S TRUE, MICHAEL! YOU DON'T KNOW EVERYTHING! [shouting] Do you think I would become a, a... a fucking terrorist for no reason? Why else would a man choose to become a murderer... a pariah? Why else would he put his life on the line... commit acts he knows to be wrong... choose a life of danger and hardship? Or, do you consider me insane?

M: Please sit down now, Professor. You're not [inaudible]... cooperate... [inaudible]...

[scraping sound]

[5.1]

P: [inaudible]... [laughter]... I am very sorry. I am of
      course lying. None of this is true. My daughter is still
      at school, as you say. She is a smart girl, no? She could
      be a professor too one day, do you not think?

M: So you weren't tortured? Your daughter didn't die in
      a bombing? Then why tell me this story... if it wasn't
      true? I don't understand your point...

P: Michael, the, ah, reason I told you this story is simply
      because... you Westerners always think there has to
      be a tragedy which drives a man to such actions...
      some kind of trauma which makes him go a little bit
      mad... which drives him to extreme behaviour... causes
      him to behave outside of established social norms, as
      it were.

      You have a sceptical look, but the truth is, in your
      cultural understanding... in your, your... your
      television-defined world... only something terrible
      in a person's background can explain their violent
      actions... like all those revenge movies where a
      once-ordinary man goes on a quest to kill everyone
      responsible for hurting his family. Or, or... or where
      the villain of the movie is horribly disfigured by some
      accident and goes on to become a psychopathic killer
      who will stop at nothing to get his evil revenge.

I find this really strange, actually. It seems as if...
despite all your actual history, your traditions... you
cannot understand why a person would fight for
freedom and justice... why someone would die for their
comrades. You seem to forget about all those people...
like your great writer George Orwell... who chose to
go and fight against Franco in Spain not because he
had some trauma in childhood, or because Franco had
killed his family, or he was personally affected by the
Franco regime... no, simply because he believed it was
the right thing to do. Because fighting against injustice
and fascism is a noble cause, the action of a responsible
man!

M: I don't think it's the same—

P: —No! You seem to have forgotten the possibility that
someone could <u>choose</u> to fight for the betterment
of others. It is as if you believe that people do not
really make decisions based on political conviction
any more... only on personal reasons... that humans
only ever act out of self-interest... or because they
are suffering from some kind of emotional trauma.
Perhaps it is because Thatcher and Reagan's
revolution truly succeeded... they succeeded in
creating a society where altruism, and, and... and
generosity... and mercy are dead values... where people
only ever act out of self-interest.

M: Mmm, I, ah—

P: —No, no! Seriously... this is your culture, Michael. I saw it when I lived here. You simply cannot understand someone who volunteers to go and fight for others... for people who are suffering... people who cannot fight for themselves... for a cause. You cannot understand someone who would risk their life and commit despicable acts... sully their own heart... blacken their very souls... to try and bring a measure of justice to an intolerable situation.

This is why whenever a martyr dies in an operation, you always ask, 'What happened to make them do this? What tragedy in their life could explain this inexplicable act?' And if a woman joins a militant movement or undertakes a revolutionary act... wow! Don't get me started! Was she raped or abused? Was she rejected by her fiancé, by her family? Did she have a miscarriage? You simply cannot conceive of any other reason why a woman would choose to fight.

You know, when Wafa Idris became the first woman to martyr herself in a, a... a suicide mission, as you call it... in Palestine, I read about it in your newspapers. They talked about what kind of make-up she was using, how beautiful she looked, why she did not have a boyfriend... about how she should have gone shopping with her girlfriends instead of conducting a mission!

It was as if they could not, ah... could not grasp the idea of a beautiful young woman choosing to give her life in this way for her people. As if a, a... a woman... especially a beautiful one like Wafa... could only be a normal woman if she went shopping!

At least when a man becomes a terrorist, they do not talk about how handsome he is, or how he should be playing football with his friends instead... But they still always want to know what is wrong with him... why he became so damaged... so abnormal... so extreme.

[2.3]

[recording interruption – extended white noise]

M: [inaudible]... keep saying 'You did this, you believe that, your government this, your culture that'. Who do you mean, exactly? You seem to be blaming me personally for everything, as if I'm directly responsible. Is it fair to generalise like that?

P: Of course, of course... normally, you would be correct. One cannot make such sweeping generalisations or lump everyone together in this way. As a scholar... or should I say former scholar... I know it. But right here, right now... in this room... with the questions you are asking me... I think it is fair to address you like this. Shall I tell you why?

[1.8]

OK, OK... in the first place, you are the, ah...
representative of your government while you are
interrogating me... trying to get me to reveal my
plans... drawing me out. I know what you are doing,
my friend. [...] The point is, you are employed by them.
You work for them in that nice building in London.
Your job is to protect this country and advance its
interests. So... yes... right here, right now, you <u>are</u> the
British government. I am talking directly to the British
government, as it were, face to face... and of course,
to the allies it is in coalition with. The British invaded
Iraq and Afghanistan in concert with other Western
countries, and they share a common set of policies and
concerns. In fact, all these countries share common
policies and approaches towards the Middle East... in
support of Israel, for example. Given this, I think it is
completely fair to speak of <u>your</u> foreign policy... <u>your</u>
actions in Iraq... <u>your</u> torture and rendition—

Public interest?
See query further
on re UK
involvement
in torture.
Suggest another
recording
interruption.

GH   M: —But there you go, exactly as I mentioned. We, the
British, have never had a policy of torturing or
rendering anyone. That was the Americans, not us!

P: Oh, come on, Michael! Do you think I am naive?
Do you think I do not know? Everyone knows! It is all
over the news! British agents were in Guantanamo.
They may not have held anyone down, and, and,

and... waterboarded them personally, but they were in the room... asking questions, going along with it. You may have been there yourself, I am not sure. No, no, no... do not shake your head. You cannot just dismiss this. Besides, people got tortured to death in British custody in Iraq. ███████████

███████████████████████████████ It is common knowledge. There are court cases going on right now... the rendition flights landed on UK soil. You were up to your bloody neck in it! It was just a part of the war which you were fighting with your American allies...

███████████████ and of course, you did it first in Northern Ireland. It is not as if you do not have a clear record in these matters...

M: Professor, we—

P: —and I might also ask... did Britain withdraw from the coalition in protest? Did the, the... the government hand over information to the human rights lawyers to help with prosecutions for the abuse of human rights? Did the British representative at the, ah... UN denounce the Americans? Has the British government tried to help the Red Cross get better access to all those <u>ghost detainees</u> in Afghanistan and God knows where else... all those people who have just disappeared?

M: Well, no—

P: —Exactly! Exactly! No, no, no... you cannot escape responsibility that easily, my friend—

M: —Please don't wag your finger at me, Professor—

P: —[inaudible] you may be personally opposed to torture, but the people you work for accept it... or at least they tolerate it as just one of the costs of working with the Americans. And not only that, your government was voted in by your people. They are the representatives of your society. They reflect your wishes, your values. Is that not democracy? This is why I lump you all together...

       Rabbena yeHra'ko kolloko bgaz wissikh.[2] [mumbled.]

M: [inaudible]

[2.3]

P: There is also the problem of the English language itself, which does not permit a singular <u>you</u> as differentiated from a plural <u>you</u>. If we were having this conversation in, ah, ah... another language... such as my own... I

---

[2] Trans. 'May God burn you all in dirty gaz.' Note: Arabic Egyptian colloquialism, refers to poor-quality cooking gas.

would be able to be a little more precise about exactly when I am referring to <u>you</u> as a representative of your government or <u>you</u> as an individual. But, given your job ███████████████████████, and given that you are part of a society that voted for the government as your representatives, it is legitimate to speak of your government's policies.

[2.3]

M: Mmm, I—

P: —There is another reason for the plural use of <u>you</u> in the context of this discussion. I am sorry... I interrupted you again... I know I always do this... but the fact is that you as an individual... Michael, the intelligence officer who works █ ██████████████████ keeping Britain safe from terrorists, and all the other individuals in your society... are connected to millions of other people in the world through the woven threads of the global economy. The oil which runs your nice Range Rover comes from the Middle East... and the coffee in that double espresso you buy every morning outside █ ████████comes from Africa or Latin America...

See further comments below. P keeps dropping in these details, taunting us with how much he knew about M.

Our counter-surveillance measures were obviously operating well below par on this. I trust this embarrassing security hole has now been sorted. I think we're extremely lucky that most of the terrorists we've had to deal with over the last couple of years have been complete idiots, and nothing like this outfit. Disturbing to think that he learned his trade in Iraq, though. How many more do you think there'll be over the next decade? *GH*

The same is true for a thousand other products which you consume every day... from the leather in your nice shiny shoes, to the cotton in that very smart white shirt you are wearing, to the smartphone you carry with its coltan components... to the prawns you love so much in your weekly Chinese takeaway. [...] In virtually every one of these cases, those products come to you through a global chain which goes back to some poor farmer, or a poor woman in a factory in Bangladesh, or a worker in Thailand who gets paid a few cents a day so you can enjoy stuffing your face while playing video games on your mobile. Meanwhile, <u>his</u> role in this virtuous chain is to work fourteen hours a day while, while... while living in a shack without electricity or running water, listening to the sound of his children coughing and being unable to afford the medicine for them.

The point is that this does not happen by accident. It is not some kind of natural phenomenon... like the seasons or a hurricane. The global economic order is the result of human actions... of, of... of policies made and enacted. It is the order of things, created and enforced by Western governments to ensure that their own societies remain wealthy and independent... no matter the cost to others. And I will not mention how the wealth of Britain and the other European powers was built on the pillage of the developing world during the age of imperialism... colonialism. How much gold

and ivory was taken... stolen... from Africa, do you
think... or hardwoods... rubber... copper? How many
billions of hours of free labour did your people get from
all those African slaves, do you think?

M: Oh, come on now—

P: —No, no, no! Do not look so sceptical. I am just making
the point that if the, ah... if the Africans came to
Europe and took all their gold back... took a few million
slaves and made them work hard for a hundred years
building roads and farming plantations... or perhaps
just levied a tax on every household in Britain... I think
that Africa would soon be quite well developed! What
do you think! [laughter]...

M: We weren't the only ones who traded in slaves,
Professor.

P: What?

M: I'm just saying... I'm sure you well know that the Arab
traders were in Africa long before the British.

P: You are correct, Michael. That is true. Many different
empires took slaves... that is how it was. All I am
saying is that now... here today... you are part of a
system which is maintained by your government...
on your behalf. You benefit directly from that system

every single day... as you have your whole life... as your parents have... and their parents... and their parents before them. That system is the result of your government's policies and actions, and unless you actively work against it... unless you try your best to withdraw from it, and resist it, and fight against it... then you signal your acceptance of it. You nourish it with your purchases, with your wholehearted, thoughtless consumption. You are like the good man who lets evil flourish by doing nothing, Michael. You are like the passive supporter of slavery in previous years... the one who just walked past... said nothing... when a black man was being racially abused. [...]

Bas la'nnak atwal,[3] you simply see none of that. [...] This is why I think I am justified in including <u>you</u> in the responsibility of your government's actions. You are a willing collaborator in the system. After all, I am not aware that you have ever boycotted a cup of coffee or tried to make sure that your cellphone does not have coltan from those warlords in the DRC in it... and you still have that nice SUV which you take your family out in ██████████ to ██████████ ... [inaudible]...

For God's sake! How did they miss all the clues – when it was right in front of their faces? The OIC should have pulled the plug on the whole operation a lot earlier. We will need a credible explanation for why the operation was allowed to continue. I'd be interested in your thoughts on a convincing position to take. GH

---

[3]   Trans. 'But because you are ignorant...' Note: Arabic Egyptian colloquialism.

[recording interruption]

[7.7]

P: Have I said how much I have been looking forward to
        talking to you like this, Michael?

M: Yes, you did, Professor—

P: —When I was hiding in Iraq, ████████████████
        ████████████████████ I imagined it so many
        times... this opportunity. The truth is no one listens to
        someone like me... no one hears what we have to say—

M: —maybe it's because people don't want to listen to
        someone who is trying to murder them—

P: —No, no, wait... even when Osama bin Laden wrote his
        letter to America, no one read it... instead, everyone
        says they do not know why he is attacking America...
        they do not understand what he wants! The fact is,
        no matter what we do... even if we stop the armed
        struggle... we can never explain our point of view...
        except in a room like this! [...]

        Even so, the point I am trying to make is... I appreciate
        this opportunity to tell you what I think... to go on
        record.

[1.8]

Anyway, it did not happen to me... this story about
being tortured by the Egyptian police. I am sorry to
disappoint you. I did not experience some particular
trauma or tragedy which made me this way... which
magically turned me into a completely new person. The
story I told you earlier about being tortured is not my
personal story... although I knew a lot of people who
<u>were</u> tortured in both Iraq and Afghanistan...
like ████████████, the man who went on to be a
Western informer... you must know him... he was
one of your agents before he was killed in, ah... 2006,
I think it was... ███████████████████████
████████████████████████████████
████████████████████████

Anyway... he told me that when he was first arrested...
for no reason he could ascertain... just a sweep... they
sent him to Abu Ghraib. They really made him suffer...
loud noise, cold, heat, beatings. [...] But the thing that
really upset him was when they photographed him
naked... with four bottles of beer. Can you imagine?
This is a devout Muslim and he is photographed
naked... with alcohol! He said they threatened to show
the photos to his family... his friends... his community...
if he did not work for them. He told me that it was the
thought that people would think he had been drinking
that enraged him the most. When he got out, he vowed

he would kill an American soldier for every bottle of
beer they had put in the photo with him. Actually... we,
ah... we helped him keep his vow...

I heard so many stories like that... and the one I
just told you. Men... and women... who joined the
resistance because they wanted revenge for the killing
or maiming of their children... or their wives, sisters,
brothers, cousins. People who had really suffered in
the most terrible ways... like another story I heard of
an old man who was kicked in the stomach by a marine
during a night raid... you know, when they break
down doors and go searching for insurgents? Well,
so... the old man was just trying to shield his women,
like Muslim men are expected to do when someone
breaks in in the middle of the night. They throw him
to the floor and a marine kicks him right in the guts. It
must have ruptured something because he died a day
later, his belly swollen with blood. As you can probably
guess, his two sons joined the resistance a few days
after they had buried their father.

These people... I met quite a few, actually... were very
angry... very determined. They really wanted to kill
Americans, soldiers... especially all those private
contractors with their dark sunglasses who shot
at people from their SUVs... as if they were playing
a video game! These ones... they wanted to make
American families drink the same cup of sorrow they

had tasted. You cannot invade a country without causing immeasurable suffering. And in Iraq, you caused so much suffering, as you yourself know...

In any case, I apologise. I, I... I never intended to mock you with a false story. That was never <u>my</u> story... I can see you are disappointed in me. You are thinking that I am an inveterate liar, as you no doubt expected. After all, one can never trust a terrorist! If they are willing to kill, they will no doubt lie. [...] What I am trying to say is... I, ah, was trying to make a small point about the preconceptions of your society. I will answer you truthfully now. You asked me an honest question, so I will give you an honest answer...

You know what set me on this path, what made me become a <u>terrorist</u>, as you call me?

[1.8]

M: What?

P: It is very simple... you did. Or, to be more precise in this instance, the government you work for in that nice building in London did. It happened slowly, of course, over many years. There was no single, special transforming event... no big traumatic experience... although there were certain catalysing events along the way... like the invasion of Iraq. I think that motivated a great many people, as I am sure you already know.

No, no... it was more of a process... a growing realisation about the true nature of the world, a kind of gradual unveiling of the truth... of reality. I started to question, to read and study, and as a consequence, I became more and more aware of what was happening. I started to understand more clearly what Western governments were doing, and how they were acting. [...] I slowly gained... what do you call it? [...] critical consciousness.

And you know, it started when I read the newspaper with real attention... when I listened to the radio... when I saw it with my very own eyes on TV. Then, as any curious person does, I began to research. I read about the history of Western intervention in my own country... and in the Middle East... Africa... Asia... Latin America... the Pacific. Later, I began talking to people who knew first-hand what was happening in these places, people who had witnessed it with their own eyes. And you know, the more I learned about all the terrible things your government and other Western governments were doing in so many countries, including my own, and had been doing for hundreds of years, the more my frustration grew. I began to feel a, a... a righteous anger and a, a... a determination to try and change things.

I began to feel a real sense of pain in my heart... pain at all the suffering of all the millions of victims of Western policies in these places. And I admit it. The pain turned into a burning rage... a cold rage at all the senseless violence, the meddling, the arrogance... the indifference to the suffering caused—

M: —I understand that, Professor, but what gave you the right to start killing people?

P: What? [...] What gave me the right? What gave _you_ the right to go around the world slaughtering people of, of, of every race, every creed? No, no... this is it. This is the point. I started to realise that I do not need your permission to resist. If you are somehow allowed to kill whoever you choose... women, children... Africans... Arabs... well, I am allowed to resist you. It is my right, no, my duty to resist you...

What gave me the right? [muttered] ... you know the thing that angered me the most was the, the... the open, sheer hypocrisy and double standards displayed by Western governments. The way they are always lecturing other countries about the importance of liberty, democracy, civilised behaviour, human rights... and all the while they are lecturing others about these things, they are _doing_ the complete opposite!

[banging]

*Mal'oun abo edemocratiya w-Ho'ou' el-ensan
bta'etkom, shwayet dowal awbash!*[4]

M: Professor! Please try to control your outbursts—

P: —Was it an expression of liberty that the US military
locked up taxi drivers in Guantanamo Bay? Did they
beat Dilawar to death in Afghanistan... punching his
legs over and over until they pulped like meat for
a kebab, every soldier hitting him as they passed...
for <u>freedom</u>? Was it for <u>freedom</u> that the sanctions
enforced by your fucking government killed half a
million children in Iraq?

[1.2]

Ya welaad el kalb![5] I cannot tell you how upset I was
when I saw Madeleine Albright on television saying
that all those dead children in Iraq were an acceptable
cost for the policy... that she believed it was a, a...
a reasonable price... to kill five hundred thousand
children in order to punish Saddam. I nearly smashed
the TV when I saw it! How can a human being say
that... much less the Secretary of State of America, the
most powerful country in the world, for God's sake?

---

[4]   Trans. 'Cursed by the father of your democracy and human rights, you,
a bunch of tramp nations.' Note: Arabic Egyptian colloquialism.
[5]   Trans. 'Sons of a dog!' Note: Arabic Egyptian colloquialism.

M: Mm, well... you have to try to under—

P: —*Mato'leesh efham. Howa ento khalleto feha magal*
     lettafahom![6] [...] I ask you again... is, is... is it in
     promotion of <u>democracy</u> to overthrow the government
     of Iran and install the Shah... who then tortured
     thousands of his own people with all his US-trained
     SAVAK agents? Or to assassinate Patrice Lumumba...
     a popular democrat... in Zaire? Or for the British and
     Israelis to invade the Suez Canal... my own country?
     Was it part of democracy promotion to support
     Karzai in Afghanistan when he stole the election...
     in front of international monitors? Is it in protection
     of democracy to provide tens of millions of dollars'
     worth of arms to dictators... to give them tear gas to
     use against their own citizens... to give them electric
     prods and pepper sprays for torturing prisoners? Did
     the international community agree that Israel's wall
     was acceptable... that it could steal land from poor
     Palestinian families and cut Palestinian villages in half,
     making life so unbearable for them?

[2.9]   *Is this in the public interest?*
          Current tensions re Israel?
          Grist for the anti-Zionist lobby?
          Suggest a short recording interruption. G.H.

---

[6]   Trans. 'Don't tell me to understand. You (pl.) haven't left any room for
     understanding.' Note: Arabic Egyptian colloquialism.

Was it for <u>civilisation</u> to make the prisoners in Iraq masturbate while the guards took photos... or put them on a leash like a dog? Was it <u>civilised</u> to shoot a twelve-year-old boy while his father tried to shield him from the bullets... while they both wept for mercy in front of the world's cameras?

M: Please try to calm down, Prof—

P: —*A'hda ezay? A'hda ezay!*[7] How would I calm down? I will not! I WILL NOT!

[banging]

[2.3]

I confess, I actually cried when I saw that little boy killed by the Israelis... Muhammed al-Durrah. There were tears running down my cheeks... I cried for this child, shot like an animal... his father trying to shield him with his bare hands.

Do you know his name? Is his story widely known in your society? It should be... He is a martyr to Western hypocrisy... a pure symbol of your true values. The Americans gave the Israelis the weapons they used to shoot him, and Britain and America

---

[7]   Trans. 'How would I calm down?' Note: Arabic Egyptian colloquialism.

block resolutions in the UN condemning Israel's appalling behaviour. Year after year, as the Israelis relentlessly take more land for their settlers, shoot more protestors, crush the Palestinians into the dust... your government does nothing but express support for Israel, issuing platitudes about how the fourth most powerful military in the world, a nuclear-armed state... needs security from the Palestinians... a people armed with rocks. My God! How anyone can be aware of what is happening in Palestine and not weep for shame, I, I... I do not know.

And, and... and your government... your own EU... your American allies... you seem to openly support the Israeli project to disappear an entire people from the land they have lived on for thousands of years, with your military aid, your diplomatic recognition, your special treatment. Did you know that Israel is the only country who trades with the EU that is exempt from human rights guarantees as a precondition for access to the EU market? They get a free pass! They can do anything they like and they will never be punished... unlike all those other countries in Africa and Asia. Muhammed al-Durrah... this tiny, unarmed, vulnerable little boy... he symbolises what is being done to the whole nation of Palestine. Boys throwing stones at a military superpower are shot in the face on TV and no one lifts a finger to help them!

M: [inaudible]... please sit down... [inaudible] █████
███
███
████████████████████████████

P: No one! NO ONE! *Ya wlad el mitnaaka!*[8]

[4.7]

[scraping sounds]

P: These bare walls tell stories, I think. What do you
       think, Michael? What are these scratches from... or,
       look, someone has made their mark here. 'W', 'A'... no, I
       cannot read it. Who was this, I wonder? [...]

       So, Michael... I told you how I became a militant... a
       revolutionary. What about you?

M: Can you sit down, Professor? I would prefer you to be
       seated.

P: Oh, yes. OK, OK. [scraping sounds]... So how did you
       become an, ah... interrogator, Michael? By what
       crooked path did <u>you</u> come to be here in this room
       tonight?

---

[8]   Trans. 'Sons of a whore!' Note: Arabic Egyptian colloquialism.

[2.9]

M: Well, it was by accident, I suppose. In my final year of
      university—

P: —What were you studying at university?

M: What? Oh, I read politics.

P: Politics?

M: Yes, politics. At Durham. [...] Anyway, my tutor in
      my final year told me that the security services could
      always use people like me, and I should give it a try.
      I mean, I didn't have any real plans, and I did enjoy
      researching about what was happening in the world,
      you know... current events, wars, and conflicts, and
      all that. So I put in an application, and, well, the rest is
      history, as they say. So here we are.

P: Yes, here we are... [inaudible] story...

[recording interruption]

[5.1]

P: [inaudible]... Western civilisation... it would be a good
      idea! That is what Mahatma Gandhi said when they
      asked him what he thought of Western civilisation.

It would be a good idea! Ha! He was so right, if you ask me... I do not know if you truly understand what I have been saying—

M: —I do, Professor. I hear—

P: —I was not tortured into being a terrorist. I did not have to have a member of my family killed to make me angry... nor did I require a preacher to radicalise me. I did not go onto extremist websites. I did not sit in my room looking at jihadi videos like some pimply-faced, sexually inhibited teenager. I was not infected by going to the mosque and discussing jihad... and I am not a sexually frustrated virgin who wants to go to paradise so I can finally have sex. As if anyone would ever become a terrorist and risk his life for that! I cannot believe some of you people actually believe that is true! Ha! [...]

You know I am a Christian by birth, do you not? A Copt... like the former Secretary-General of the United Nations, Boutros Boutros-Ghali? I am certainly not a secret Muslim. To be honest with you, I am not very religious at all. No, no, no. I do not go to church... I do not pray... it has been many years since I read the scriptures or heard a priest give a sermon... humanity... justice... that is my confessional faith. And I never emailed Osama, in case you were wondering... or Anwar al-Awlaki. I have not been brainwashed.

No, I just watched CNN, the BBC, al Jazeera. I read the New York Times, the Washington Post, the Guardian, the Independent, Le Monde. I read the works of Robert Fisk, Mark Curtis, John Pilger, Noam Chomsky, Naomi Klein... all those... and I studied. I learned the truth... and the truth set me free, as it says in the holy Bible. The truth turned me into an activist. It was the truth that, ah... radicalised me, if you still want to use this word. The truth of what your government... and what other Western governments... did.

[4.7]

I do not know if you remember... you might not have seen it at all, given what you were doing at the time... but in 2003, a short time after the initial invasion of Iraq, there was a, a... a picture on the front page of one of your newspapers... I forget which one. It was of a man holding the body of his little daughter. She was wrapped in a kafan. She had been killed in the fighting. But the man's face, oh my God! You have never seen anything like this before. It was a grimace of pain... sheer, pure agony. You have never seen anything so painfully intense. He was weeping with such a, a... a look... like his, his... very heart was being torn into little pieces! It was as if all of the pain of all the families in the history of the world was concentrated in his face right at this moment.

That picture was, ah... I was just... [inaudible]...
ah... when I saw that picture, I really felt his pain so
deeply... right inside here. I felt that man's pain... and
the suffering of all the nameless families burying their
nameless children in Iraq at that time. And I felt rage...
real, incandescent rage. It started to flow up in me like,
like... like a volcano! Rage at the callous indifference of
all the suffering... at the hallow platitudes which just
wiped away all the suffering by blaming Saddam... or
al-Qaeda... or 9/11! Rage that a respected American
leader can say live on television... to the whole world,
'yes, the lives of half a million children in Iraq is an
acceptable cost'! I felt rage that your government went
to war even though the UN did not allow it, and even
though millions of people around the world marched
against it. So much for democracy or the will of the
people... or the fucking international community,
for that matter. Your leaders obviously care nothing
for what the people want... or the authority of the
international community... except when it suits them,
of course.

Most of all, I felt rage at the fact that no one in the
West would ever recite the names of all the victims of
your invasion... or make a memorial to honour their
memory. I bet you do not know the name of a single
Iraqi victim of your invasion. Am I right? Can you
name one? [...] Even one single small boy?

[3.8]

No, I expect not. To you, they were just unworthy,
nameless <u>collateral damage</u>. [...] Well, it was then
that I knew I had to do <u>something</u>! I could not just go
on with my life as if all that suffering and pain and
violence did not exist... as if it did not matter to me. I
could no longer be indifferent to the suffering of my
fellow human beings. So I guess you would say that
that photo... a photo of a man's suffering... is what
<u>radicalised</u> me.

[2.3]

Seriously though, would you be surprised if the man
in that photo became a terrorist... after you killed his
daughter and devastated his country... after all the
killing, the torture, the chaos? If he was sitting here
instead of me, could you really ask what <u>radicalised</u>
him? Would you seriously look him in the eye and ask,
'Why do you want to kill us? What did we ever do to
you?' [...]

Ohhf... for me, the real surprise is not that there are
what you call 'terrorists' in Iraq and Afghanistan
and Palestine, but, but... but that there are not more
of them! Given how many fathers and brothers, how
many sisters and mothers there must be in those
countries who have lost family members, victims

of <u>collateral damage,</u> I am surprised that al-Qaeda
is not a million strong! Huh... It is amazing that so
many people can forgive... or at least... refuse to take
vengeance. This really surprises me.

What I am saying is, your unit, when it was stationed
in ███████████ and your sergeant ███████ was
████████████████████████████████████

M: What the fuck! How did you know [inaudible] sergeant
        [inaudible]...

> We probably need to chop this recording interruption
> back even further. Someone might be intrigued to know

[recording interruption] what Staff Sergeant CB was caught doing and

> try to follow this up. We have to head off any

[2.3]   more efforts to revisit what went on over there
                – for HMG's sake. I'm sure you agree. GH

M: [inaudible]... get that you are angry about certain
        events, but can you honestly say that you had a
        normal childhood? That you never had any bad
        experiences growing up which might have influenced
        who you are today... experiences which might have
        affected you negatively? Egypt's not exactly Sweden or
        Switzerland. I can't imagine that you didn't see some
        terrible things during your childhood... experienced
        some injustices... tragedies. Egypt is not the kindest,
        most fair-minded society, I imagine... and anyone who

experienced that would be affected by it... damaged, even... traumatised at the very least.

P: You are right in one respect... it was a hard life... much harder perhaps than the life of a middle-class child in the Home Counties, or the suburbs of Copenhagen, I expect. But it was probably no harder than growing up chronically poor in a sink estate in one of your big cities... or, or... or a former mining town in the north-east... or Wales... somewhere like that. Poverty and all its violence and degradation will leave a mark on anyone, diminish them permanently. But as you undoubtedly know, this is not an explanation for why someone chooses a particular path in life. People are not just products of their upbringing. They are not like computers that get programmed a certain way... blank slates to be written on.

M: Oh, I know. That's not what I'm suggesting. I'm just trying to understand why you turned to a life of violence.

P: OK, OK. I see. The truth is that I had a pretty good childhood, especially compared to my peers. My family, as you already know, was part of the established middle class in Egypt, and my parents loved me very much. I had many friends, and a strong community. The Copts in Egypt are very tight-knit, you know... they look out for each other. And you know that my father was a schoolteacher in a private school for expats. We always had enough money for a pretty good life... not a lot, but enough, you understand... and I was very well educated comparatively. Also, my family was not really involved in politics, so we did not get harassed by the national police, the Al-Amn al-Markazī... Mabahith Amn ed-Dawlah... you know them? The State Security Investigation Service? I am sure you know them well... But no one in my family was ever tortured or imprisoned... not like some I knew.

I do remember the poverty and the racism, though... and I know it must have shaped me at some level. I certainly reflect back on that now... I am going to stand up for a minute and walk a little, if you don't mind...

M: No, no. That's fine. Please...

[scraping sounds]

P: I get very stiff... since the injury in Iraq. I assume you know about it... and I have nervous energy. I have to keep moving around. [...] What you do not know... what your files do not tell you... is that at my school... you know, the, ah, private international school I was allowed to attend because my father was a teacher there... anyway, the European students would call me a 'dirty Arab'. They would take every opportunity... whenever the teachers were out of earshot... to make fun of Egyptians... to mock them. They would play cruel jokes on the janitors and canteen staff. But the worst was when we would go to other schools to play football. I was quite good in those days... a striker. I scored a lot of goals... [inaudible]...

I remember it so vividly... we would all cram into the team minibus and drive across town to the other school. Do you know what the European boys would do to amuse themselves along the way? [...] They would lean out the window and spit on people. Huge gobs of saliva saved up in the mouth until an old man in traditional dress... or a woman in a hijab was standing by the road in the path of the van. If they were, ah... successful... if their spit landed on someone's head or back... they would all laugh and cheer and claim points. It was disgusting! I was so ashamed to be on that bus. Later... I realised that this racism was just an expression of what the children had picked up at home, from their parents... and their parents had picked it up from their own societies. Europeans have felt superior to other races for hundreds... thousands of years... it was nothing new. I came to realise that people of colour have been spat upon for centuries.

[2.9]

But what about you, Michael? What was your upbringing like? Did you have a happy childhood?

M: I... ah... yes, I suppose it was. I was an only
       child, so my parents, ah, you'd have to say they
       lavished all their attention upon me. And much
       like you, we were not poor by any standards...
       solid upper-middle class, I guess you'd call us. We
       had a decent standard of living... good schools...
       a nice home. And like I mentioned before, I have
       fond memories from my childhood... especially
       when I went fishing with my grandfather. He
       really doted on me. ███████████████████
       ███████████████████████████ I was his only
       grandchild and he wanted to be a real part of my life. I
       was really sad when he died...

       After he passed away... when ████████████████...
       it did leave me with a certain sense of... well, ah...
       aloneness I guess you'd say. During my teens,
       my father was away a great deal of the time █
       ██████████████████, and my mother was a little...
       distant, shall we say. But, no... I wasn't deprived
       in any way... and I can't remember any particular
       unhappiness during my childhood.

To be completely honest, I hate reading this – laying out all his
dirty linen – like he's talking to a damn shrink. I know it's part of
his interrogation technique – building rapport and all that.
But it still seems so undignified for a British officer. Why can't he
make something up, like he did with the earlier stuff?
    Does it really need to be included in the public record?
                    Can we get away with expunging it?   GH

P: You were lucky, Michael. There are so many who
       could not say the same thing... especially during the
       same years you were growing up. There was so much
       real poverty in Britain then, following the Thatcher
       revolution... not to mention all across the developing
       world. Well, that has still not really changed, has it?

       Looking back at my childhood, I am somewhat
       ashamed of my ignorance... and by my, ah... reaction
       to the poverty in my country. Oh, wait, yes... here is a
       story for you... when I was small... maybe ten... I used
       to go to the end of my road where the shanty town
       began... where the people from the rural areas would
       come to live, hoping to escape their destitution and
       strike it rich in the city. I liked to explore and try to
       find small animals. I once had a collection of snakes,
       you know? I kept them in boxes in my room and fed
       them small lizards.

       Oh, and... ha! I had forgotten this! I once had a desert
       sand snake... beautiful patterns on its skin... Then
       I found a small brown house snake... they are very
       common in Cairo houses... and I put it in the box
       with the sand snake. But, to my consternation, the
       next day it was gone. I thought it must have escaped,
       even though I could not find a hole in the box. The
       next week, I found another house snake and again
       put it in the box with my sand snake. Once again, it
       disappeared... ha! Can you guess! Yes, yes! It turns out

all I was doing was feeding the sand snake... the big one was devouring the little ones...

I am sorry. That is not the story... I digressed again. What I was saying... once, when I was exploring the shanty town, I found some other children there. They had no shoes and their feet were dirty and cracked... and they only had rags for clothes... just a dirty and threadbare shirt and pair of shorts. But what made me laugh at the time were their massive bellies and skinny limbs. You know what I am talking about? Swollen bellies protruding out, but really stick-like legs and arms? I thought they were, ah... fat... like pregnant women... I would laugh and tease them.

[3.9]

It was only later that my mother told me that this was a sure sign of malnutrition... that, and the way their hair browned at the ends... I never felt so ashamed... I still feel ashamed when I think about it... laughing at malnourished children... laughing at the victims of extreme poverty.

M: But you were just a child, Professor. You couldn't possibly know—

P: —I know, I know! It is illogical to feel so bad about something when I was too young to know any better...

but I just cannot help it... I still feel like a complete shit... like a typical spoiled rich kid...

It gets worse, though. [...] One time, I saw one of these ragged little boys. He had mucus running down his face. He sneezed, and a tapeworm came out of his nose. You know what a tapeworm is? Yes? He tried to flick it off, but it stuck to his lip. So he began to pull on it. I could not believe what I was seeing, but it began to stretch longer and longer out of his nose. He was choking and gagging as he pulled at it. It must have been in the back of his throat. When it had finally come all the way out, it must have been ten feet long!

M: That's disgusting—

P: —Yes! Yes! I did not know what it was at the time, but I was so, so... so, ah, horrified... so shocked to my core. I remember I asked my mother if one of those worms lived in me and if I sneezed, would it come out like that? She told me that the worm ate the boy's food, which was why he was so malnourished, but that it could be easily cured by taking medicine which would kill it inside his stomach. I asked her why his parents did not give the boy medicine. Of course, she told me that they were too poor for medicine, or they did not understand what to do.

[1.2]

It was my first real experience... my first direct
confrontation, really... with real, hard-core poverty.
Can you imagine such poverty in your own country...
in today's world? There are people with their own
jetliners... people with more than a billion dollars... and
yet some children not so far from here are sneezing out
tapeworms? It's so unbelievable! [...]

Anyway, as I said... difficult experiences in childhood...
or at any other time... are not an explanation or an
excuse for a person's behaviour. It is the reaction to
those experiences which is important... the choices a
person makes in response to them. One man can see
such abject poverty and be completely unaffected,
failing to see how it affects him, or is any concern
to him at all. Another can become afraid and try to
ensure that he will never be poor like that. Or, or, or...
a man can choose to try and help his fellow man... try
to end the suffering he sees in the face of another... he
can try to erase the affront to human dignity that such
poverty represents—

M: —But that's no excuse for violence, Professor.
You can't blame the existence of poverty for why you
chose to take up violence. There have always been
poor people—

P: —I am not blaming poverty for my choices, Michael.
I am not blaming that at all... I am merely answering
your question about my childhood. I really do not
consider I had a traumatic or unhappy childhood.
Despite what I just told you, I have a great many very
happy memories... of my mother and father... my
friends... the community we were in... the holidays we
went on... ah, yes, the stories we would tell around the
table... As I said before, we were comparatively well off
and we lacked for nothing, materially.

But looking back, I can see that these experiences
of the reality of poverty in my country... the reality
of racism... shaped my outlook. I always hated
inequality... unfairness... since I was a child. I expect it
explains why I went on to study economics. I wanted
to understand how we could have a society... an entire
world order... where some people can own land the size
of a city, and eat from gold dinner plates... while others
live in shacks and cannot afford a simple medicine for
killing the tapeworm that lives in the bellies of their
children. I wanted to do something with my life that
would make a difference.

M: Mmm... I suppose you have a point—

P: —You know, I once went back to Cairo, just a couple
of years ago... oh, you look surprised! You were
unaware of this journey? Ha! Well, I went to the same

neighbourhoods that I used to explore as a child.
It really depressed me because I could see right away
that nothing had changed. I mean, a lot of people had
cellphones... everyone... always on the phone... and all
those hawkers trying to sell phone credit. That was
one difference from before. But the roads were still full
of potholes... dirt and rubbish everywhere... unreliable
electricity... shoddy buildings... you know, the ones
that fall down like a pack of cards when the earth
shakes? I was shocked, frankly. And out in the villages,
ohhf... it is even worse. How can this be?
How can people be living in the same conditions in
the same shanty town after twenty-five years?
How is this possible? Where did all that money for
development go?

Would Britain tolerate this, Michael? Vast areas
where people lived in poverty for generation after
generation... not a single sign of progress?

M: I think you'd find that there are areas like that in
       Britain...

P: I suppose you are right... but I am guessing it is not
       quite on the same scale... and a different type of
       poverty. There are not thousands of homeless children
       in your big cities... forced into child labour... or those
       armies of poor people who live on rubbish dumps
       rooting through the garbage for scraps?

The point I am trying to make is that these experiences made me want to try and understand how such a system is maintained... which is why I studied economics. I suppose they stimulated a desire within me to engage with the world and try to do something positive to make a change... But in those days, I was mainly concerned with helping my own country. The thought of taking up arms was the furthest thing from my mind... I would not have dreamed of it.

It was only much later, when I learned how really brutal this system is... how it is rooted in racism and oppression... how throughout history it has taken sustained violent resistance from the oppressed to bring about real change... that I began to see the need for direct action... But in the beginning, I just wanted to study economics so I could help developing countries escape their poverty.

[2.9]

[banging]

M: What are you doing? Can you please sit down now?

P: [inaudible]... check ███████████████ [inaudible]... side ██████

M:

[recording interruption]

[2.3]

P: Michael, let me ask you a question. Do you know
       where I was exactly when your army invaded Iraq...
       when you started slaughtering thousands of Muslims
       for what we all know was a, a... a pack of lies? Do you
       know what I was doing? I do not mean that I was in
       Egypt, as it no doubt says in the file you have... but
       what I was doing that very day?

       Surely, you must know when I was born? [...] March
       20, 1963. I was celebrating my fortieth birthday on
       the day you and the Americans invaded Iraq. Shock
       and Awe... that was my present. Or, should I say...
       the birthday present for all those poor Iraqis! There
       we were, trying to eat the beautiful food my wife
       had prepared... Baba Ghanoush... chicken tagine...
       ta'amiya... tehina... basbousa... macaroni béchamel...
       all my most favourite dishes! My wife had been
       cooking all day... my friends were there... my extended

family... my colleagues from the university... notable people from the community.

But all that delicious food just tasted like ash in our mouths... like dirt! We simply could not stop watching the TV... seeing all those bombs raining down... knowing all those poor people... people just like us... families... were dying. People just trying to live their lives... just trying to survive... while your air force blew them to fucking pieces! It was the absolutely worst birthday I ever had! It was that night actually when I knew I would go to Iraq... when I knew I simply had to do something. I could not stand by another day and just do, ah, ah... ah, nothing... just pretend that I had no responsibility.

[2.9]

I am curious, Michael. After what I have just told you, what good do you think your so-called de-radicalisation programmes are? Would they have worked on me? Would I have been dissuaded from going to Iraq?

He's right, of course — those programmes are probably not worth the level of resources we currently put into them. But we have no real choice. There'd be absolute hell to pay if we couldn't show we were doing everything possible to prevent terrorists! We must prepare a position in case anyone asks about the effectiveness of HMG's current programmes in the light of this material. I'd welcome your thoughts on a possible angle to take. GH

M: Well, I'm not sure they're aimed at someone—

P: —The fact is, <u>nothing</u> would have stopped me from going! I would have laughed in your face. Not unless George Bush himself had come on television the next day and said that it was all a big mistake and they were packing up and going home... after rebuilding all the things they had smashed, of course! The truth is that you cannot stop people like me from taking up arms against you... not unless you close down all the television stations in the world... all the newspapers... the entire Internet. Not unless you find a way to completely suppress the truth of what your government does in the world.

Do you hear what I am saying? The problem is not the extremist preachers, or the jihadi websites. It is not al-Qaeda propaganda or disaffected young people. The issue is that your government has committed so many wrongs and injustices... and keeps committing them every day. And what they really want is for people like me to do nothing about it! They want to be free to keep doing all these things, and for no one to fight back or try and resist them... Or, they want us to engage in <u>non-violent</u> action like signing petitions or peaceful demonstrations. This is the real aim, I have come to realise... to make people everywhere into sheep who will never fight back... especially in the Middle East... and especially Muslims! Anyone who disagrees with your wars... or your torturing... your overthrowing of regimes that no longer suit you... your control of the international economy... you want them to sit back and basically do nothing.

M: Again, I'm not sure that—

P: —I decided that day that I was not going to be a sheep... *AHHA*,[9] not now! I would not go quietly into that dark night, my friend, but I was going to rage against your oppression. *Le'en elly byorbot fe ra'abetoh habl, alf meen yoggoroh.*[10]

And do not think that this is just about a few nasty little wars and some, ah, ah... weapons sent to the Israelis. I have hardly mentioned the way your government oppresses the world's poor through its economic practices... and why it is that the Middle East has so much valuable oil but also mass unemployment, poverty, illiteracy, debt... inequality. I was an economics professor, for God's sake! I know how this works... how the rules of the international economy consistently favour Western countries and keep developing nations poor. How the IMF and the WTO are used to protect Western producers from competition,

---

[9]   Trans. 'I truly object.' Note: Arabic Egyptian colloquialism.
[10] Trans. 'Because that who ties a rope around his neck, there will be thousands to drag him.' Note: A famous Egyptian proverb.

and Western consumers from paying prices that
would allow for savings by Third World producers
that could stimulate development. How so many
valuable resources... coffee, bananas, hardwoods,
copper, coltan, rice, many, many more... come from
the developing world but never seems to bring them
prosperity... because the prices are kept down by
Western manipulation of the commodity markets. The
fact is, anyone who can read can know this. You do not
need to be an economics professor... just a concerned
human being!

M: Please try and control your temper, Professor! You're a
very angry ma—

P: —Yes, I am angry! I have good reason to be! Don't I?
[...] Sorry, I will try and talk calmly. The question is...
I am angry at why, I mean, what about the story of
how so many Western pharmaceutical companies
lobbied against allowing poor countries in Africa
and Asia to use generic AIDS drugs because they
could not afford twenty thousand dollars a year <u>per</u>
<u>person</u> to buy them from Western companies? How
many millions were there, would you say, that died to
protect the profits of your pharmaceutical companies...
like when ███████████████████████████
███████████████████████? And do you
think the poor of the world will just die quietly...
without ever rising up... without so much as a

whimper? Do you think you can oppress them forever and they will not fight back one day?

M: But it's not the poor fighting back, is it, Professor? You're not poor, you're a well-off university professional... or at least you were. Why do you care so much about the world's poor? Why don't you let them fight their own battles? It's not really your problem, is it?

P: That is very, ah... Western of you, Michael... very egoistic... self-interested. You seem to think that every individual would only be interested in themselves... that they would only care about themself and their own family, as if no other fellow human being mattered. Maybe it is true that Westerners only care about themselves, what do you think? [...]

M: I think you're playing with words, Prof—

P: —To be honest with you, I do not believe this at all... nor do I believe that you, Michael, really think like this. I mean, look at the, ah... the job you do. You could be a banker in the city, I expect... you are an intelligent man. You could be making a lot of money for yourself... or be a businessman, a CEO. But instead, you are here... in this nasty little room in the middle of the night, dealing with dangerous men... trying to keep your country safe. That tells me that you are not a selfish person, Michael...

And your government keeps sending peacekeepers to save strangers in faraway countries who are suffering... Rwanda... Somalia... Sierra Leone. Putting to one side that very fascinating story about how you went from university straight into the intelligence service, did you not go as a peacekeeper to Bosnia? Why would you do that if you did not believe that every person has a responsibility to help their fellow human beings? [...]

Shewayet ensaneya ya'eny.[11] [mumbled]

How did he find out M's deployment history?
This was not publicly available information. Clearly, they have better counter-intelligence than we thought. It is imperative we learn how they did it in order to regain security for all relevant personnel. Check with JS. GH

[2.3]

M: *Ana lasto hajaran bettab'e, ya Professor.*[12]

P: Ha! *Helw a'wi! Enta btetkallem 'Arabi aho?*[13] I thought as much! Where did you learn Arabic, I wonder? Perhaps in Iraq... or maybe it was on those little trips you took to Morocco... Algeria? Did you need it for interrogating al-Qaeda, huh? [...] It is no mind—

---

[11] Trans. 'A bit of humanity for instance.' Note: Arabic Egyptian colloquialism.

[12] Trans. 'I am definitely not a rock, Professor.' Note: Classical Arabic.

[13] Trans. 'How sweet! So you speak Arabic as I can see.' Note: Arabic Egyptian colloquialism.

M: —Yes, yes. I speak a little bit of Arabic... enough to understand what you say. It's not important. Tell me how you know about Bosnia, Professor. [...] It's just that it's not something widely known about me. [...] I'm curious how you came to possess this information.

[2.1]

Seriously, how do you—

P: —Tell me this, Michael. If you had a friend who was being beaten every day by a group of local skinheads... or if your cousin had no food and could not feed his family... or you knew your neighbour was suffering alone in his house... would you not help him? Would you really say, 'It is not my problem. I can only take care of my own'?

M: But you're not fighting for your relatives or friends, Professor. It's not really the same thing. Getting back to my question, how do you know—

P: —No, no, no! It is the same! This is what you do not understand... with your individualism... your selfish materialism. [...] To you, every man is a solitary island, cut off from his fellow human beings. But I believe that we are all brothers and sisters... we are all part of the same human family, the very same body. The Palestinians are my brothers... and so are

the Iraqis... the Afghans... the, ah, Darfurans... the
Tibetans... the Chechens... the Tamils... the, ah, ah,
Basques. [...] And when one of my brothers suffers,
I suffer too. When one of my brothers is beaten and
oppressed, I feel the pain and shame of it too. Like the
Apostle Paul said in the holy scriptures, when, ah, ah...
one part of the body is sick and feels pain, the rest of
the body is sick too.

I consider you my brother too, Michael. If someone was
oppressing you and your people in the same way that
the Palestinians are being oppressed, do you know, I
would go and fight for you too.

[6.3]

M: Professor, with the greatest respect, this is an
interesting argument and one you express quite
eloquently... as I would expect from a highly educated
person. And you know, I cannot but sympathise with
your reasons for frustration. I get very upset too when
I see some of the very real problems in the world—

P: —Problems! You are calling them problems? As if they
just occur by themselves... like some kind of natural
phenomenon... like a storm or an earthquake... as if
they were not caused by people... by human actions?
[...] As if no one has responsibility for them! These
are not problems I am talking about, Michael, they are

injustices! Injustices caused by policies and actions...
which are caused by people! Someone is responsible
for them! [...] Murder is not a <u>problem</u>, is it? You
would not say, 'It is a <u>problem</u> that people are being
murdered,' would you? You would say, 'It is a <u>crime</u>
that someone is murdering people!'

M: So you think Western governments are the cause
of all these problems... that they're responsible for
everything? That seems rather naive, simplistic...
especially for someone as educated as yourself.

P: As I have already explained, Michael, you cannot
deny the role your government has played and the
deliberate choices they have made—

M: —OK, OK, yes, my government and other Western
governments have made many mistakes in the past...
and their actions have not always made things better...
although we can debate whether they really had the
freedom of action that you attribute to them. The
point is, you can't expect me to believe that you read
the newspapers, got upset, blamed certain Western
governments, and then just decided to become a
terrorist! Millions of people... hundreds of millions
of people! [...] read the same newspapers and watch
the same television news every single day. Injustice,
poverty, war, death... the fact is, they've always been
with us. It's a fact of life. We all know this! Everyone

knows it! But how many people decide to become
terrorists as a result of it? And why target the UK?
Why come here? What I'm saying is that there has
to be more to it than this. It's simply not normal
behaviour.

P: No, no, no... you are right... most people do not become
terrorists from reading the newspaper. In fact, most
people do nothing from reading the newspaper. They
just turn to the football pages... or they switch on
the TV to Coronation Street. Most people are sheep,
Michael, as you know. Most people will just let the
government shit all over them... [inaudible]...

M: As I've already said, I can tell that you're very
angry, Professor... that you hate what you believe my
government has done to you... or to your people, as
it were... the people you want to help. You hate our
policies, and you hate our hypocritical actions. Is that
why you're doing this? Are you so driven by <u>hate</u>? I
can't really see how you could be a terrorist, trying
so hard to kill us, unless you really hated us. I mean,
when you see the bloodshed, the carnage that a bomb
causes on innocent people who were just going about
their business... well, that involves pretty strong
feelings to be able to cause that... especially the women
and children, old people, handicapped, whatever. You
have to have some real rage in your heart to do that,
surely?

P: *Gaatak niila, wala-nta fahem Haga!*[14] [mumbled.]—

M: —No, Professor! Don't... it's... at the least, try telling that to the victims... the people with their legs blown off. [...] It's a perfectly legitimate question—

P: —No, no, no! It is a cliché! And I know you are a much more intelligent man than this. Frankly, it is unbecoming of you, Michael. You know very well that <u>hate</u> has nothing to do with this. [...] Anger, maybe, at the injustice... but not hate. And certainly not hate at individuals. You have been a soldier. Do soldiers hate the people they shoot at? Did you hate the Iraqi child you shot... I mean, personally hate him? Did you ███████████████████████████████████ ██████████████████████████████?

I'm still amazed the field commander missed this. You'd think he'd never read M's file before the op. Or was the shooting incident even in M's file? And if not, why not? I hope someone has noted this for the Review of Procedure hearing. GH

M: [inaudible] fuck did you know [inaudible]—

P: —Do air force pilots hate the people far away on the ground when they, ah, ah... press that button to release the bombs? Did Britain invade Iraq because they,

---

[14] Trans. 'May a disaster hit you, you understand nothing!' Note: Arabic Egyptian colloquialism.

ah... hate the Iraqi people? Do they hate Afghans... Libyans? Did you hate the people of Sierra Leone when you sent in soldiers to rescue your comrades—

M: —Wait! How do you know—

P: —Hate has nothing to do with this, Michael! Despite what your movies always show, we never stood around chanting 'Death to Britain! Death to America! Kill the infidels!' [laughter]... We do not even have names for you... unlike the names your troops always seem to have for us! 'Hajis'... 'camel jockeys'... ah, 'ragheads'... you know. I am sure you had others...

To be honest, we do not much think about you, either personally or collectively. Seriously, I do not hate you at all. Actually, you could say I love you! [laughter] Yes, I know... it is a paradox. What I mean is, I love your movies... your country makes fantastic films... even Hollywood makes good films... occasionally. And your comedy is so wonderful... Monty Python... Ben Elton... Mr Bean! Oh my God, that guy is so funny! Ha! [...] Little Britain. Seriously, you guys have the best humour in the world. And writers... do not get me started! Chaucer... Shakespeare... Hardy... Orwell... Rushdie. Oh, and I love your classical music! Britten... Vaughan Williams. Ah... it is like being transported to another world. [...] And to be honest, I have hardly met an Englishman

I did not like... including you, Michael. I find British people to be so, so... so, ah, polite... friendly... interesting.

The truth is that there is so much I love about your culture and your people. What angers me is not your culture or your values, but your actions... your foreign policies... all your wars and invasions... all the wicked governments you support... all the weapons you sell... your complete lack of honour...

[2.3]

I am not doing this because of hatred, Michael, no matter all the crimes you have committed.

M: So what <u>do</u> you think about, Professor... when you press that button? When you're about to blow some young lads away?

P: What? You are asking me... [inaudible] you... wait... no... what do <u>you</u> think about, Michael... when you shoot an innocent child on the street... when you drop a huge bomb on a wedding party... or, or... or open fire on a pregnant woman and her husband driving towards a checkpoint? For God's sake—

M: —I did not mean to cause—

P: —I will tell you what I think about, Michael. I think
about the hundreds of thousands of dead people...
innocent, nameless dead... and the mutilated bodies of
children lying in the rubble of the houses smashed by
your bombers... and the blameless men being tortured
in your prisons... I think about how I am helping the
oppressed, the voiceless, the beaten... [inaudible] [...]
Now, you tell me what you think about—

M: —OK, OK, OK. I'm sorry to have mentioned it. What
about simple revenge, then? Are you trying to pay us
back a little for what you believe we've done to you? Is
this your retribution... for the bombs, the shootings?
Because if it is, then I can understand it. Really, I can,
Professor. I've been there. My cousin... she, this was
when I was at school. Anyway, she started going out
with this older guy, a real loser, thought he was proper
hard... a player, as they say. The thing is, he introduced
her to drugs, got her started. Soon she started using
pretty heavily, and next thing you know, she's missing
school, getting into trouble, you know, staying at her
boyfriend's place for days on end. Her parents are
beside themselves. It's the talk of the whole family.

Well, one night I was walking through town and I
saw her, lying on the ground in the entrance to an
alley, covered in vomit, barely breathing. I mean, at
first I didn't even recognise her, she was so dirty and
dishevelled. But then I saw it was her. I had to roll her

on to her side so she didn't choke. She was groaning, and twitching, retching. I mean, she was in a terrible state. They said it was bad smack. He practically poisoned her! After I called the ambulance, I started to get really angry, you know... seeing her like that. How could someone do that to her... degrade her like that? Endanger her life? Why wasn't he looking after her? She was just a kid, for fuck's sake!

So I went looking for him. I was so fuckin' angry. I was going to smash his face in!

[2.3]

P: Did you find him? What happened?

M: Yes, I did find him... the same night, down his usual pub. He had some mates with him... There was a confrontation, of course... only he and his mates knocked the stuffing out of me. I was only sixteen, mind you, and there were three of them. The point is, Professor, I know what it feels like... to want someone to pay... to crave a little revenge.

P: What happened to this man?

M: Oh, the usual. I think he went to prison briefly, petty crime, small-time dealing. He's still around, as far as I know... still causing shit.

P: And your cousin?

M: She's OK now. Married... kids... the usual thing. I guess
it was one of those teenage rebellion things... a wake-
up call. Luckily, there was no lasting damage.

P: But you see... this is not the same thing.

M: What do you mean?

P: Your feeling of revenge, I mean, it is natural... to want
justice for your cousin. But, but... ah, would you give
up your life for some revenge against this, this... little
man? Would you renounce your family, your friends...
would you choose to live without pleasure... without
the love of a woman... without security, normality...
all for revenge against one man? No, this is insane. No
one will choose this life for a feeling of revenge. Do you
know that I have lived with constant fear since I went
to Iraq? Ten years of being fearful every day... that I
would be arrested, tortured by the Americans, killed in
battle... or, or blown up by one of those drones circling
in the sky. Do you know this fear? [...] I can tell you, it
sits on your shoulders like a heavy blanket... pressing
down on you. And you think I chose this kind of life for
myself, just for revenge?

No, no! It is not about revenge, Michael. Besides, do
you really think there could ever be enough revenge...

that all those millions upon millions of people in
Africa or India or Iraq... wherever... who suffered so
much... could they ever be satisfied? How many of your
citizens could we kill, do you think, to revenge the one
million people who have died because of Iraq? [...] And
I am not saying that it is not cathartic to fight back...
that you do not feel a certain amount of satisfaction.
Oh, no! The truth is that it makes you feel like a real
man again... like you have some control over your own
life... that you are in control of your own destiny. You
feel like you are really making a free choice, whatever
happens... whether you live or die. You feel like a real
citizen should, I imagine, not just a subject, blindly
following what he has been told to do...

You are the ones who do revenge. You are like the
God of revenge... ah, ah... Nemesis himself! How many
had to die in your little colonial wars whenever a
British settler was killed by a native, do you think?
Or when a soldier died... like in Denshawai? We all
know this story in Egypt... how the British took
revenge on the villagers, telling lies... hanging the
villagers. Do you know about this atrocity? [...]
And what about 9/11? Three thousand are killed,
and how do you respond? A million dead in Iraq
and Afghanistan... countless thousands tortured...
imprisoned... disappeared. Israel is the same.
Hezbollah captures a couple of their soldiers... to try
and make an exchange for some of the thousands of

people Israel captured before, I might add... and Israel launches a full-scale invasion killing thousands... blowing up tens of thousands of homes... sowing hundreds of thousands of mines across southern Lebanon to ensure that Lebanese children will get their legs blown off for decades to come.

He's like an angry little child stamping his feet and throwing a fit. The shrinks should be able to make something out of this – narcissistic rage or something equally nasty and medical-sounding. At the very least, we need to focus attention on this kind of material, rather than his arguments. GH

[1.8]

Actually, Western countries remind me of a boy I knew at school. He was a real, genuine bully... big... muscled... flat face... completely insecure. You know the sort? You had a bully at your school? Yes, yes... so you know.

Well, whenever someone stood up to him... after they had been tormented to the limits of their patience... even if they would hit him softly or slap him in the face with an open hand, he would respond by holding them on the ground and punching them with full force for ages... in the body... on the face. He would always leave them bloodied... bruised... sometimes with lost teeth. It was so completely ah, ah... disproportionate. We would all be so horrified to witness it... so terrified by its, its... its uncontrolled ferocity.

Thinking back, I can see now that it was a very pure example of your philosophy of deterrence... the approach your government seems determined to live up to. Always try to so terrify, so damage, and so humiliate your opponent that they will never be tempted to fight back again, even against the most outrageous injustices.

M: Mmm, this is an interesting perspective—

P: —Of course, this theory completely misunderstands human psychology, in my experience. The fact is, when someone does this to you... when they take away everything you hold most dear, especially your dignity... your sense of self-worth... you simply have to fight back, even when you know it will result in your own destruction. At least you will not be cowed into submission... at least you will die on your feet, not on your knees.

No, no, no, Michael, I am not doing this for revenge... or hatred. On the contrary, I would say that I am doing this for <u>love</u>. Does that surprise you? Well, it should not, as I know you went to kill people in Iraq because you loved your country... because you believed in the truth of your cause. I know you loved your comrades... the men who fought alongside you... and you loved your family and your people... the people you thought you were fighting to protect. You

were not there because of some kind of hatred
of Arabs...

There is a quotation from Che Guevara about this
which I like. He said, 'the true revolutionary is guided
by strong feelings of love'. I think—

M: —[inaudible]

P: Sorry? What did you say?

M: I said, didn't Che Guevara also say that hatred was a
key part of the struggle... that you needed relentless
hatred of the enemy to transform you into an effective,
cold killing machine?

P: So, you know Che, Michael. I am impressed. [...] Ohhf...
I think this statement is more about, ah... hatred of
injustice... hatred of oppression... at least, this is how
I see it. All I know is that I do this for the love of my
fellow human beings... for the love of justice. I do this
so my children... and my friends' children... and the
children of all those living in Palestine, and in Iraq,
and in Afghanistan, Libya... wherever... can breathe
the same free air you do... so they can be proud of who
they really are... so they can have the same chances
to succeed in this life as your two children have. I
actually just want some fairness... a level playing field,
as you call it... for you as well as me.

M: OK, OK. I can see what you're saying. Sure, everyone wants that... but not everyone goes out and slaughters civilians... no, please don't shake your head like that, Professor...

[2.3]

P: I suppose you might think it is ironic that I am actually undertaking this, ah... campaign of mine because I believe so much in your own, purported values, should we say. I actually take all this talk about... ah... about freedom and justice seriously... unlike most of your own, and I must say, my own, fellow citizens... with their flat-screen TVs, their Gameboys, their football, their endless pints in the pub... or, in my case, their sweet tea and water pipes! The truth is, I, I... I actually believe it when George Bush or Tony Blair says that it is our love of freedom... our commitment to justice... which defines us as civilised people. I hear that and I want to try and make it actually <u>true</u>. I do not want to be someone who is all talk, talk, talk, and but then never gets out of his comfortable chair. I want to make justice real... for the Palestinians... for the Iraqis... for the Afghans... the Chechens... the innocent men in Guantanamo... for all the people being crushed down by the actions of your government and the other governments who collude with them.

M: OK, yes, so you're right about some things, Professor.
Tony Blair and George Bush were somewhat two-faced
and rather unscrupulous. Typical politicians, if you
ask me! They talked a lot about justice, and freedom,
and democracy, and keeping the world safe from evil
terrorists... all the usual things politicians say... and
then they went out and did some very bad things.
Fine... it's undeniable. You can have that. But is that
really a reason to become a terrorist? Do you really
help to bring justice by murdering people? Are you
advancing democracy... or the well-being of the poor...
or a solution to the Palestinian issue... by coming to the
UK and blowing things up?

Again, I understand that he's trying to build rapport with P by agreeing with him – getting him on side and all that. But it's so undignified to be agreeing with a terrorist about the failings of a British leader. Do we really need to include this in the official public record? A short recording interruption? GH

[4.7]

P: Michael, what would make you turn to terrorism?
What could turn the tables... make you the terrorist
and, and... and me the counter-terrorist?

M: Nothing. I'm sure I could never do anything like that.

P: Nothing? Are you sure? Can you <u>really</u> be so certain?
Mmm... what if a foreign army... say the Egyptians, for
argument's sake... people with a different complexion...
a different language which your people could not

understand... a strange and different religion... came and occupied your neighbourhood with their army? What if they came and smashed down the front door to your house ███████████ in the middle of the night, frightening ██████████ ... your lovely wife... and then, ah... took you away with a hood and plastic handcuffs, and, and, and held you for a month without any legal representation... and they did not even tell your wife where they were holding you? And she had to try and find out where you were with people who would not speak to her in her own language, and who looked down on her with suspicion and disdain.

And what if they killed your seven-year-old daughter, little ████████████ with a phosphorous bomb... and you could watch the phosphor particles sinking deeper and deeper into her flesh, all the while you can hear her screaming... and if they bashed ████████████ with rifle butts, your teenage son, for throwing stones?

Looking back, this is so bloody obvious now. Why didn't the field commander intervene sooner – and what's the potential fallout? Could the wife sue the Agency for negligence? Is there a duty-of-care issue to be considered here? Check with Legal before release. Do we need another small recording interruption here?

GH

M: Wait! Wait! How the hell do you know—

P: —If they took away your job and made you submit to humiliating searches every day on the way to work... work which involved cleaning the toilets in a factory, even though you are a highly qualified and experienced professional? And what if they denied you any legal or political means to express your frustrations or get justice for the killing of your daughter? You could not even speak the language of their laws... and there was no one to speak on your behalf? And what if, in the end, this foreign army confiscated your house ██████████, just told you one day to leave and never come back... and you had to live in a refugee camp with just the clothes on your back... in a, a... a whole other country where the local people hated you, and, ah, resented your presence... with your terrified wife and your broken, damaged boy?

M: No! Wait! Go back to... how do you know about my family? Are you threatening them—

P: —What if you then had to live there for year upon year... with no end in sight... nothing but weekly food handouts from the UN? [...] Are you telling me that after all this happened to you and your family and a man came and whispered in your ear, 'Hey, you were once a soldier, were you not? Why don't you join us in driving these occupiers out? It is the right thing to do... you would be helping your people... you could really help us. And one day, you might get your house back... and your old job. You might get your old life back... your remaining son might have a chance of a proper life... a future. You might be able to visit the grave of

your daughter again and walk the streets of ███
███ , instead of living in a foreign land, surrounded by
hopelessness'—

M: —Professor!—

P: —are you telling me that you would say 'no' to them?
       Do you expect me to believe that you would insist
       on non-violent political struggle... some kind of
       political solution from the politicians? If you said that
       I would say you are a liar, my friend... to yourself if no
       one else—

M: —just stop a minute! How did you know █████
       continue with this████████████████████
       ████████████████████████

[recording interruption]

M: [inaudible] ███████████████████ died, you don't
       have to tell me, Professor! No, sir! ██████████
       ████████████████████████

P: ████████████████████████████████
       ████████████████████████

*Why is this still in here? Can't we get the break in the recording a little
cleaner? Someone might be able to work out what this refers to – and we
simply can't have that. On the other hand, I suppose it adds authenticity
to the electrical disturbances explanation – GH*

[6.9]

P: Ohhf, I am so tired... I slept so badly last night... and
        the air in here, it is foul, is it not? Like a mortuary...
        not even one window, this fluorescent light... and it is
        starting to flicker...

        Can I tell you something? The first time I saw a
        corpse in Iraq... a real dead person... it was a kind of
        revelation. It made a very strong impression on me.
        It confirmed to me the rightness of my decision. After
        that, I was really sure of why I was there...

        It was the body of a man... not a boy, you understand,
        but a full-grown man... a man who must have had a
        family... friends... colleagues... neighbours. And this
        body... this corpse... was just lying by the side of the
        road in a ditch... like a stray dog run over by a car...
        like roadkill. It was kind of twisted, curled up... like the
        man, whoever he was, had tried to curl himself into
        a little ball but then he'd died. Or maybe he had just
        taken a bullet in his guts, you know... some shrapnel
        from a shell... and crawled in there to die.

        The flesh on his limbs, it was all dried out. It was
        the same colour as the dust it was lying in. All his,
        ah, ah, ah... teeth were exposed... and his mouth was
        wide open... pulled back by the skin contracting as it
        dried, I guess. His clothes were in tatters... like rags.

That body must have been there for several weeks or
more for it to be in that condition... like old leather
left out in the elements. I can still picture it... every
detail. It is like yesterday to me... I cannot forget that
horrible, dried-out face... that curled-up corpse of a
man.

I was shocked because this was a pretty major road...
people walked past all the time on the way to the
town... military patrols drove past every other day...
cars... bicycles... ambulances. What I am trying to say...
how could so much traffic go by and no one saw the
body... or if they did, no one cared to give it a burial...
find out who it was... contact the man's relatives? How
could a human being just remain unburied like that?
I mean, how could someone... a person! [...] be that
insignificant... that unimportant?

My question is this. Could this ever happen in a
Western country, do you think? Of course, I have heard
those stories of old people dying in their homes and
not being found for weeks. But this was on the side of a
major road... *Tshofo youm!*[15]

[banging]

---

[15] Trans. 'May you (pl.) witness a similar day.' Note: Arabic Egyptian
colloquialism.

Rabbenah yekhreb boyotko, ya-wlad el...[16]

It was at that moment... as I was staring down at that dried-out husk of a human being lying in a pile of rags... that I completely understood the, ah, ah... moral hierarchy of the world we live in. It was like a ray of light that came down... like Saint Paul on the road to Damascus... I suddenly understood that for all the pontificating... all the endless verbiage about human rights... and equality... and democracy... and how much we value human life... the fact is that some lives are truly worth much less than others... that a man walking down a road in Iraq is worth nothing... even less than nothing... just roadkill... just collateral damage... compared to someone in New York or London or Madrid or Oslo.

I realised that this man would remain forever unknown. He would never be mourned. His name would never be read out at an official ceremony... or, or, or... be etched into a public monument. There would be no commemorative plaque for this man. Unlike those people who died on 9/11 or 7/7, his story would never be recounted... he would just vanish into the sands of history... an unknown victim of Western values!

---

[16] Trans. 'May God ruin your (pl.) homes, you sons of...' Note: Arabic Egyptian colloquialisms.

As I collected his body and took it to the morgue, I knew that it was my duty... my calling... to try and change the twisted moral hierarchy of this world... this absolute outrage in which some lives can be tossed aside, unnamed and unacknowledged... forgotten. I knew I had to deploy my whole being... all my energies... to turning this world that you had made on its head.

I knew then that I had to do something... anything... which would make your government treat the lives of others with some fucking goddam respect! To make you consider them as a little bit more than just roadkill, or, or... or collateral damage! I mean, imagine if a group like mine killed someone in the UK and they lay unburied by the side of the road for weeks... and then I sent a letter to the newspaper and dismissed him as just some unfortunate collateral damage. Can you imagine the outrage this would cause? How would that man's relatives feel, do you think? How would you feel, Michael, if I killed one of your comrades ██████████████████████ and left his body to rot by the side of the road and then said, 'oh, you are talking about a little bit of collateral damage'?

Do you understand me, Michael? Do you hear what I am saying? I had to do something that would make you remember the names of the people you murdered! At the very least, you should have the decency to know

the names of your victims! *Deh a'al Haga!*[17] [...] You
could say that I am the voice of all the unremembered
dead of your imperial wars. [...] Or, as one of those
Russian writers put it... I forget who... I feel that it
is my duty to speak on behalf of those who lie in the
earth... I can tell you, the silent cries of the dead for
some kind of justice, they, ah... help me to fulfil my
duty... they give me the strength I need to keep going—

M: —not to blow your own trumpet... [mumbled].

P: What? What did you say?

M: Well, I'm just saying, Professor... it seems to me like
you've maybe got a slightly inflated view of your
own importance, don't you think? A bit of a martyr
complex? You, leading the oppressed of the world to
freedom?

[2.3]

P: Ha! A martyr complex... I suppose you could be
right, Michael. You have to have some belief in your
historical role to make this sacrifice. No one does it for
peanuts. The point is... I am trying to fight back. Your
very own Shakespeare said it well... 'if we bleed...'... no,
no, wait... How does it go? [...] Oh, yes... 'If you prick us

---

[17] Trans. 'That's the least to do.' Note: Arabic Egyptian colloquialism.

do we not bleed? If you poison us, do we not die? And if you wrong us, do we not revenge? If we are like you in the rest, we will resemble you in that...' [inaudible]... What is it? [...] Oh, I remember... 'The villainy you—

M: —'teach me I will execute, and it shall go hard, but I will better the instruction'—

P: —Yes, yes! You have it! That is it... [inaudible] ██████

██████████████████████████   .

[3.9]

M: Professor, you mentioned my family. How did you come by that information? Are they... at risk?

P: No, they are not at risk, Michael. This is between you and me.

M: But you know their names... where they live—

P: —Do not worry, Michael. They will not be harmed...

[recording interruption]

[1.2]

M: You mightn't believe me, Professor, but as I have said before, I really get it. It was a mistake to go into Iraq.

On a personal level, I never believed those claims about Saddam's WMDs, and I suspected it'd be a complete balls-up. And I certainly didn't believe we should just follow along like America's lapdog. But the question I have to ask is... is this the right way to respond? Why employ extreme violence? Aren't you just making it worse, adding further violence to all the violence that already exists? Doesn't that make you the same as those you condemn? Doesn't it bring you down to their level? I mean, how are you any different from Bush and Blair if you're willing to do the same kind of things you condemn them for?

P: Ohhf... I, ah... I have heard this question many times before... from my wife, ███████, among others. I have even asked it of myself in my many moments of doubt...

I presume our friends in Egypt have picked up the wife and put her through the appropriate paces? Check the resulting intel.
There may be something we can use to our advantage when this all goes public. GH

M: And what did you tell her... your wife? What do you tell yourself?

P: I told her that it would be a wonderful thing if the West decided to lay down all its weapons... if the Israelis, the Americans, the Russians, the Chinese... and the British... melted down all their tanks and aircraft carriers and made them into ploughs and computers and heart machines instead. I told her that if writing a letter or going on a demonstration made a real difference, I would do it. I also told her that if these things made a real difference, the world's governments would immediately outlaw them! Ha!

[2.3]

You might not believe it, but I used to believe so strongly in non-violent political activity. Really. I went on demonstrations... signed petitions... voted... wrote letters to the newspaper... shouted slogans. I joined political groups at university... community groups... NGOs... protestors... all kinds of things! At the time, I believed that politics could be a force for change... a way to really improve society. But you know what all that non-violent political activity achieved? Nothing... absolutely nothing...

M: It's worked now, though, hasn't it? Mubarak is gone in your own country. Elections are on the way. The Arab Spring... Tunisia, Morocco... all that?

P: Maybe you are right, Michael. We will see. I wonder if anything will really change in the long run. In my own country... Egypt... it seems like the protestors have simply overthrown one part of the military so another can take its place. The faces have changed, but the power is the same... and the protestors are still being beaten.

The point I am making... is that at the time
when I was protesting, not one thing changed
in my country, and all it got me personally was
insults... beatings... arrests... my name on a
blacklist... boycotts of my classes... my family
harassed... so much unwelcome attention from
the authorities. I am guessing that this is probably
how you know so much about me... UK-Egyptian
intelligence cooperation... ███████████████
███████████████████████████████ Certainly, those
SSI bastards know all about me from the days when
I was a political activist... when I was struggling
to bring some small semblance of democracy and
accountability to my country.

M: So was that where you first got your training... the
Egyptian opposition?

P: No, no, no... [inaudible] [...] What I am saying is... when
a government responds with repression and violence
to any and all demands for change... to peaceful
measures for political reform... or when it does not
respond at all... when it is completely indifferent...
like when, ah, ah, ah... two million ordinary people
marched through London and they ignored all of it and
attacked Iraq anyway—

M: —But didn't your lot kill some of these very same
people, the very ones who agreed with you?

P: What? What are you talking about?

M: I'm just saying that when terrorists blow up people
       on the Underground, some of the people you're killing
       actually agree with you... they support your cause!
       How the hell can you justify killing people who are on
       your side?

P: Well, I can see your point, but it was not me... we... my
       group... never targeted civilians in this way. Besides,
       I could ask the same thing about all your country's
       bombings and invasions! Out of all the hundreds of
       thousands of civilians killed by your bombs, how many
       do you think were actually on your side... people who
       welcomed you when you first invaded?

M: But we didn't deliberately try to kill them, Professor.

P: Ohhf! That is just semantics, Michael—

M: —No, it's not—

P: —the point I am simply trying to make is simply that
       after protesting, and demonstrating, and making
       arguments... what are you left with? When everything
       you do is met with indifference? Direct action...
       violence... force... revolution. That is it! That is all that
       is left! Violence is the last option remaining when non-
       violent methods fail... when you have tried everything

within the law. The fact is... when, ah, democracy
fails... or, or, or... when it is not even an option, like
in my own country... then you have to force change
through the exertion of direct power. You simply
cannot trust politicians to make the right choice... it is
not in their interests... they will only do the right thing
when they are forced.

I can see you agree a little bit... I think you know
what I am saying... It saddens me, but after all I have
seen and learned these past years, I have to confess
that I have completely lost faith in politics... look at
the issue of climate change. Are the politicians going
to make the necessary changes to avoid disaster on
their own... will they really challenge the power of
the energy companies head on... after all, those oil
lobbyists take them to expensive dinners and fund
their election campaigns? Will politicians vote to spend
the hundreds of billions of dollars needed to change
the entire infrastructure of the nation so electric
cars can charge anywhere and all the trains run on
clean electricity? Will politicians take money from
business or the military to invest in green research?
Will they fund green research at the same level as
weapons research... or, or, or... force industry to be
carbon neutral if it means losing jobs in the short
term? You are a dreamer if you think so. The only time
politicians... governments... will make the right choices
are when they feel forced to... when they are backed

into a corner and they realise that they have no other option. They will only do the right thing when they are afraid not to! That is the law of politics today, my friend.

M: You could be right on that, Professor. But still...

[2.3]

P: I told my wife, and I am telling you... non-violent, political struggle is exactly what your government would like us to do... and what the Israelis would like the Palestinians to do... what the Russians would like the Chechens to do... and the Indians the Kashmiris... the Chinese the Tibetans... the Sri Lankans the Tamils... the British the Irish. What every government wants its own people to do... lie down like lambs! Become sheep! Stop resisting! Stop fighting back! Watch TV... read a celebrity magazine... go on Facebook... click a 'like' button... stop being citizens!

He's actually wrong about this – it's actually a lot easier to crack down hard when they're violent. And the public accepts stronger measures against violent thugs than peaceful protestors – not that we could ever make such an argument in public!

I know you know this from your own personal experience... it is so much easier to occupy a country if the people do not fight back... to take their land if they will only write letters and shout slogans... to extract their oil and minerals if they will only engage in protracted negotiations. Seriously, did the first intifada stop the Israelis from building their settlements on the West Bank? Did the millions who marched against the Iraq war stop the invasion? Did the monks chanting their prayers in Tibet stop the Chinese from massacring them? Did the protestors in Syria stop the tanks from running over their bodies?

I told my wife that non-violence does not always work... especially when you are facing an enemy who will not respond to reason... who will listen but then do nothing... an enemy who pretends to respect freedom and justice, but who in reality refuses to compromise unless they are pushed... unless they are forced by reason of arms!

Besides, there are other reasons to use violence, you know... like when a people have been crushed and beaten down, until they themselves come to believe that they deserve their suffering... until they accept that they must be inferior to their masters... that they cannot make their own destiny. You know, if a man in this condition acts... if he takes his own life in his own hands and makes a choice... or forces a choice on his enemy... he becomes a true man again. He is empowered! He changes history... and he finds a reason for his life... or more importantly, for his death—

M: —*Beyadi la beydi 'Amr*[18]—

P: Yes, yes! Exactly, Michael! You have it!

M: What I mean is, you don't have to quote Fanon at
       me, Professor. We're not in the British Empire any
       more, and you're not the leader of the anti-colonial
       movement!

P: I am very impressed... you know Arabic history, as
       well as Fanon. But then again, I suppose it is not
       surprising that a counter-terrorism officer would
       study Fanon... and Che. I expect you also read Mao...
       Marighela? [...] The point is... did he not speak the
       truth? Would Britain have left Palestine if the Jews
       had not killed so many of them in their terrorist
       campaign? Would the people in the colonies of Africa
       or Malaya have risen up to throw out their oppressors
       without using revolutionary violence? I think you are
       underestimating the power inherent to the simple act
       of fighting back... resisting... how it can empower a
       man... make him the master of his own destiny, even
       just for a brief moment... how someone who is beaten
       down can become a whole person again by standing
       up for himself. I think you also underestimate the
       importance of vengeance... although after the revenge

---

[18] Trans. 'In my own hand, not by [an enemy called] 'Amr.' Note: Classical
     Arabic proverb which means 'I control my own destiny'.

which America has made on the Middle East since 9/11, maybe not, huh?

[1.9]

M: Do you feel like a man when you kill, Professor? [...] In your personal experience, is it really cathartic, would you say?

P: Michael, do you really want to ask <u>me</u> how I felt killing someone? [...] You are the one who refuses to talk about that. ████████████████████

[3.8]

Michael, let me ask you another question. [...] If I was not a, a, a... lowly economics professor formerly of Cairo University sitting here in front of you, but was just a regular citizen and it was 1939? We are in Germany and the Nazis are killing so many people already... mental patients, children with deformities, Communists, gypsies, Jews, homosexuals... anyone who speaks against them. Would you really ask me the same question? 'Why do you use violence against Hitler? Why fight fire with fire, adding to Hitler's violence?'—

M: —I don't think you can compare—

P: —No, no... wait... seriously... I mean, would you
really suggest that I use non-violent political means
to oppose him instead? That I write a petition, or, or...
hold a demonstration? Would you really ask this? I
mean, yes, yes, yes... I know what you are going to
say. I know that there are few, if any, regimes today as
bad as the Nazis... and that democracies like Britain
cannot be compared. But the question relates to
the possibility that sometimes non-violent political
struggle is not enough... that in some situations it will
simply fail.

Besides, you do not really take your own advice,
do you? Your government uses this very argument
all the time... practically whenever they go to war.
'Non-violent methods will not work in such-and-such
a case,' they say. Saddam... Gadhafi... Milosevic...
Noriega... the Taliban... Ho Chi Minh... the Soviets...
whoever it is we are fighting this week. 'The evil we
are facing today is the same as Hitler and the Nazis.
We cannot negotiate with them. It will only appease
them!' Et cetera, et cetera.

The fact is that you use violence all the time... and you
claim the right to use it whenever you feel like it. But
what gives Western nations the right to use violence
whenever they decide they want to... and then to ask
me why I choose to use it... as if the whole world should
just lay down... should become like sheep... while you

can do whatever you like? As if it is only everyone else who must use non-violent methods?

My question is... where do you get this right from? Who gave it to you? Did I agree that you should invade Kuwait to throw out Saddam... or bomb Milosevic... or smash Afghanistan to find Osama? Did I vote somewhere that you should attack Iraq for the second time to find those non-existent weapons of mass destruction which the UN inspectors had already said were not there? And I am not even going to talk about Libya... the Philippines... Korea... Vietnam... Cambodia... the Suez... Lebanon... Grenada... Panama... Colombia... and so on, and so on...

Was there an election? I missed it? I mean... [inaudible]... ohhf... No! Do not shake your head like that... it is a real point! Some... [inaudible]... The fact is... I have only scratched the surface of all the examples of when you and your, ah, ah, ah... <u>enlightened</u> Western countries have used violence to settle your disputes. I know my history, Michael. What about the Falklands, if I might ask—

In the light of current tensions with the Argies over the Falklands, would it perhaps be prudent to clip this section a little? As always, your input would be most welcome.

GH

M: —Oh, well, now you're—

P: —Argentina puts some soldiers on a few barren rocks near the South Pole... islands which Britain took from them by force not so long ago, I might add—

M: —That's a little bit of a—

P: —and rather than negotiate... rather than have a
        non-violent dialogue about it... or go to the ICJ... write
        a petition... your government's first resort is to use
        violence... to start a war. Talk about extreme violence!
        You are willing to kill hundreds of your own men...
        and even more of theirs... all those young conscripts...
        who did not even want to be there! And for what...
        national pride... honour... a symbol of your imperial
        possessions? It certainly was not for anything really
        tangible or so important it was worth all those lives.
        Your government could have given every person on
        the Falkland Islands a million pounds to relocate to the
        south of France and it would have cost less than the
        war... and no one would have had to die!

M: Actually, they've found oil there recently—

P: —Oh, I know, I know. This is why they will never give
        them up now... but they did not know that then. Back
        then, they were willing to go to war over some wind-
        blown rocks and a few sheep! My point is... why is it
        that you are allowed to settle your conflicts with war
        whenever you like... with intervention... and yet you
        tell me I should not use the same violence? A few
        sorties by the air force... some night bombing with
        your Stealth jets from forty thousand feet... a little
        no-fly zone here and there... or maybe just a quietly

engineered coup, like Allende in Chile... or Iran? An assassination raid... some drone attacks on a village? [...]

M: Mmm... I don't think you—

P: —Hey, you know that the CIA-assisted coup against the democratically elected Allende in Chile took place on September 11, don't you? That violent little intervention later led to more than thirty thousand innocent deaths... thousands tortured and abused... and one of the nastier regimes of the twentieth century. That was Chile's 9/11... a special gift from the American government.

[scraping sounds]

But when people like me choose to fight back against real oppression... *A'ouzo be-llah!*[19] Invasion of our lands... thousands tortured... people disappeared... Western-trained death squads... pregnant women shot at checkpoints for not understanding English. Then, then, you have the impudence... the gall... to ask why must we be so violent... why we are so bloodthirsty... why can't we try and settle our grievances peacefully... don't we know that violence never solves anything? [laughter]... My God! Sometimes, I cannot even take

---

[19] Trans. 'God forbid.' Note: Arabic Egyptian colloquialism.

it in how absurd it is! How perverse it is for you to be asking me why <u>we</u> are so violent! It is like a lion asking the lamb in its jaws why it is fighting so violently to break free! 'Look out there, lamb! You might chip one of my teeth!' I mean—

M: —Wait! Can you sit back down, Professor? Or stay over there... you're making me nervous agai—

P: —OK, OK. I will sit... even though this seat is putting splinters in my ass! [scraping sounds] What I am saying is... it is as if... I mean, ah... what exactly has your society been doing for the last five hundred years... except killing millions? It is as if you are not even living in the same world as me... as if you have a different history to everyone else! As if you did not kill literally millions of ordinary people in Africa... in India... in Indochina... in Iraq... or, or, or transport millions of human beings around the world in ships during the slave trade, throwing them overboard to drown if they showed signs of illness or resisted in any form... as if all these things never actually happened! [...] But perhaps you do not know your own history—

M: Oh, I know my history, I can assure you. As I said, we weren't the only slave traders—

P: —yes, yes... but maybe they teach you a <u>different</u> history in school... I bet you do not learn the story about how your government caused the deaths of tens of millions of peasants in India by deliberately causing famines... or, or, or at the very least, refusing to take the necessary action to prevent them... or Ireland, where your government's actions caused millions to starve to death. Maybe you do know that particular story because of your heritage... You are of Irish origin, are you not?

M: Yes—

P: —And I expect you are not told about how your colonial officials would go out in Africa and burn entire villages down, killing old men... women... children... just so they could warn other villagers to send their young men to work in the mines or on the plantation... to pay their taxes on time. What about the, the, the, ah... West Indies? Did you learn in school about how the colonial officials would hang slaves for minor offences like talking back, or, or... or burn them alive? How they would cut off their lips... eyelids... their genitals! [...] as punishment? Or tie them in sacks and throw them into the sea... flay the skin off their bodies? I mean, they did this to thousands of people... people just like you and me... just like your own family... your young children...

And they kept a record of it! Can you believe it?
They wrote it all down... lists of all the creative
punishments. You can see the documents in the British
Library! And all so the people of Britain could have
their morning cup of coffee and sugar to go in it! Do
you learn about these things in your history of the
great British Empire?

*And what about all the good the British Empire did? The roads, railways, education,
development, parliamentary democracy, English, cricket! P offers a very one-sided view
of history which we must be prepared to contest in the most rigorous terms.* GH

M: Mmm... [inaudible]

P: I am also guessing you do not learn the story of all
those lovely British massacres... like the, the, the...
ah, Amritsar massacre in India where British troops
opened fire on women and children, killing hundreds
of them... or Batang Kali where your troops massacred
plantation workers in Malaya. I bet you were never
required to memorise the facts about how millions
of workers were transported from India to South
Africa... the Pacific Islands... other places... to work
in plantations... all those 'coolies'. I bet your average
British schoolboy knows nothing about how British
troops kept a million Kikuyu in camps in Kenya...
torturing thousands to death... gang-raping the
women... tearing off the testicles of suspected Mau
Mau... holding them upside down and ramming sand
into their rectums... My God, you people were fucking
savages, weren't you?

And what about the German attempt before the
First World War to completely wipe out an entire
people in Botswana to clear the land for settlers... do
you teach that in your schools? And I would happily
bet that your schoolchildren are not taught about
British concentration camps... the first recorded
concentration camps. Your country invented them,
my friend, not the Germans, in South Africa, and then
again secretly after the Second World War for holding
Communists.

Are you telling me that you learn... you are taught...
about the history of Western intervention in other
countries... about how the United States has tried
to overthrow more than fifty governments... fifty!
[...] many of them following democratic elections
where they did not approve of the winners? And
how it has bombed more than thirty countries in
the decades since the Second World War? How, how,
how, ah... America has tried to assassinate more than
fifty foreign leaders... and tried to suppress popular
movements in at least twenty countries. Are these
facts widely known? Do you teach your students about
how General Suharto in Indonesia... the tyrant so loved
by Margaret Thatcher... killed half a million people
suspected of being Communists... and how the CIA
provided Suharto with detailed lists of those it wanted
eliminated?

This is your history, Michael. All this killing and
maiming of your fellow human beings is what you
have been doing for hundreds of years... even if <u>you</u>
have forgotten it... even if your country has no real
memory of all these misdeeds... even if your scholars
and politicians just talk instead about cricket...
parliamentary democracy... railways... the English
language... the ethical foreign policy. Ha! What a
fucking joke! [...] Even if Tony Blair... *el behema*[20]...
and those stuck-up Cambridge professors say they are
<u>proud</u> of the British Empire.

The fact is... you act today as if your, ah... record
is completely clean and you can just decide... oh,
this year... we, ah, do not like Libya... or Syria... or
North Korea... or whoever... so we are going to kill
tens of thousands of their citizens in a little bombing
campaign! 'And don't worry people of the world, we
can make good decisions because it is not as if we
have ever done anything bad before! Don't worry,
we are doing the right thing this time! It will work
out, you will see! No, ha, ha... we do not have a
history of violently devastating other countries!
We did not ruin Iraq just a few years ago... the same
way that we ruined countless other countries in Africa
and Asia!'

---

[20] Trans. 'Mindless, no-thinking animal.' Note: Arabic Egyptian colloquialism.

[4.1]

[scraping sound]

> Can you not see now why your question is an insult...
> why your words mean nothing to me? Can you not see
> why a man might choose to act against you... why he
> might try to resist you with force? I tell you, you might
> have forgotten your history, but we have not... we
> remember everything. We live our history, Michael...
> we do not suppress it.

M: Professor, I get what you're saying, but you're talking
     about things that happened so long ago... ancient
     history... the really distant past. Why do you insist on
     living in the past? Haven't we improved as a world...
     advanced somewhat from before? Don't we go through
     the United Nations today... NATO, the EU? It's not like
     we're in the days of the British Empire and we're just
     running around all over the place playing God, killing
     natives, as you maintain.

     Besides, I don't really see the connection to what
     you're doing today? How can you justify blowing up
     innocent people, all this horrible killing, by referring
     back to things which happened hundreds of years
     ago? What would be the point of that? Isn't life
     about making progress, finding better ways to solve
     disputes... manage difficulties? Don't you want to live

in the present... or do you think everything was better in the past, when the Ottoman Empire ruled the Middle East, perhaps... or maybe under the ancient pharaohs?

P: How can you say that... ancient history? You British live surrounded by history, as all Western countries do. The public rituals of your people are all impregnated with history... like, like... ah, when your royals marry... or, or, or when the Queen opens Parliament... when everyone wears red poppies in their lapels... all those statues in every street of every town and village... all those flags and plaques in every single church. History is all around and you want me to just forget it? You, in particular, given your personal ancestry... you know better than anyone what history is. I bet you have been to a rugby match at Croke Park... maybe a Six Nations match, I expect? Did you sit in the Hogan stand? Do you know what the name means? Do you have some memory of what happened there? [...] You know you do.

M: Jesus fucking Christ, Professor! How do you know about—

[banging]

This is disturbing when you see it in black and white – the extent of P's knowledge of M. I hope the instructors at the Farm have noted the appropriate lessons and instigated counter-measures. GH

P: —Well, I remember too. I remember Suez and I remember 1967... I remember Mai Lai and the bombing of Cambodia. [...] And I remember the Israelis

shooting a little boy... and Bloody Sunday... and
Kosovo... and British soldiers beating Iraqi youths...
and Abu Ghraib... Guantanamo... Fallujah... the death
of Dilwar. I remember the shooting of Jean Charles de
Menezes, the Brazilian electrician. Your colleagues
shot him eight times in the head from close range. I
still cannot believe it. And he was innocent...

M: That was a tragic accident—

P: —the point is that you cannot escape this history... and
you cannot tell me to forget it... to, to, to just forgive
you once more and trust you that this particular war...
today's bombing campaign... or the next one or the
one after that... is justified and will turn out for the
best. Your violent history, my friend, precludes such
generosity. You have proved what you are really like
too many times for anyone to trust you again. You are
a violent bully through and through, and I am so sick
of it! Millions are sick of it!

[4.7]

KIFAYA! Kifaya kidb![21] Somebody has to stand up
to the bully... someone has to say, 'No! Stop!'
Somebody has to fight back... someone has to stop
<u>appeasing</u> you—

---

[21] Trans. 'ENOUGH! Enough lying!' Note: Arabic Egyptian colloquialism.

[banging]

M: —And that's you, is it? You're going to stop the bully?

P: Exactly! Yes... that is me. Why not? You could say that
I follow in the footsteps of the rebelling slave... the
renegade native... the revolutionary on the street. My
forebears... my, my, my revolutionary ancestors... are
the, ah... slaves on the Amistad, violently taking back
the ship which was transporting them into slavery...
the plantation slaves revolting in Haiti against their
owners to win their freedom... the, the, the... ah,
Zulus charging Boer cannons in South Africa... the
Maori renegades harassing the colonial militia in the
rainforests of New Zealand... Ho Chi Minh fighting
the French in Indochina... Che fighting imperialism
in Latin America... Arafat fighting Israeli colonialism
in Palestine. [...] So many who came before me... all
fighting for the right to be free... for the right to have
a little human dignity and equality. [...] This is my
confession... my faith.

And it is not only me... others too. You are going
to find out that there are a lot more of us than just
me... because you cannot keep grinding your boot in
someone's face forever... even if you put a British flag
on the sole of the boot! You cannot beat someone like a
dog every day and they will not get angry. Eventually,
they will stand up and fight back. That day has come,

my friend... that is what I am doing. I am fighting back against you.

M: With the greatest respect, these still sound a lot like excuses to me, Professor. I can understand that you might go out and join the insurgents, as you did in Iraq and Afghanistan... ███████████████████████ ████████████████████████ that you might feel you needed to fight against the invasion, which was, I concede, a poor decision. It may even have been strictly illegal under international law—

P: —the same international law you keep insisting other countries should follow, but then you are happy to ignore with your invasions and renditions—

M: —maybe you do have the right to fight against an invader, especially if it's a fair fight between soldiers on the battlefield... and if you follow the accepted rules of war. But you're a terrorist, Professor! You deliberately attack and murder innocent civilians, which is wrong. And what's more, you're trying to do it here in my country! Don't I have the right... the duty... to protect my citizens, just as you say you're fighting for yours?

[4.7]

P: Are you an innocent civilian, Michael? What exactly is your crime? Tell me...

Is this more evidence of P's psychopathic sadism – taunting M this way? Can we use it to discredit his political statements? Make sure the shrinks come up with something we can use. GH

[1.9]

Actually, I have two questions for you. First...
what about all the civilians who died in Iraq... in
Afghanistan? Were they not also innocent?

M: Oh, for God's sake! You know that's not the same
thing! We did not set out to deliberately kill civilians.
In fact, we take all necessary precautions to try and
avoid killing civilians. We try to protect civilians...
unlike terrorists like you. Are you aware that we
employ lawyers to check our targets to make sure
that all measures are taken to ensure that civilians
are protected and no operation breaks the laws of
war? To make sure we're not endangering civilian
lives? [...] I've seen missions cancelled because they
were worried that they'd result in civilian deaths...
███
█████████████████████████████████████ and then
we lost some of our boys in attacks as a result! It's
completely different.

P: This is a very nice argument, Michael. You do not
intend to kill civilians... and yet it seems your
intentions are betrayed by your actions, because you
consistently kill so many civilians! You did not intend
to, but somehow you managed to kill nearly one million
civilians in Iraq.

M: You're deliberately exaggerating, Professor. It was not a million—

P: —a million... half a million... a hundred thousand! What difference does it make when you are talking about so many lives? Your country went mad when fifty people were killed in London! Imagine if it was ten thousand! A hundred thousand! *Bas enta mosh 'awiz tefham. Ba'olloh toar be'olly eHlebouh!*[22] [...]

My point is... how is it possible that you did not <u>intend</u> to kill any civilians, but you still managed to kill a hundred thousand... or six hundred thousand... a million? I mean... are you stupid, is that it? Do you not know... does it not occur to you... that invading a country... dropping bombs on their cities... you do not expect anyone will actually die from this? [...] Or is it that your weapons are not as accurate and discriminating as you believe? Or maybe you are just not very good at fighting wars... maybe you are not the best military force in the world like you always think you are. Is that it?

If we're asked, I think we'll simply have to keep stressing the accuracy of modern weapons and the comparatively low level of collateral damage compared to previous wars. There's not much else to say, really. Don't you agree? GH

---

[22] Trans. 'But you [deliberately] don't want to understand. I tell him it's a bull, he tells me to milk it!' Note: Arabic Egyptian colloquialism.

Actually, I believe that if a man throws a grenade in a crowded market, he cannot turn around and say... 'I did not intend to hurt anyone!' This is ridiculous! And if a man shoots a, a, a... ah, machine gun in a house full of people, he knows some of them will die. It is the same with war... if you attack in this way... if you use these weapons... you know it will kill many civilians... as it has done every single time before for the last thousand years!

This is why I simply do not believe it when you say you are different and you do not want to kill all those innocent civilians. If you already <u>know</u> for a fact that it will happen, then you <u>accept</u> it will happen. If you accept it will happen and go ahead and do it, then how is that different from intending it to happen... really? Can you explain this difference to me... because from a moral point of view, it does not seem that great? I mean... if you are so concerned about limiting civilian casualties in your wars, why do your bombing campaigns target civilians so often?

M: What are you talking about?

P: Well, OK... let us examine it. In Germany and Japan, Allied bombers would drop tons of explosive on civilian areas, sometimes killing hundreds of thousands in a single night—

M: —Oh well, the Second World War was a completely different time, a different context entirely—

P: —and did NATO not target electricity plants... war treatment plants... television stations... bridges... in Kosovo... Libya? I heard your air force say they had run out of targets in Afghanistan...

In the public interest? Questions in the House about NATO targeting strategies? Suggest another brief recording interruption to avoid difficulties. GH

[1.9]

And if the West is so concerned about civilian casualties, why do they not count them?

M: What do you mean?

P: Why do Western military forces not keep an official record of all the civilians who have died in Iraq and Afghanistan as a result of the occupation? Why did the Americans ban their own officials from counting the Iraqi dead?

As above – do we really need questions about why we don't count civilian casualties in Overseas Ops? I'm sure that Legal can come up with a credible-sounding legal opinion, but it would be easier not to have to deal with it at all.
     I suggest a short file interruption to avoid potential difficulties. GH

M: [inaudible]... say.

P: Is it perhaps because they do not want it known how many civilians have actually been killed... because they know it will contradict all their statements about how few civilians have died? As I understand it... it is, ah... part of the laws of war that the occupying power is responsible for the civilians under its control. For most of the last century, records were kept of the civilian deaths during an occupation. It was only in Iraq... well... first Afghanistan after 9/11... when so many were being killed that they stopped counting and said they would no longer keep a record. ███████████████████████ ██████████████████████████████████████ ██████████████████████████████████ They would leave it to the Iraq Ministry of Health... or the Afghan Ministry of Health. Ha! What a joke! Since then, they have spent so much time trying to deny how many have died... but not always successfully, hey? All those medical studies cannot be wrong, can they? Even if we look at the most conservative counts, over a hundred thousand civilians have been killed in Iraq. That is more than all the, the... those killed by terrorists put together for the last one hundred years!

Can I tell you something? When I hear Western leaders saying that the civilian casualties of their wars are, are... are lower than in any other war in the past, I cannot help but think that it sounds a lot like a Nazi concentration camp commander defending himself by saying that he is doing a good job because he has the lowest death rate among his prisoners—

M: —Don't be ridiculous—

P: —The truth is, Michael... all your talk about the laws of war... and not targeting innocent civilians... and taking care to avoid civilian casualties... well... it all looks very hypocritical and suspicious when you look at the real numbers of those killed. To be frank, you are deceiving yourself if you think these arguments convince anyone any more. The dead do not believe you... I believe their silent voices accuse you from the cold, hard ground in which they sleep.

[2.3]

I, ah... I know that you know, because you have been trying to catch me for a long time, [but] some of my group's operations in Iraq, and later in Afghanistan, killed innocent civilians. But we never intended it, either. We always tried to only kill the coalition forces or those mercenaries... the security contractors with the dark sunglasses. But you know... we had, ah... very primitive devices... not like your high-tech, laser-guided weapons. We had to improvise... always... with what was at hand. Sometimes we used timers, sometimes primitive sensors. Using a cellphone was the best, because then we could wait until a patrol

was close by the place where the bomb was. The point
is... we did not <u>intend</u> to kill civilians, as you say... but
sometimes the people would be in the wrong place
at the wrong time. This was war. I have heard you
and your leaders call it 'collateral damage'. But... you
know... we... my group... we killed far fewer civilians
than you did.

Have you seen what a five-hundred-pound bomb
can do in a city neighbourhood? I know you have.
[...] We never dropped a bomb like that... much less
ten or twenty of them in one go! No, no... we tried
to only attack soldiers... or, or, or, ah, politicians...
mercenaries... people who were armed... not like some
of the groups we sometimes fought with, of course. I
always believed they were wrong to do that, but they
did not listen to us. They argued that sometimes killing
civilians could be justified... especially if it hastened
the end of the war. They believed that killing a small
number of civilians—

M: —A few? They murdered <u>hundreds</u> every month!

P: I know, I know... it was a disaster... a real crime. But
        they argued that if it led to a state of chaos... of making
        the country ungovernable... then this would hasten
        the end of the occupation and shorten the war. They
        thought that in the long run, this might actually save
        more lives than if the war dragged on for many years...

or if the occupation continued without end. It was a similar logic, I believe, to the bombings in Madrid and London... kill a number of civilians in those countries to save even more civilians in the countries under occupation.

Actually, this is the same kind of moral logic the Americans used to justify the use of torture... commit an act of evil against one person in order to prevent a greater evil against many others. In fact, I believe it is the same logic behind all of your wars... the sacrifice of a little 'collateral damage' for the greater good of whatever this week's cause is... overthrowing Saddam... establishing democracy... capturing a narco-criminal like Noriega... saving some civilians by killing others... whatever.

The truth is... I found it hard to argue against, to convince them otherwise. I can only say that my group... then as now... chose only to target those who were involved directly in the fighting somehow... like the soldiers who were fighting... the armed mercenaries... the militias... the politicians who gave the orders. You could say, actually, that I am trying to follow your own Western 'just war' theory, as it is called. It is more difficult these days to decide who is really a civilian or a non-combatant... what with armed settlers in Israel shooting and torturing peasants... or people who work in the arms industry... military contractors... private security. [...] But like you and your lawyers, we always would discuss carefully who is a legitimate target and then try and ensure that civilian casualties were minimised.

The question is, Michael... if I limit my attacks to your military and security personnel... to the politicians who give the orders... the armed response units... the ones who shot that Brazilian in the Tube... or the workers who make the bombs... does that still make me a terrorist? Is my struggle still illegitimate in your eyes? After all, these are the rules of war that you always insist on. If I fight by your own rules of killing, will you still consider me a terrorist?

I presume GCHQ has had this intel by now and all UK-based armed personnel are on heightened state of alert? It's too late now for the poor buggers at Shrivenham, obviously, but everyone else needs to be on heightened alert with maximum precautions. GH

[5.3]

I feel really bad for the innocent people who died because of us. I also feel bad about some of the people we had to work with. I wish we had not had to rely on them. But the fact is... sometimes it is the case that in a revolutionary struggle, you have to make allies with a variety of other groups... some you would not normally want to be associated with.

M: Yes, you did work with some very... unsavoury characters, Professor... people who were pretty savage

in their attacks on civilians... who did terrible things
to some of the humanitarian workers who were
only there to help. I mean, cutting off people's heads
on the Internet? Bombing the UN headquarters?
Slaughtering pilgrims on their way to pray? These
were your allies, Professor. How do you justify this?
Aren't you tarred with the same brush? I can't help
but think that it rather undermines your claim to
keeping to just war principles, as you call them.

P: Yes, you are right, Michael... it was a painful choice.
I knew they were bad people, and I tried to avoid
cooperating with them... but in a war... ah, well... you
sometimes have to make difficult compromises. It is
inevitable. In war, the blood of children and old people
will always water the earth... this is a reality. [...]
Anyway, you have no right to judge me... your record
is no better than mine! In Iraq, the British were allied
with the US who engaged in some pretty horrible
torture themselves. All those photos and videos from
Abu Ghraib and God knows where else? Does this
mean that the British are tarred with the same brush?

Is the following really in the public interest? It has the potential to reignite questions about the Afghan mission – and I know our special friends over the Atlantic would appreciate these events not being dragged up again. Strongly suggest brief recording interruption. GH

There were also those fucking death squads working
out of the Iraqi Ministry of the Interior. They were

the allies of the coalition. [...] In fact, everyone knows they were trained and armed by coalition forces. In Afghanistan, you are allied with groups from the so-called Northern Alliance, ████████████████████████████ ████████████████████████████████████ ████████████████████████████████████ ████████████████████████ Ask Amnesty International what their record on human rights is like. One of those guys... is known for tying people he does not like to the treads of his tanks and then running them over until they are hamburger meat.

M: He denies it, you know.

P: Of course, he does! He's working for the West now. He knows the value of a good reputation. But you're dreaming if you think these guys are pure like the snow... Anyway, I am sure you know the story about the 'caravan of death'... as it is called... where Afghan soldiers and CIA agents put five thousand foreign fighters in containers and then drove them into the desert and slaughtered them all. And yet... in, in, in, ah... order to overthrow the Taliban in 2001... the Americans gave those unsavoury people, as you call them, millions of dollars... arms... and a free pass for their crimes. We will not even mention the killer squads the Americans had operating in Afghanistan... those guys who went out killing suspected insurgents, some of whom were just Afghan farmers that they blew up for the fun of it. And then they pissed on their corpses! *Haga tsem el badan!*[23] And you talk to me about the nasty people I was allied with! [...] *'Amal teddeny f-moHdrat me-sobH.*[24] [mumbled]

The fact is... your record is disgraceful. Should I mention how British forces trained the Mujahidin in Scotland to fight the Russians during the Cold War... or those nice Protestant paramilitaries you worked with in Northern Ireland? What about ███████████████ ████████████████████████████? And we will not even talk about the Contras in Nicaragua... UNITA in Angola... all those vicious death squads across Latin America... Suharto in Indonesia... the support Western countries gave to Pol Pot, the butcher of Cambodia, when he fought against the Vietnamese... the brutal right-wing regimes the West supported against Soviet expansion... like Baby Doc Duvalier... the support for Saddam when he was fighting Iran and gassing Kurds... Noriega... the Haitian death squads... the support for Gadhafi before you turned on him this year. *We LESSA! Elly gai keteer!*[25] The truth is... you have a much worse record than me of choosing bad allies.

---

[23] Trans. 'It's something that poisons the body.' Note: Arabic Egyptian colloquialism, meaning: 'What an awful thing!'

[24] Trans. 'You, lecturing me since the morning!' Note: Arabic Egyptian colloquialism.

[25] Trans. 'And still! There is much more to come!' Note: Arabic Egyptian colloquialism.

But I understand it now... I do, I do! I get what
happens. In a war or a struggle, you sometimes have to
make common cause with people you would not want
as your friends at any other time. The important thing
is the cause... and you will do what is necessary to
achieve your goal.

M: I will concede that sometimes, yes, you do have to work
with people you'd rather not. But that's politics—

P: —Your politics, for sure.

M: What d'you mean by that, exactly?

P: OK, so... your government allies with Saddam one
day because it is a way of supporting opposition
to Iran who have just expelled the Shah, and the
Americans are helping him to use poison gas against
Iranian troops... but then just a few years later, you
are bombing Saddam and getting him hanged for
crimes against humanity! And to think that the
Americans said they were invading Iraq because
Saddam used chemical weapons... after they helped
him to gas the Iranians! Ha! What an irony! [...] The
same thing happened with Noriega... one day he is on
the CIA payroll and a solid ally against the spread of
Communism... and a nice little conduit for CIA drug
running... and the next he is being kidnapped and
taken for trial in America. And then there is Gadhafi.

One day he is the mad dog of the Middle East and you are bombing him, [the] next he is a solid ally against Islamist terrorism and you are giving him arms and sending people to his torture chambers for interrogation. Then a short time later, you are bombing him again!

M: You're being too—

P: —No! No! Listen to me! This is <u>your</u> kind of politics. You have no moral centre, Michael... no sense of honour. Despite all your fine words about how much the West values human life... and promotes democracy and freedom... blah, blah, blah! [...] the fact is, whenever it is in your interests, you will ally with, and provide support to, any dictator or violent group... no matter how bad they are. You are guided solely by expediency. You will support a dictator one day, and bomb him the next... only to support him again the next day. This is the sign of a society with no sense of morality... no code of honour. Surely you can see that it is a dishonourable kind of politics which will openly support a dictator like that guy in Uzbekistan... you know... the one who boils people in vats of oil...

███████████████████████████████ simply in order to maintain a military base for operations in Afghanistan... and then tries to discredit anyone who speaks out about this hypocrisy... even your own ambassador!

I thought we'd seen the end of the whole Craig Murray fiasco! What a cock-up that was! If we keep this section in the document, we may need to have a revised statement on Murray. Check with JP. She will dig something up.

GH

M: You're the same, Professor. You made the same strategic choices we did—

P: —That is true, but I only did it once... in the heat of a war. It is not something I do as a habit. I will not take that path ever again.

M: You might be right. Politics, especially international politics, can be a very dirty business. [inaudible]... no, please don't scoff ████████ I'm ████████████████████████████████████

[2.9]

Anyway, at least we fight fairly, Professor... out in the open. Not like you... planting bombs and then running away. Using ambushes and snipers and then melting away. Why don't you ever stand and fight like real soldiers?

P: Michael... I am so surprised to hear you ask that. Do you know anything about war? I thought you were once a, a... a soldier! No nation goes to war if it is a fair fight. No, no, no... do not shake your head at me! War is not a game where you go on the field of play with equal capabilities and a set of rules and then fight until one side surrenders. It is not cricket! The whole point of war is to overwhelm your opponent... smash them to pieces... crush them utterly. This is why

Western nations only attack small, militarily weak countries... why they would never risk attacking a capable country like Iran or North Korea, even if they really wanted to. The whole point of war is not to fight fair, but to fight to win.

Now, for the side being crushed... the ones on the receiving end of this unfair fight... the point is not to commit suicide and, and, ah, lose in an instant... but to use tactics that suit your position and which might even up the fight a little. We would never engage in open battle with you, because that would be completely irrational. War is not irrational... <u>we</u> are certainly not irrational. The fact is... if we attacked you in the open, you would not fight fair, you would call in your air support and bomb us to pieces and then pour in so much fire that no living thing would survive!

[loud banging]

Ana feyya rogola tkaffy setteen waHed zayyak![26] [...] But what you are really upset about is that we do not stand out in the open and wait for you to blow us up from ten miles away... that is your idea of a fair fight! One where you can fire easily at us with everything

---

[26] Trans. 'I have courage that suffices sixty people like you.' Note: Arabic Egyptian colloquialism.

you have, while we cannot do anything except fire
harmlessly over your heads!

M: No, I'm not saying—

P: —*Ya 'Eeiny!*[27] You are not in a position to talk to me
about being cowardly! What is more cowardly, would
you say... ah, ah, dropping five-hundred-pound bombs
on flimsy shacks from 40,000 feet knowing that
they cannot even see you... much less fight back... or,
or, or trying to fight back against an army that has
thousands more troops than you... full control of the
air... a variety of massive weapons that you can only
dream of having... all the very latest technology?
Is it more cowardly to try and fight with a few
Kalashnikovs and some home-made bombs... or with
the latest body armour... tank support... full air cover?

Let me ask you a personal question, Michael... be
honest now... would you be brave enough... or would
all those soldiers moaning about how cowardly the
insurgents are... be brave enough to get rid of all
your, your, your body armour... your radios... your
air support... your special explosives and hand-held
drones and grenade launchers... and just a few of your
guys with a rifle each fight against a few of my guys

---

[27] Trans. 'Oh dear!' Note: Arabic Egyptian colloquialism, with a mocking
meaning.

with their rifles? We could meet in a small forest or an abandoned industrial area and creep around... a bit like the, ah, ah... Ultimate Game... but with real guns! Now that would be a fair fight... that would show who has the real courage!

M: Any day, Professor! Our lads would—

P: —Let me ask you another question then. If you and a few of your friends were up against an invading army who had more than a hundred thousand heavily armed soldiers... plus an equal number of mercenaries... and they had all the latest equipment... complete air superiority... a network of informers... drones in the sky all day and night... a set of prisons where it was known that they would torture you if you got caught... would you be brave enough to take them on? Would you have the courage to go up against them with a few handguns and some home-made explosives?

Or... how about this... could you take a rifle and a few grenades and attack a heavily fortified embassy... knowing you would most certainly die in the attempt?

M: OK, OK. I take your point, Professor. Yes... you are a brave man. I don't doubt your courage. But then what is your goal then, here... in the UK? What are you planning, exactly? This isn't Iraq, after all. You can't really set up an insurgent group and engage in guerrilla warfare, can you? So you must be planning a, a... terrorist campaign.

P: You will not get any operational details out of me that way, my friend. I will never reveal details of ongoing operations, as I have told you. I took an oath to protect my comrades... and that is what I will do. You could even torture me... but I will not tell you anything. All I will say is that there is now a serious campaign underway in this country. It is not like what has come before... a few lone individuals... small groups... taking it upon themselves to make some kind of statement... like the 7/7 bombers. This time, there is a real strategy. There are others like me... serious people... determined people... people committed to the cause and committed to the strategy we have chosen to pursue. And it may surprise you, but it is not only Britain. There will also be operations in several other European countries... in America... Israel. We will fight in all those countries who believe they rule the world and act with impunity.

I assume this section has been shared with the relevant allied security services? There's clearly an international network out there we have not got on top of. Inter-service cooperation will need to be stepped up significantly – and fast. GH

M: With the greatest respect, I expect you are, shall we say... stretching the truth, Professor? The fact is, it's in your interest to create the illusion that you're a much bigger force than you actually are... that you

have much greater power and capability than you
really do. That's the nature of terrorism after all... to
create a psychological effect... to spread fear through
the illusion of omnipotence. What I'm trying to say is, I
expect you're exaggerating somewhat.

P: Fine, Michael. Believe that if it gives you comfort...
although I know you are a skilled interrogator and you
can probably tell when someone is lying to you. [...]
Look in my eyes... am I lying, Michael?

[5.1]

Anyway, it means nothing to me... I speak the language
of deeds... the whole world will soon see what our
capabilities are.

How's the investigation into P's associates and the wider network proceeding?
We'll need to demonstrate significant progress to avoid public alarm
when this gets released. Get a briefing from RS. GH

M: OK, Professor... why are you here... specifically in the
UK? Why come and fight here and not back in Iraq or
Afghanistan? I mean, if the point is to drive us out of
those lands, what're you doing in the UK? That's not
where the troops are.

P: It is quite simple, Michael. Like the IRA before me, I
have come to the conclusion that one bomb... or, or,
or one successful operation... on the UK mainland is

worth a hundred bombs in Iraq or Afghanistan. For so
many years, we have seen that no matter how many
soldiers die overseas, your government will always be
able to convince the public that the sacrifice is worth
it. You have a powerful set of national rituals and
myths to achieve this... like the parades of respect for
the coffins at Wootton Bassett. No one protests... no
one screams to bring the troops home. It is an article
of faith that everyone should support the troops...
support 'our boys', as you say... and do not make any
political statements about why they are overseas. I
suspect that the anti-war movement is a spent force
in this country. They cannot put across their message
without being seen to betray the troops... without being
viewed as, as... ah, unpatriotic.

My belief is that only when attacks take place on your
own soil... only when your people feel unsafe in their
own country... will they begin to question why they
are in Afghanistan... why they are bombing people
in Libya... like, like, like the Madrid bombing! If you
bring the fight to the homeland... to the very centre
of power... then you have a real chance to change the
policy... to alter history. I think that when you start to
suffer here like others are suffering over there... then
you will take our message seriously.

M: And how exactly will you do this? [...] You are not
intent on sending your message using any... shall

we say... umm... unusual means, are you,
Professor?

P: I do not follow you...

M: What I'm asking is, uh... whether you might be
planning to use weapons of mass destruction...
chemical or biological agents, for example? That's not
the kind of spectacular you're planning, is it?

Have any relevant connections been discovered in this regard – or any reported thefts of materials? Do we need a specific alert for the WMD hazards agencies – or would this be unnecessarily alarming? Suggest you consult with PL. GH

[laughter]

P: You sound like someone in a bad movie, Michael.
La' begad! Helak helak lato'a'a[28]—

M: —I think it's a fair question, Professor. You seem very
determined to send the most spectacular message you
can, and the fact is that terrorists have used WMD
before... and groups like al-Qaeda have been trying to
obtain them for years, ███████████████
███████████████████. It would send a
real statement, as you well know. I just want to know if
you're planning on using it here in the UK.

---

[28] Trans. 'Seriously! Watch out, watch out. You may tumble down.'
Note: Arabic Egyptian colloquialism.

P: Ohhf... what do you mean by WMD, Michael? Are you talking about those missiles and bombs which can turn a country's history back to the Stone Age in a few hours? Or do you mean those small arms... the SLRs, the Brownings, RPGs, all the thousands of different pistols, rifles, grenade launchers... all six hundred million of them out there... made in your factories... in the hands of children and drug dealers? Talk about weapons of mass destruction! You should see what small arms do around the world! Half a million people a year killed by them! That is more people dead than all the WMD attacks of the last sixty years!

M: You're being pedantic again, Professor.

P: No, no, no... it is not pedantry. It is entirely legitimate to question your racist, value-laden terms. The truth is... the bombs and guns that you manufacture and sell to the whole world... and which you use in your interventions... they are <u>our</u> WMD! They kill millions and lay entire societies to waste. Meanwhile, based on your movie-inspired fantasies about some kind of ah, ah... fanatical Arab-type person smuggling a mythical nuclear weapon in a suitcase into one of your cities, you get all worried and upset by your fantastic nightmare... completely oblivious to our daily real nightmare! [...] *Danto khalletona nshof ennogoom fe 'ez edhohr!*[29]

---

[29] Trans. 'You have shown us midday stars.' Note: Arabic Egyptian colloquialism, a famous saying indicating that one's world is turned upside down.

[banging]

M: We might manufacture the weapons, Professor, but
       there's no shortage of customers like you who actually
       use them to kill people [mumbled]—

P: —Oh, don't be ridiculous, Michael! What are you talking
       about? You sell your weapons to dictators... regimes
       like Saudi Arabia and Indonesia. The point I am
       making is... I mean, I already told you... we will always
       only attack legitimate targets. WMD in any form are
       completely indiscriminate, which means they cannot
       really be effectively targeted. If we used them, there
       is no doubt that civilians would die... they are simply
       not suitable to our purposes. Besides, we are not
       irrational, you know. We are fully aware that if we used
       such weapons, the reaction from the government...
       from every government and organisation in the world,
       actually... would be so extreme, and so devastating...
       worse than the reaction to 9/11, I expect! The point
       is... not only would we cease to exist, but many
       innocent people would no doubt suffer in the process.

       There is also a real taboo against such weapons. I think
       our message would be lost in the horror people felt...
       and we would lose any possibility of being understood.
       To quote your own aphorism... we want a lot of people
       watching and listening to what we say. We do not
       want a lot of people dead... and I am sure that our

supporters would abandon us if we did anything like that. No, no, no... it would not be advisable or useful. You can be assured, Michael... we are not going to attack your country with WMD.

Do we have a profile or general indication of who P's supporters are likely to be yet? It's clearly not the usual local jihadi wannabes. It's a priority to track down every last one of them to prevent another royal cock-up like this one! GH

Actually, I do not think al-Qaeda or any other group is likely to use them either... not if they are rational... and I know they are quite rational. I met members of al-Qaeda in Iraq, and even though they were pretty ferocious... trying to kill as many civilians as they could in their efforts to destabilise the society... they were not in any way irrational. They knew where the limits were, and one of those limits was WMD. In fact, I believe that bin Laden himself said in an interview... I remember reading it somewhere... that they decided against flying one of the planes into a nuclear power station on 9/11 for this very reason... using WMD did not suit their purposes. I think he realised that it would be a kind of Rubicon to cross that line, and too much of a risk. The other point, of course, is that these things are expensive... and really difficult to use. You are either killing yourself because you make a mistake and get contaminated... or, or, or you are killing no one at all because the sun comes out or the wind blows the wrong way!

No, no, no... I do not think any serious group considers using WMD. I mean, look at how many amateurs tried it to no effect. Those crazy Japanese guys in Tokyo... Aum Shinrikyo... even with all their labs and scientists they could not make anything that destructive. They would have done more damage with a few coordinated backpack bombs. No... why would any serious group try something so impractical and unreliable when all you need is a gun or some home-made explosives... both of which are commonly available? Hey... why use WMD when you could kidnap and execute someone with a kitchen knife and then put the video on the Internet?

It's shocking every time I read this. Pure savagery. We need the shrinks to use this to show his mental state. GH

M: [inaudible]... for God's sake [inaudible]

P:

[recording interruption]

[2.1]

P: [inaudible]... total bullshit, and you know it! ████████

██ He was

██

—

M: —[inaudible]... respect, you're lecturing me like one
        of your students! Preaching like one of those bad
        American evangelists! You're giving me a sermon,
        not an explanation... a set of pre-thought-out
        rationalisations and justifications. And nobody likes to
        be preached at, Professor!

[2.3]

P: Michael, you are absolutely right... I <u>am</u> preaching at
        you. I freely confess it... I am lecturing you the same
        way that your government has, has, has... lectured
        everyone else for the past five hundred years... and
        continues to do so, I might say, whenever it, ah, feels
        the need to invade a country or bomb it into changing
        its leader... especially when the so-called international
        community does not fall over itself to give you a rubber
        stamp of approval! Of course, when other countries
        want to organise an intervention in Rwanda or Ivory
        Coast or somewhere small, then you lecture them
        about the need for caution and letting countries take
        responsibility!

        Yes... I am lecturing you the same way you lectured
        the people of the Empire that what was being done

to them was for their own good... that they were
savages who needed Christianity and civilisation in
order to advance and join the community of advanced
nations! That was after they had handed over all their
minerals and crops and hardwoods and everything
else the Empire and its profiteers wanted to pillage,
of course...

Yes, yes, yes... I am lecturing you in the same way
you lectured the people of the colonies about how
they were not ready for self-rule because they
were uneducated and lacked a proper grounding in
democratic rule. I am lecturing you in the same way
that you lecture other countries about democracy...
human rights... civilised values... all the while, as we
know! [...] you were torturing and murdering Muslims
in Afghanistan—

M: —Oh, come on—

P: —The fact is that you have been lecturing... no, no...
that is not quite the right word... what is it? [...] mmm,
yes! You have been hectoring us... yes, that is the
word! Hectoring us, for hundreds of years... and we
have had to listen to you in quiet submission... like a
little schoolboy... like a child. Well... right here... right
now... it is my turn to speak and you have to listen to
me for a change! I am going to sermonise you for once
in this life... for one time in history... so that maybe...

for once... *Ana hatkallem, we enta hatesma'eny kwayes!*[30]

[1.8]

Don't I deserve a voice? I just want someone to hear me. When is someone like me ever heard?

M: Not if you use violence, Professor... if you accept the rules of civilised behaviour... act appropriately.

[8.8]

Professor, have you ever considered that you might be a little bit psychologically unbalanced... that maybe you're suffering from delusion? A touch of madness? I mean, how else does a respected university professor end up in a place like this... as a terrorist? It's simply not normal. It indicates some kind of mental, ah... disturbance.

P: Ah, yes... I was wondering when we would get to this most predictable of questions. I am fully aware that this is the most common perception in your society. [...] Terrorists... or militants, as I would prefer to call them... revolutionaries... whatever... must be

---

[30] Trans. 'I will talk, and you will listen carefully!' Note: Arabic Egyptian colloquialism, used by protestors in el-Tahrir square.

insane or abnormal in their thinking. After all, they commit horrible, extraordinary acts... so they must be mentally unbalanced by definition. Certainly, this is how they are portrayed in all your films... the wide-eyed fanatic... the diabolical Dr Evil type... the cruel Arab willing to commit any manner of atrocities... played by an Indian actor, moreover! Ha! The truth is, you cannot conceive of someone joining a violent group unless they are mentally disturbed.

Actually, I find the contrast with the attitude towards joining the military very interesting. Soldiers also join a violent group to go and kill people for a cause, in a way... but this is not how it is generally understood.

M: That's completely different!

P: No, no... listen. Soldiers are considered selfless heroes for their killing. No one questions their sanity... even if they do subsequently go and act like a psychopath! Even if they go absolutely crazy like those soldiers at Mai Lai... or Haditha... or those really sick fucks at Abu Ghraib! My God!

[2.3]

Actually, you raise an interesting philosophical point, Michael... how does anyone really know he

is not insane... especially if he does not conform to
the accepted norms of his society? We really only
know our thoughts and behaviour fit the society-wide
norm... that which we have decided to call 'sanity'...
by comparing it to those around us. But, who exactly
should we compare ourselves to... who among us is
the norm? Let me ask you another question... if I
may? [...]

M: Please... by all means—

P: —Is it a sign of madness to continue in the same
actions over and over and over again... even when the
same bad result is produced every time... like, like...
ah, when Homer Simpson reaches for that six-pack
of beer hanging over the electricity lines and it gives
him a shock... but he just endlessly keeps reaching,
believing that this time he will be successful and
actually get the beer?

What I am asking... is it a sign of sanity or insanity
to try and bomb a whole country into democracy...
especially when you have tried it so many times before,
always to the same disastrous effect? Is it sane to
think that sending in tanks to crush the same people
you have sent in tanks to crush a hundred times before
will work this time? Is it a sign of mental health to
believe that God told you to invade Iraq? You know,
I sometimes think that if I compare myself to certain

sections of the population... American leaders or
Israeli politicians, to take one example... I probably
come out far ahead in the sanity stakes!

M: You're deflecting the question, Professor.

P: No, no, no. I do not agree... I am making a perfectly
intelligible point.

M: No, you're avoiding the issue. Do you sometimes look at
your own behaviour, your own beliefs, and think that
there's something wrong? That you are so far from
those around you in society that maybe you're... well,
you know... mentally unbalanced?

P: Oh, I see what you are saying... it is a stupid question,
nonetheless.

M: Really? You think it's <u>normal</u> to go around randomly
killing people... blowing things up?

P: So you think I am insane? I seem crazy to you?

M: Well, given your behaviour, and your views, you do
seem quite... unusual, Professor. It's not normal, what
you're doing.

[2.3]

P: So... mmm... so you do not agree that madness can be
        political?

M: I don't follow.

P: What I mean is that violence... and oppression...
        injustice, it can drive a person insane. The prisoners
        held at Guantanamo Bay, many others held in solitary
        confinement... with sensory deprivation... declared
        innocent but then told they could not be freed...
        some of them were driven completely mad. And the
        Palestinians, humiliated every day... trapped in a huge,
        open-air prison, denied the right to take their sick
        children to hospital... attacked by settlers... denied the
        protection of the law. [...] Or, or... your own soldiers,
        coming back from Iraq with depression... killing
        their wives... committing suicide every week. What
        I am saying is that with enough oppression... with
        enough brutality and violence... you can crush any
        man's spirit... twist his mind. Even if I was mentally
        unbalanced by what I have seen with my own eyes...
        this would not detract one iota from the justice of my
        cause. [...] If I am mad... if <u>we</u> are mad to fight you... it
        is because you made us this way.

        In any case, I am not mad... and I am not the first
        professor or university-educated person to take up
        arms or get involved in militant activity, as I am sure
        you know. Ramadan Shallah. Do you know him? He

is the leader of Islamic Jihad in Palestine. He got
his PhD in 1990... he used to teach at an American
university. Angela Davis. Do you know her? No?
She was a militant in America. She was a professor
of philosophy at the University of California. In the
IRA there are many with PhDs. And Hamas! Ohhf...
practically the entire leadership of the movement
are doctors, engineers, university professors... very
highly educated people, very qualified. Actually, so
many militants throughout history have come from
the educated classes. Maybe it is because the more you
learn about how the world works... how it really is...
the more you realise that you have to fight the system.
[...] On the other hand... or at the same time... maybe
it takes a little madness to fight for revolution against
the most powerful forces in the world! Ha! [...]

Seriously, though, if you think about it logically,
it simply makes no sense that terrorists would be
insane or mentally ill... they would not be able to plan
and carry out complex and dangerous operations...
all the while keeping it secret and avoiding the
attentions of the authorities... if they were mentally
unbalanced or unstable in some way... if they suffered
from depression... mania... irrational behaviour...
schizophrenia... whatever. Seriously... the sort of
people who are prone to mental illness are more
likely to blow themselves up! [...] At the very least,
they will ruin the operation... and give it away. They

will certainly get caught because of their unusual behaviour.

Let me ask you a question. What kind of person are you? Are you sane... emotionally balanced... intelligent?

M: OK, I suppose—

P: —Of course you are. They would not want you in the army if you were not... or, or, ah... the intelligence service. The fact is, any armed group needs a certain kind of person to be successful... and just as the army tries to make sure that their recruits are intelligent... mature... stable... et cetera... so does any serious militant group. Of course, unlike the military or the intelligence services, militant groups cannot always be as choosy... and there are probably a lot more loopholes for crazy people to get in. But in principle, the fact is that we choose our members the same way you do... with the same qualities that you choose for your soldiers... agents... police officers... anyone really, who has responsibility for life-and-death actions.

No, no, no... it is a complete myth that terrorists are insane or mentally abnormal... criminals, maybe... but not militants or revolutionaries. I know this for a fact. In my experience, it actually takes emotional stability and intelligence and a, a, a disciplined personality to be a successful insurgent... not to mention courage!

You do not send disturbed individuals or immature children up against the most powerful militaries in the world with just a rifle or a home-made bomb! That is a recipe for total failure!

Of course, I did meet some pretty crazy people among the insurgents... in other groups, mind you. [They were] strange individuals who had often travelled from some far country because they wanted to conduct jihad. I suppose this means that there are always exceptions... But then again, I am sure you met some crazy people in the military? Yes? It has its share of psychopaths...

Anyway, in our group... we would carefully weed out anyone we thought was mentally unstable, or, or... or emotionally scarred... the depressed... the homicidal... the unbalanced. It was just too dangerous to have them involved... Hey! You do not need me to tell you this, do you? You have been hunting militants for so many years now. Did you ever meet one who you really believed was insane?

M: No, not really... at least not from the organised groups, as you say. There've been one or two sad, lone individuals who obviously had deep personal problems. I did meet quite a few who were pretty intense in their beliefs... others who seemed very angry... a bit like you. [...] But no, none who were what

you'd consider properly... you know, psychologically,
medically... insane.

But then again, I never met a real suicide bomber. They
must be pretty screwed up, don't you think, to want to
kill themselves? Staying alive is the most basic instinct
human beings have. Wanting to die... to throw your life
away for a belief or even just being so willing to die...
it's not normal behaviour. I think you have to be either
extremely depressed and pretty unhappy with your
life, or some kind of brainwashed fanatic to undertake
a suicide mission.

You must have met some in Iraq, I imagine? What was
your impression? Can you explain why they did it?

P: Yes, you are right... I did meet some of these people
in Iraq... quite a few actually. We conducted a few
martyrdom operations ourselves... but you are wrong
to call them suicidal. That is not how we saw them...
and it is certainly not how they saw themselves.
Suicide is a very Western term... and very misleading
in my view. As I mentioned before... you cannot get
a depressed, unstable person to carry out a complex
operation. You cannot rely on them to keep their nerve
and go to a new target if the first one is too difficult...
or, or, or walk away from a threatening situation.
The same is true for a fanatic... they are just too
irrational... too emotional.

The fact is, to strap explosives on your body... to have an electronic switch or a mechanism to operate at the moment of detonation... and then to travel somewhere... with people watching you... knowing for certain you will die in the attempt... knowing that one small mistake will result in you being shot or blown up... well, that takes real discipline... real nerve, my friend. You have to be so calm... so in control of your emotions... so at one with yourself... otherwise you will panic and blow the whole thing... excuse my pun!

No, no... you cannot give this mission to a depressed person... someone who is really unhappy and morose. It is too risky. An operative needs to be able to make good decisions as they go along. If the target has moved... or, or, or if it is not possible to mount the attack without killing lots of civilians... or if someone becomes suspicious... or if the mechanism fails and needs to be fixed on the spot, they have to be able to change the plan... make a quick and rational decision—

Well, this is going to throw the cat among the pigeons – if there's no way to profile individuals at risk of becoming suicide bombers. We will probably need a statement on this – or at least a response to potentially tricky questions. Any suggestions? GH

M: —But they're still killing themselves, aren't they? There's no getting around that. Their lives are still over—

P: —*Maheya mota waHda mesh etnein.*[31] [...] But back
      to your question... yes, that is true... but just because
      you undertake an action in which you know you are
      going to die does not mean you are committing suicide
      because you are depressed and <u>want</u> to die. Think
      about the soldier who throws himself on a grenade in
      order to save his comrades. He knows he will die, but
      he is willing to sacrifice his life to save his friends.

M: But I would argue that's a kind of instinctual action in
      the heat of the moment... it's not pre-planned, which
      seems so much more cold-blooded. I'm certain those
      soldiers would much rather stay alive, but they know,
      in that second, that if they don't act, a lot more people
      will die.

P: True... but simply being a soldier or a militant is a risky
      occupation... you accept that you may die at any time.
      Besides, there are plenty of other cases where soldiers
      volunteer to go on missions which they know, to a very
      high degree of certainty, that they will probably not
      come back from... or, or, or, ah... what about when a
      soldier is injured and decides to stay behind and die to
      give his comrades a chance to escape? You would not
      call this <u>suicide</u>, would you? It is not an act of despair...

---

[31] Trans. 'Because you die once not twice.' Note: Arabic Egyptian
colloquialism, meaning that they make the decision knowing the
consequences.

it is a <u>sacrifice</u>... it is giving your life in a positive way for others... actually, it is a selfless act...

Suicide, on the other hand, is a selfish act... you want to die to make the pain go away. You are willing to destroy yourself rather than continue to live with your pain. [...] Whereas this is the complete opposite... it is about giving your life, not taking your life. It is as you say... they do not necessarily want to die, but they perceive... at that moment in history... in those circumstances... that if they do not sacrifice their lives for the cause, many more people will die... things will never change... the oppression will continue. At least... that is how our volunteers saw it. They felt they were giving their lives as a gift to the people they wanted to save.

M: But why use suicide bombers... or martyrs or whatever you want to call them? Why not just plant bombs or mount an ambush or something? Why kill yourself? For one thing, you lose a trained operative. If they die, they can't exactly fight for the cause any more or mount another operation. Also, suicide missions—

P: —martyrdom operations—

M: —martyrdom operations are viewed, shall we say, rather negatively. Most people see them as abhorrent, evil even. It's just <u>such</u> extreme behaviour.

My question is... why use a tactic that everyone disapproves of? Doesn't it lose you support? I mean, if you're going to lose your best operatives, and public support, why do it? Isn't that irrational behaviour?

P: I suspect you already know the answer to this question, Michael. You know that a walking, thinking bomb is a very powerful weapon... even better than a, a, a guided missile! I mean... this is a bomb which can get into places and attack in ways which no other method could achieve... and the psychological effect of such a bomb! Wow! Can you imagine how frightening this is! When any man... or woman... could be a walking bomb and you just do not know. They move around among you, and then... boom! I mean... this makes such an impact. In a way, it helps to even up the psychological battlefield... we do not know when one of your drones or your high-altitude bombers will kill us instantly with a surprise attack... but you also do not know when one of those people walking up to you will explode himself and kill you all...

The other advantage, of course, is that a human bomb is very cheap... much cheaper than any of your high-tech weapons. It costs us a lot less to launch a martyrdom operation than it costs you to launch a drone attack... or helicopter attack. You could say that a human bomb is the poor man's drone! Not that we would not prefer to have some of the weaponry you have! The truth is... if we had helicopters and bombers and tanks... missiles... drones... all the things you can use... that is how we would probably choose to fight. We would not <u>need</u> to use home-made IEDs or human bombs. We would not need to ambush and hide and live underground. We would fight you in the open. We use the weapons of the poor because we are poor soldiers fighting a very rich enemy. [...] In a way, we are David to your Goliath.

This is somewhat ironic now, isn't it – in the light of the Shrivenham incident? What are we doing to follow up on how they managed that? It will be a complete nightmare if any other nutters follow suit. The PM will need to provide public assurance. GH

[3.8]

M: But Professor, do you really believe that what you're doing will actually work? I mean, it never <u>really</u> worked in Iraq. The surge managed to quash most of the insurgent activity there and there are still fifty thousand US troops there and a US-backed regime in power. And... as you yourself alluded to... you can't really say it's working in Afghanistan. NATO forces kill a lot more insurgents than insurgents kill NATO forces. The Afghan army is slowly being trained and equipped. The main contributing nations seem able to absorb the losses... And it certainly hasn't worked in Israel. The Palestinians have been using terrorism against Israel for more than fifty years and what have they achieved, exactly? It didn't work in Sri Lanka, did it? They lost in the end. The Basque country? Colombia? Kashmir? Chechnya? Pakistan? I could go on.

P: Afghanistan... I am not sure—

M: —The point I am making is simply... if you keep persisting with a strategy that doesn't really work, which has such a poor record and, clearly, a very low probability of success... is that really rational? Aren't you acting like Homer Simpson, then... reaching for that prize but getting stung, over and over and over again? And is it moral to do so? Should you engage in a violent campaign knowing that it's likely to fail? I mean, if you know that the only outcome will be a lot of people dead to no effect, isn't that an immoral action to undertake?

I suppose I'm questioning how rational your strategy really is, and why you keep persisting with it? More to the point, why not switch to something else? Isn't that what the definition of rationality is? Re-evaluating your actions and adjusting them when they fail? [...] The simple fact of the matter is, terrorism doesn't really work. The state... the society you're fighting... it's just too strong... And randomly murdering people like that just makes everyone hate you. Any message you think you're sending gets lost in the shock and horror of the act itself. No one listens.

[4.1]

P: Mmm... [inaudible]—

M: —And I haven't even mentioned the high personal price you pay for choosing this strategy. How costly has it been for you, especially as you could always work in a more positive way for reform? You've lost your family, your home, community, seeing your daughter grow up... hearing your wife's voice. ██████████████ ██████████████████████████████ You live on the run... hiding... eating bad food... wearing bad clothes... always a few seconds away from death or capture... not knowing who to trust. You're hated and despised, vilified... instead of respected and valued. If you'd chosen a different path... if you'd pursued your struggle through building a political movement, winning international support... you could've been a respected man. You could've been another Nelson Mandela... or Aung San Suu Kyi. This is what I can't understand! Why keep going like this? You're a clever, committed, charismatic man! Anyone can see that! Why give that all up to be a hunted, hated terrorist!

P: I find it so interesting that you mention Mandela... I am sure you know... before he became the leader of South Africa and the respected world figure that he is now... before he won the Nobel Peace Prize... he was a convicted terrorist. It is amazing to think about it now, but the Americans had him on their list of terrorists. They once described him as one of the worst terrorists in the world! Can you imagine? And do you know what is so funny? [laughter] They forgot to take his name off the official list of proscribed terrorists. When he tried to visit America just a few years ago, the State Department had to admit that he needed a special visa because he was still on their books as a terrorist. Condoleeza Rice was so embarrassed. [laughter] She had to publicly apologise. I laughed so hard when I saw that.

Even I have to admit it – that was just embarrassing. Poor Condi!

[laughter]

M: Yes, I did see that... institutional [inaudible]...

[2.3]

P: The fact is, Michael... that Mandela took up the armed struggle for exactly the same reasons that I have... because all the years of non-violent struggle did not work. All those years of, of... of marching and writing letters to the British government... and burning their identity cards... well, it simply did—

M: —But he renounced violence and entered the political
process later on, didn't he? And then he achieved
his goals of liberating his people by dialogue with his
opponents. Isn't that the point? He didn't achieve his
goal through the kind of violence you are engaged in.

P: I think you have it the wrong way around, Michael.
He never renounced violence when he was in prison.
That is why they would not let him out... even when
he became a martyr... when he was a symbol of
resistance around the whole world... even when it
became embarrassing for the government to keep
him locked up. The fact is that it was only when the
South African government realised that they could
not win... when they knew they would lose the armed
struggle against MK... when they were being strangled
by the sanctions... that they came to Mandela and
asked to negotiate. I am sure you get what I mean...
ma yo'khazo belqowa, la yostarado ella belqowa.[32]

The truth is that it was not Mandela who needed to
renounce violence and engage in political struggle, it
was the oppressive South African government! They
needed to stop trying to crush people with force...
to finally allow justice and freedom. As I have said
before, it was only after the armed struggle forced the

---

[32] Trans. 'What is taken by force, can't be regained except by force.'
Note: Classical Arabic with Egyptian accent.

government to change that they started to negotiate
and freedom came to South Africa.

This is simply what I want... Western governments to
stop their violence and embrace justice and freedom...
to engage in a, a.... a <u>political</u> process, instead of always
using force... to open up dialogue and talk to those of
us struggling for a better world... to use democratic,
political means instead of bombs... to become political
actors instead of military, imperial actors... But I know
they will not do it voluntarily. The powerful do not
surrender their power voluntarily... which is why I
am prepared to keep fighting until they give in to the
inevitable march of history... Is this too much to ask?
Is this a hopeless, irrational struggle in your eyes? [...]

I have to stand again, Michael. My back. [scraping
sounds] This room is so filthy... dirt everywhere...
peeling paint, rust... I wish we could have been
somewhere else. I am sorry you have to be detained so
long in this squalid little room.

M: No, please. Don't concern yourself, Professor. It's the
job... we have to do this.

[2.9]

P: Indeed we do, Michael. We have to do this. [...] You
mentioned Aung San Suu Kyi just now. I believe she

also illustrates <u>my</u> point more than yours. I mean... hmph... what has she achieved, exactly... apart from becoming an international symbol that everyone talks about? She has been fighting for democracy in Burma for so many decades... thirty years, something like that... and to what effect? Nothing! She is still under house arrest... her party is still excluded... there are no free elections... no political rights. The generals are still in power... raping the country... exporting drugs... enriching themselves while people starve. They continue to brutally crush even the smallest sign of protest! The Rohingya Muslims are still slaughtered. Her non-violent struggle has achieved virtually nothing!

M: And you think things will never change in Burma?

P: Ohhf... not likely... not without some kind of armed struggle. [...] You know, it is so interesting that you bring this example up, because I would have thought that if there is one country in this world that needed some <u>humanitarian intervention</u>, it would be Burma. What I mean is, if the West, ah, ah... <u>really</u> cared about human rights, or, or democracy, or freedom... if all their talk was anything more than hollow platitudes designed to justify all their meddling in oil-rich countries... then they would have bombed Burma long ago! At the very least, they would have started a campaign and instigated some major sanctions or something. Instead, they make speeches praising the Burmese opposition and then go back to bombing Libya in the hope that the regime which comes after Gadhafi will give oil concessions to American and British oil companies... instead of the Chinese and Russians!

[4.7]

I am sorry. I got a little side-tracked there... You were asking whether I thought that armed struggle was a moral course of action if it did not have a realistic chance of success. OK, so... the first thing I would dispute is your suggestion that armed struggle does not work—

M: —Actually I was restricting it to terrorism. I know that other forms of armed struggle can sometimes work, but terrorism seems like a very limited strategy.

P: OK. Let us adopt your understanding of what terrorism is. We can even, ah, differentiate it from a broader armed struggle. I still think it can be successful... because it depends what the terrorism is intended to do. If it is the sole means of winning freedom... ending an occupation... overthrowing a repressive government... something very major like that... of course, it is unlikely to be successful. But the fact is that terrorism never takes place in isolation... it is never the only tactic of struggle.

We might need to prepare our own interpretation of the following cases, one that emphasises terrorist atrocity and failures. Suggestions for an angle? GH

It is one tactic of many, usually by one small group. Other groups... other individuals... are fighting in other ways... spreading propaganda... fund-raising... organising a movement... demonstrating... writing petitions... consciousness-raising... a thousand other things.

What I am saying is that in concert with all these other struggles, terrorism can be a part of a successful movement. It certainly worked for the, ah... Zionists... in Israel. They forced you... the British... to hand over Palestine to them. The Irgun... the Stern Gang... Lehi... Haganah... all those Jewish terrorist groups... blowing up hotels and assassinating British officials... you cut and ran. Then they terrorised the Palestinians into leaving the land... Plan B, as I am sure you know... the planned massacres... Deir Yassin, all those towns wiped from the map, from history. [...] Most people would say it worked for the Irish... at least in part. They got an agreement and the end to direct military rule. It worked in Spain in 2004... it forced the government to withdraw Spanish troops from Iraq. The mujahidin in Afghanistan used terrorism against the Russians... terrorism supported by the Americans, who also supported the successful terrorism of the Contras in Nicaragua, I might add!

[scraping sounds]

The other point is that terrorism may not always have such grand aims. It may not necessarily intend to overthrow a whole government... start a revolution. Sometimes, terrorism is intended merely to draw attention to an issue... to make a statement. We are here! We want to be heard! You cannot ignore us! Actually, this was the strategy of the Palestinians when they started to hijack planes and undertake operations in Europe in the 1970s. They wanted to make the international community take notice, because they felt they had already been forgotten.

And you cannot say that did not work. My God, it really worked! The whole world stood up and noticed... everyone knows them now... everyone has heard their cry, and knows their struggle—

M: —But it hasn't got them any further to getting their land back, or even to getting them a separate state, has it? They're in a worse position now than ever before... and the whole world sees them as terrorists!

P: True, true. They are fighting a powerful and entrenched enemy... an enemy with very powerful friends... Britain, for one. In effect, they are fighting the Israelis, the Americans and the Europeans all at the same time. You are all deploying your forces together to ensure they are slowly disappearing off the face of the earth.

The point is... there are many other purposes for
terrorism. Sometimes it is a warning message. If you
try to repress us, we will strike back... if you make us
suffer, we will make you suffer.

M: So, it's about revenge? We're back to that?

P: Ohhf... OK, yes... I suppose, in a way... but at the same
time... a warning... a kind of... deterrence, if you
like. It is a way of trying to stop a government from
undertaking a particular policy by demonstrating
that it will be very costly to do so. On the other hand,
sometimes it is a provocation... a carefully calibrated
strategy to make the government react with violence.
What I mean is... by committing a, a... an outrage, the
terrorists hope that the true nature of the regime will
be revealed by the way they respond. This way, the
people will see the truth of the power that oppresses
them, and then a broader political struggle can be
more easily organised... can emerge...

This was the particular strategy of the 9/11 attacks,
I believe... as well as being a way to get noticed, of
course. Not only did Osama manage to get the whole
world talking about all those things which he had been
saying in so many interviews, and letters... for so many
years... his grievances about the military forces in
Saudi Arabia... the support for the Israelis... which no
one had really listened to... but he knew that America

would react with great repression and violence... and
he believed that this would finally convince Muslims
and oppressed people all over the world of the true
nature of American power. Once the Americans really
started to oppress Muslims in revenge, he truly
believed it would galvanise a great movement to
oppose America.

In a way, I think you have to say he was pretty
successful. No, no! Listen! You look sceptical, but
America did respond by immediately going out and
killing a million Muslims in revenge... devastating
at least two Muslim countries... the torture of
thousands... renditions... death squads... oppressive
laws... Guantanamo... bullying countries to cooperate...
all those things which showed its true nature. Bin
Laden succeeded so well in making America react as
he hoped. It was kind of amazing. He had discerned
America's nature perfectly!

Of course, I do not believe al-Qaeda has managed to do
anything else since. In fact, it is pretty much finished
now, which is why I knew we needed to re-evaluate and
continue the struggle in a new way... But you cannot
say they were not successful! [...]

Oh, my back is so stiff now. These chairs... they are
so uncomfortable... they must be an instrument
of torture, don't you think? I can't even sit for

a minute! [...] How is it that you can sit so still,
hour after hour? Do they train you in sitting, or do
you have a steel backside? Ha! It reminds me of
[inaudible]

The point I am trying to make, Michael, is that it is
too simplistic to say that terrorism does not work. It
depends on what that particular act of terrorism is
trying to achieve. It also depends on which case you
are looking at. Sometimes, terrorism is nothing more
than a statement... a, a, a... clarion call to others to
take up the struggle... a cry which says... 'I am ready to
die rather than be a helpless sheep who does nothing.
I am ready to lay down my life. What are you prepared
to do?'

It also depends on whose terrorism you are talking
about. We could say that it has worked very well for
you over the years. It has certainly worked well for the
Israelis... and the Americans.

M: What? I don't understand.

Is it really in the public interest to highlight state violence and terrorist successes? See previous note. Suggest another small recording interruption.
                                                                                GH

P: Are you being deliberately ignorant, Michael? *Eh?*
      'Amel nafsak mosh fahem?[33] Did you not keep all those
      colonies... all those tens of millions of people in Africa
      and Asia... under your control through terrorising
      them into submission? How else could you stop them
      all from rising up and throwing you out?

M: So we're back to ancient history—

P: —And did the Americans not stop all those left-wing
      movements... all those peasants struggling for a little
      land... those unions fighting for a fair wage... from
      succeeding in Latin America through their support
      of terror by the dictatorships they armed? Through
      supporting death squads... disappearances... daily
      murders of regime opponents?

M: You're twisting the—

P: —No, no! Listen! They undermined the Sandinista
      revolution in Nicaragua by supporting the Contras...
      a terrorist group! They used total terror in Operation
      Condor to crush leftists all over South America...
      assassinating people on the streets!

---

[33] Trans. 'Seriously? You are acting as if you don't understand it?'
     Note: Arabic Egyptian colloquialism.

And what about the Israelis? Do not get me
started... but they use terror every day to keep the
Palestinians down. They fly over Gaza in their jet
fighters every single day... creating sonic booms
to make people... children... afraid they are being
bombed... buzzers flying overhead day and night.
They kidnap Palestinians... torture them... break
the legs of protestors... in order to terrify them into
submission. For God's sake, they send in tanks and
full-scale invasions every few months just to show
the Palestinians what happens when they dare to
resist... assassination teams all over the world to kill
their enemies... to warn them what will happen. Like
Operation Galilee...

M: [inaudible]...

P: And it really works! For decades they have slowly
taken more land... built more settlements...
constructed a wall to take in more land and imprison
the Palestinians. Israel is bigger and stronger than
ever and it has not had to make a single significant
concession! I would say their terror has been highly
successful... as has the terror of the Chinese in Tibet...
the Russians in Chechnya... the Indians in Kashmir...
the Colombians... so many governments who terrorise
their own people to keep them in line.

The simple point is, Michael, terrorism... or armed
struggle... whatever you want to call it... has worked
in the past... for you and for groups like mine! It
is not an irrational strategy! I truly believe it will
work again. Just imagine if there are attacks in the
UK over several years with real, sustained losses...
soldiers blown up... police officers shot... politicians
assassinated... counter-terrorism officers being
kidnapped and killed—

M: [inaudible]... come on [inaudible]...

Highly inflammatory and potentially dangerous, in my considered opinion.
Various groups – jihadists et al – are likely to take encouragement from this.
Suggest recording interruption to circumvent potential problems. GH

P: —time, do you not think that after a few years of this,
the pressure to withdraw from Afghanistan and stop
bombing countries like Libya would be so intense?
I mean, if Britons were dying overseas and here at
home... well... I think there would be a change in policy.
Is this a rational expectation, Michael... or am I crazy
to think that? And what if these attacks spread to
Europe... America... every country that was oppressing
other countries or had military forces in another
country?

Michael, I believe that when this happens, there will
finally be a real debate about foreign policy in this
country. Your political elite... your media... all those

commentators who shape public opinion... they will start to reconsider if the price of these policies is really worth it. And when we also release the facts... the reasons for why we are attacking in this way... this is why we are recording this conversation on that video recorder over there... so I can explain all our reasons... answer all your questions... Anyway, you will see what happens... there will be a real conversation... a real debate. And that is when the opportunity for finally changing your government's policies will happen.

Are we any closer to getting the video recording back?
Does anyone know where it ended up – or rather, who it ended up with?
I don't have to tell you how damaging it will be if it surfaces on the Internet, released by bloody Wikileaks – or, God forbid, it gets sent to al Jazeera!
We'll be doing cartwheels to try and limit the fallout if that happens. GH

M: I think you're being naive, Professor. Whatever you do, you'll be publicly vilified as an insane, fanatical terrorist. Your message will be ignored. This is how the media works. It's been the same way every single time. [...]

P: Well, you may be right, Michael. In any case, a principle that I try and live by says that doing the right thing is not determined by its chances of success. Otherwise, few would have the right... or the responsibility... of resistance, would they? Did Britain, facing up to the might of Germany and the Axis powers, know for certain that they would prevail? No, they only knew that it was the right thing to do in the situation. It is the same for all oppressed people. They face a much more powerful enemy, and by rights, they know that they probably will not succeed. But they resist anyway, because it is the moral choice... in that place... at that time. The truth is that I do not think I could live with myself... or look in my daughter's eyes again... if I did not try to make this world a better... more just... more equal place. If I do not do anything, then I am guilty too! And even if I fail, it does not matter, because at least I tried! I can live with my conscience because I know I have acted rightly.

You never know, my example might also be an inspiration to others... and maybe those others who come after me will succeed where I have failed. This is the thing, Michael... it is a long, historic struggle we are involved in. It is not one of your short wars where you swarm in with hundreds of thousands of troops and then declare victory a few weeks later. We are prepared to fight for fifty years... a hundred years... even a thousand years, if necessary. Justice is a never-ending quest, not a strategic goal. One day, even if it takes a hundred years... justice will come....

[2.3]

M: Professor, there are political avenues for pursuing your aims. Democracy is not perfect by any stretch of the imagination, but it does provide a means to organise, build a movement, exert pressure and see change happen, albeit slowly. There are numerous examples of citizens organising themselves and getting new legislation passed. And, in reality, society is gradually getting better.

P: Getting better for whom, Michael?

M: For everyone. We're all better off now than we were a hundred years ago—

P: —Is that why your poor people riot and go looting in the streets, Michael? They are so happy because their lives are better? Is it why so many of your citizens are occupying your public squares and marching every day... why income for the ninety-nine per cent declines every year while the one per cent gets richer and richer by the day? Is it true for the thirty thousand people who die <u>every day</u> from poverty?

M: You know how to twist everything with your words, don't you Prof—

P: —No! Listen! You are making empty slogans, Michael. You are not being entirely truthful... either that or you are hopelessly naive. Sure, society has gotten better overall, but most people are trapped in cycles of poverty and deprivation which have passed down

from generation to generation. Have you spent any
time in a poor council estate? I have, while I have
been keeping away from your radar. I have seen the
hopelessness and despair with my own eyes... the
barely suppressed anger... the envy... the general
everyday powerlessness. I have met people who are
third-, fourth-, maybe even fifth-generation poor.

And it is not just a question of absolute poverty. Of
course, the poor these days have access to welfare
provisions and enough food to live on... health care...
you know. It is not like the days when poor people
literally died on the streets... although people still die
on the streets every day in parts of the developing
world, as I am sure you know. But here... in Western
countries like Britain... it is relative poverty. It is
being poor and knowing that just up the road there
are millionaires... maybe even billionaires. It is seeing
how fabulous life can be when you have a sports car...
a private yacht... seeing it on television and in the
newspaper every single day... but then knowing that
you will never even have enough to buy the shoes your
child really needs.

The point is that this is not just a simple question of
material wealth or economics, Michael, but a reflection
of the state of your democracy. Democracy does work,
but only if you are wealthy enough. The rich and the
middle classes... with, ah, ah... time on their hands and

the ability to mobilise resources... they can organise
and get a campaign going. And if they are lucky to
get a sponsor from the political classes, they might
be able to make some changes. Certainly, the rich can
employ an army of lobbyists and take out ads across
the media... buy a candidate or two... and then they
get whatever they want! *Edemokratiya bas le-elly
ma'aah!*[34]

[loud banging]

Ma'elesh! Ma'elesh![35] I did not mean to startle you. I
get a bit worked up about this kind of thing.

M: It's OK, Professor. Stay calm. I'm just starting to get a
bit tired now—

P: —I know, I know. I am sorry this is taking such a
long time. We are working to a specific timetable... a
deadline. It will not be too much longer before we can
complete this, ah... transaction...

*Do we have any idea yet why P was waiting – what the deadline was?
Was it something to do with web-broadcasting or al Jazeera?
And then why didn't anything happen? It's a mystery, I must confess. GH*

---

[34] Trans. 'Democracy is only for those who have money, wealth, power,
etc.' Note: Arabic Egyptian colloquialism, a general saying about how
democracy is for the 'haves' not the 'have-nots'.

[35] Trans. 'It's OK', or 'Take it easy.' Note: Arabic Egyptian colloquialism.

Anyway, the point I am making is that democracy...
as you yourself say... is far from perfect. Most times it
cannot bring justice, because now it works mostly for
the entrenched powers in society. It is the democracy
of the rich, not the democracy of everyone. When
everyone tries to play a part, like when millions of
ordinary Britons marched to stop the war in 2003, it
failed miserably... or when people march against the
austerity measures. It is unresponsive... politicians
are completely cut off from the people they represent.
Most of them are millionaires themselves. They all go
to the same rich schools... the same elite universities.
They are from the entrenched classes and so naturally
they work to maintain the interests of those classes.
They are not interested in real change. Change would
not benefit them at all.

And you know, it is even worse when the policy that
you want to change involves foreign policy... people
overseas... because they have no voice in your system.
There is no MP for Afghanistan! They cannot come
over here and organise a movement... elect some
representatives... engage in public debates. Unless
someone here in the UK acts on their behalf, they have
no way of influencing your government's policies.
So what can the people of Afghanistan... or Iraq...
Libya... somewhere else where they are oppressed by
a government who receives British weapons to beat
them with... how can they <u>democratically</u> change your

policies? How can they influence your policies? If I
am a, a, a... an Afghan farmer who wants the foreign
troops to stop bombing his village... and stop taking
away his sons for interrogation... what can he do
<u>democratically</u> to end the NATO occupation?

No, no, no. Democracy is a poor tool for bringing about
change, my friend, and I think you know it. These days,
politicians only respond to two things... money and
violence. If you have enough money, you can change
things... or, if you use enough violence. Well, I do not
have any money, ha [laughter]... so I speak in the
only language I have left... You know, I met a man in
Ireland who explained it to me like this. He said that
when words no longer have meaning, when you speak
and no one hears you, your voice is so unimportant...
well, then it occurs to me that maybe the British
government will listen to a bomb. [...] Listening to a
bomb. I like these words... Or, as, ah... Martin Luther
King put it... violence is the language of the unheard.

Well, I am going to speak now... we will speak... and you
will hear us! I wish it did not have to come to this, but
that is just the way it is. If democracy really worked...
if it was really responsive... if justice could be made
through it... I would go down that path. But it does not...

M: Be that as it may, Professor, I can assure you that as
long as you employ terrorism in this country, you will

never be listened to, and the British government, or any other Western government, will never make a single concession to you. They will never negotiate or concede, and as I've said, the media will simply brand you as insane fanatics. You will simply be crushed... eliminated. █████████████████████████████

and your message will go unheard.

P: This may be true at first, I agree. But I am hopeful that history will repeat itself, as it always does.

Public interest?
Will this raise difficult questions for HMG about current negs in Af–Pak?
                    Strongly suggest recording interruption here. GH

M: What do you mean? What history?

P: Ohhf... I, ah... as I am sure you are aware, governments have always negotiated with their enemies... even when they call them 'terrorists'. Of course, they have to say in public that they never talk to terrorists... but in private... secretly... they do negotiate with them. The British government was negotiating with the IRA, even when the IRA tried to blow up the Cabinet in Downing Street with a mortar! ████████████████

The Israelis negotiated with the PLO while they were still fighting. The Spanish negotiated with ETA... the Colombians negotiated with FARC... the

British negotiated with all their 'terrorist' enemies when they withdrew from their colonies... as did the French... the Portuguese... so many. In fact, I would wager that Western states are currently in secret negotiations with the Taliban... the Iraqi insurgents... Hamas... probably even the Iranians! ███████

HMG will need to prepare a statement in case someone asks for clarification on these allegations. I suggest a flat denial – followed by deflection and obfuscation. GH

My point is simply this... in the end, you will have to talk to the likes of me... or the people and groups who come after me. But I say, why wait? Why wait until the list of the dead is so long and so much suffering has occurred... on both sides? Why not stop the inevitable killings which will follow and start a dialogue now? Why not cut out all the death and destruction in the middle and go straight to the part where the talking occurs?

[3.8]

M: There are good reasons—

P: —I cannot really understand why America did not talk to al-Qaeda before now... or at least talk to someone who could talk to al-Qaeda. Do you know what I mean? They could have avoided so much suffering. In the end, they will have to negotiate an exit from their war on

terror, anyway. But it is the same old story of every
oppressive power in history. The delusional belief that
if only you apply enough force... if only you kill enough
of them... you can... eventually... crush all opposition.
It is not just the Western powers that believe this... or
Israel. The National Party in South Africa believed it...
the leaders of the Soviet Union believed it... Saddam
believed it... Mubarak believed it, backed up by billions
of dollars of American weapons. But look at him now!
Humiliated... cowering in a hospital bed... being tried
for his crimes in front of the whole world. It is an
endless list... Milosevic... Pinochet... Idi Amin... the
Shah... Suharto... Duvalier... Somoza... Marcos... so
many throughout history. How many tyrants fell in
the Arab Spring? How many after the fall of the Berlin
Wall? The fact is... you cannot crush freedom forever,
my friend...

M: You might be right, Professor, but it's not really for
       me to say who the government should be talking to.

       ███████████████████████████████████

       I'm a lowly public servant. I just follow orders.
       It's my responsibility to try and stop those individuals
       and groups who would seek to harm the people of the
       United Kingdom.

P: Taking orders is no excuse, Michael... as I am sure
       you know. Since Nuremberg, no one can claim that

they were just following orders. If you know that what
you are doing is morally wrong, then you are morally
responsible... whether you are following orders or
acting on your own. Besides, you still have a personal
opinion on this, no matter who you work for! Do you
not think that negotiating with al-Qaeda... or whoever
it is you are fighting with this week... the IRA...
Islamists... would be more effective and less destructive
than all the killing... and rendering... torturing?

M: I'm not sure... maybe... hmm, at one level you might be
right. But sometimes you can't negotiate. The reality
is that there's a big difference between trying to talk
to groups like the IRA or ETA... or you, for example,
who seem to have a recognisable and understandable
set of political demands, someone with a political
organisation, a hierarchy, you know, military and
political branches... and groups like al-Qaeda who
aspire to converting everyone to Islam, destroying all
unbelievers and re-establishing the Caliphate. These
people don't actually have any recognisable political
demands, do they? What would you negotiate with
them about, exactly? And who exactly would you
talk to? And, unlike the IRA or the other nationalist
groups, they don't have a constituency they are
responsible to. They seem to just answer to God.

I'm just not convinced that it is even possible to
negotiate with al-Qaeda and their ilk. How do you

reason with someone willing to kill themselves in an attempt to murder as many innocent civilians as they possibly can? To my mind, they're a kind of mindless religious fanatic which we haven't seen before, at least not in the UK, probably not anywhere in the last century. They're beyond negotiation, in my book.

P: Ohhf... you see... this is where I think you... and your government... are mistaken. You are looking in the wrong place at the wrong things... and it blinds you. I met so many mujahideen, or jihadists as you call them, in Iraq... including members of al-Qaeda. And in one way, you are right... they are extremely religious, many of them. They speak in a religious language and they use the Koran to justify their actions. They are very devout... very committed. But you know... my impression was that this religiosity... this embracing of their faith... was not the reason they joined the struggle, but more a way of strengthening their resolve after they joined. It gave them courage and the strength they needed to do what had to be done. If you have decided to become a guided bomb... to end your life... it would be strange if you did not try and give your death greater meaning by seeing it as a sacrifice to God... if you did not think about your religion and whether you have given it proper attention during your life. But the point is, this embrace of religion is the consequence of their decision to join the jihad, not the cause of it. I believe it comes afterwards, not before.

Besides, when you talk to these people, you
find that they are both highly rational and highly
political... as well as being very religious. It is
one of your delusions... or maybe a necessary
myth... that they are fighting you because they are
religious fanatics and not because they oppose your
invasions... tortures... bombings... you know. When
I spoke with them... and actually... if you read bin
Laden's letter to America... or any of his interviews
with Western journalists... you will find it is the same
thing.

What I am saying is... the ones I spoke to said they
fought to end the occupation... overthrow the puppet
government... stop the oppression of Muslims... show
solidarity with the Palestinians... stop Western support
for all the dictators... and in Iraq, sometimes to
prevent other groups from challenging their position.
A local power struggle... actually, against the Iranians
who were backing the Shia groups. Hey, is this not
ironic? Al-Qaeda in Iraq fights to limit the influence of
the Iranians... the West's number one enemy today!
I wonder if the CIA are already giving them covert
support to blow up Shias... it would not surprise me for
one single minute!

*We might need
to get clarity on
this from our
cousins over
the pond.
Ask MG.
GH*

My point is... these are all political grievances,
Michael, not religious demands. They are perfectly
normal political issues... strategic questions. I never
met a mujahid who was fighting simply to convert the
world to Islam... or to bring back the Caliphate... or
because he just wanted to kill unbelievers. They
often spoke about how the world would be more just
and more peaceful if it lived in submission to Allah...
and how, ah... Muslims would be free from oppression
and violence if they lived in the Caliphate... But this
is also politics, is it not? It is an aspiration for a more
just and equitable society which is the essence of
politics!

Actually, I have a related question for you. Why is
it, do you think, that when the Jews argue that they
want a special homeland where they are free from
persecution... where they can practise their religion
without any interference from others... that the world
nods its head and says, 'OK. That is a good idea. We
will help you establish this Jewish homeland'? But,
when Muslims say the same thing... 'we would like an
Islamic homeland, a Caliphate, where Muslims can be
safe from persecution and free to live under their own
sharia law'... oh my God! Then the world says, 'No, you
must be fanatical terrorists to want such a thing'? Why
is this, Michael? Why [inaudible}... home [inaudible]...
double standards...

M: [inaudible] probably got something to [inaudible] the
       Holocaust [inaudible] Europe [inaudible]

[recording interruption]

[1.8]   *Can we use the following section to demonstrate how mentally unbalanced YS was? Check with PT. It could be useful as a means to deflect criticisms of government policy. Brief the PR lads. GH*

P: I used to have this dream... regularly for a time.
       Strangely enough... or perhaps it is not strange at all,
       considering... you were in it, Michael.

M: Really? I was in your dream? How perfectly strange.

P: It started in Iraq... the first time I really came
       close to being killed... an American patrol. We
       never saw them until they were practically walking
       past. There was a sudden fire-fight... several of my
       group were killed... others were badly wounded. I
       barely escaped through an alleyway. I had bullet
       holes in my clothes. Can you believe it? Three holes
       where bullets passed through my shirt and my
       trousers without touching my skin! I was in shock...
       amazed... in a state of total disbelief. I kept putting
       my fingers through the holes in my clothes. I had
       to touch my skin where the bullets passed... It was
       like I expected the blood to start gushing out any
       minute... like my skin was just waiting to burst open...
       like I was actually dead but my body had not realised

it... so surreal. [...] That night, I tossed and turned for hours. My heart was racing like a drum. I thought I was going to have a heart attack! I could not stop replaying the shooting... the scrambled escape... over and over in my mind.

Anyway, just before dawn... as the horizon started to glow and the animals started waking up... I finally fell to sleep. That is when I had this dream... we were in a room... you and me. It was a bit like this one in terms of its neglected, oppressive atmosphere... but more like a cheap doctor's waiting room, you know... like a typical National Health Service waiting room... There were black and white checked vinyl tiles on the floor... and dusty plastic pot plants... and really old-fashioned posters and notices on the wall warning you to avoid STDs and check your skin for changes in sun spots. The light was one of those fluorescent tubes which buzzed loudly and flickered every now and then... like it was going to go out. The chairs were vinyl... in pastel colours... a bit greasy... and really low and sagging, so when you sat in them, your knees would come up around your ears. They were arranged around the walls of the room... a Formica coffee table in the middle...

I remember that it was so stuffy and warm... and there was nothing to read except really old, dog-eared copies of Woman's Own. You know this magazine?

I do not know if it even exists any more, but for a
while in the seventies it was in every doctor's... every
dentist's... every hairdresser's waiting room... every
public waiting room in the whole world! It must be
the most boring magazine in the world... especially for
a man. I really do not know who bought it and read
it... seriously! I guess that is why there were so many
abandoned ones... donated to every doctor and dentist
on the planet. Oh... and there were ancient copies of
Reader's Digest...

The dream started with a very matronly and officious
woman ordering me to take a seat and wait. She said
that the Director will see me soon. Then she disappears
quietly through a door... I sit down and you are already
there... in a clean, crisp army uniform, you know... but
with sweat patches under your arms. You are leafing
through a magazine without reading it. You do not
even glance up at what is happening. I can tell that you
are really irritated... and probably bored.

It is strange, but somehow... I know I have just been
killed... I'm recently dead. I remember shooting...
lots of noise... smoke... but I cannot remember dying
exactly, and I do not know how I got here... this room. I
appear to have no wounds or bullet holes in my clothes.
In fact, my clothes are perfectly fine... although I smell
like I have been travelling in them for forty-eight hours
in what must have been a very sweaty train, or, or...

an unventilated car. I catch the smell of my own body odour every now and then, and I am a bit embarrassed about it, frankly. I really want to wash and change into some clean clothes... a lot like right now! [laughter]...

I have no idea what I am doing here, or what is going to happen. The Director will see me? Who is the Director? Is this not a doctor's waiting room? I am confused... and uncomfortable. I feel unwashed... uneasy. I sink down into a fake leather sofa chair, and immediately the heavy, suffocating heat wraps around me like a giant blanket. I cannot breathe properly. The heavy air is crushing my chest. I wish for nothing but a glass of pure, ice-cold water.

I have had this dream so many times now... every few months for many years... like clockwork. Along with those anxiety dreams where you are naked in public but only you seem to notice and you feel really exposed...

Anyway, after what seems an age of discomforting silence, you and I start to talk. I ask you how you came to be here, and you say it was a roadside bomb, no doubt planted by one of my lot, thank you very much! Well, you look pretty good, considering, I say, and give a laugh. You are not amused and ask me how I got here. Well, in a fire-fight with a bunch of your lads, you murderous bastards. Then we start to argue about who

is going up and who is going down... when we finally get
to see the Director, of course!

You accuse me of being a, a... a fanatical jihadist who
kills innocent women and children! I am seriously
going to burn in hell, according to you. I say that
you are a, a... a Godless atheist who rapes and burns
entire countries in the search for your oil supplies,
and you are the one who is going to burn... hopefully
in a cauldron of burning oil! Now that would be ironic!
Besides... I am a Christian by birth, while you are a
materialist, hedonistic atheist. You respond that you
are Anglican. You have been baptised as a child. Well,
I am fighting for justice and equality, while you are
fighting for resources and imperialism, I say. Bullshit,
you say, I am fighting to protect my people... and
your people, thank you very much... from murderous
fanatics like you! [...]

It is at this moment, when the argument is at its most
heated and we are both at our most angry, that the
matron steps back in the room and quietly says that
the Director has been delayed and we will have to wait
a little longer. We stop and look at her for a moment as
she waddles out of the room... and then we start back
in again! You evil bloodthirsty terrorist! You blood-
sucking imperialist! You crazy religious fanatic! You
greedy, torturing scum! We go on and on and on...

[2.9]

Wasn't this the clearest indication that P knew exactly what was going on? Did the OIC note this at all in the log? I can see we are going to have to juggle and do cartwheels to explain this. Any suggestions about a credible angle gratefully received. GH

M: And?

P: Oh, I thought you were not even listening. You looked a bit distracted there, Michael. Are you expecting something to happen? [...] No? [...]

Anyway, I am sure you can guess the rest. We argue ceaselessly and without resolution... two enemies locked in combat. We scream at each other and all the, ah, ah... bile and hatred we feel for each other pours out like a, a, a... stream of molten lava. We blame each other for starting the war... and for continuing it... for being a terrorist... and a state terrorist... a fascist... and a fanatic. And every once in a while, the matron woman comes in and interrupts us to say that we will have to wait just a bit longer...

Meanwhile, the seats get more and more uncomfortable, and the room gets stuffier and stuffier... and hotter and hotter...

So... eventually... after a thousand angry words and a hundred more visits from the matron... I wake up covered in sweat... and the next thing you know I am sitting here talking to you in a similar airless, shitty little room!

[4.7]

I wonder if we are already there, Michael... in God's little waiting room. What do you think? Maybe we are not in this old factory storeroom at all...

M: [inaudible]... me go and not [inaudible]...

[recording interruption]

P: why we left it there, right out in the open.

the hillside day.

[3.8]

M: [inaudible]... would it take to make you stop this campaign? What I mean is, what do you expect the British government to do... exactly? What are your terms, Professor?

In the public interest? It could cause public alarm to release evidence of another planned operation, especially given how badly this one reflects on the ability of the service to respond. Plus, we don't want to have to answer awkward questions about this arsehole's list of demands. You can just imagine what some members of the House – not to mention the press – will say! There's also the Israel question. Suggest recording interruption to avoid embarrassment.

GH

P: I am glad you asked, Michael. Do not fear... there will
        be a published list of demands sent to all British media
        outlets very soon... after the completion of the first two
        operations of our new campaign. This way, the British
        people will know we are serious... and that we will not
        stop until the government... at the very <u>least</u>... begins
        a dialogue with us on these issues. Of course, we do not
        expect them to be publicly humiliated and seen to cave
        in to our demands—

M: —But exactly who is the 'we' you are talking about,
        Professor? Who should we talk to? What are the names
        of your colleagues?

[1.8]

P: All in good time, Michael. It will become clear later.
        I was going to say that we can negotiate out of view
        and try and come up with some... shall we say?...
        creative ways in which your government's policies
        could be altered and adjusted. But there has to be
        some real expression of regret... at least in private, but
        preferably in public so the world can see it... and some
        evidence of a determination to make amends for all the
        suffering.

        Having said that... there are a number of steps
        which... if taken immediately... <u>could</u> lead to
        a suspension of the campaign. At a minimum,

and Britain should withdraw its forces from Afghanistan immediately and announce an end to involvement in any further NATO or US interventions in the Middle East. In particular, the government ███████████, and should announce it will not support any military action against Iran... It should announce the end of its unquestioned support for Israel, and expel Israeli diplomats to demonstrate its seriousness about the peace process. The ███ Related to this, it should take steps in the European Commission to force Israel to sign the same human rights guarantees that other importing nations have to abide by... and instigate a ban on the importation of Israeli goods until the Israelis dismantle their settlements back to the 1967 borders... At the least, Israeli products from the Occupied Territory should be subject to an immediate import ban. [...] Why are you shaking your head?

M: The government will never agree to any of this... it's totally unrealistic.

P: OK... you may be right... but you asked me what would make us halt our campaign, and I am telling you. As I was about to say... the most important thing we demand is policy changes and measures which will allow the Arab revolution... *Al-Sawra*... to succeed. Support must be offered to the protestors. Governments who resist the calls for democracy must be warned. Sanctions must be imposed... economic and military... on those regimes like Syria and Bahrain who use violence to suppress the demonstrators. In particular... and this is very important, Michael... the British government must end all exports of military weapons to those authoritarian regimes.

We will clearly have to prepare a response to possible questions about current British arms exports.

And crowd control products... like teargas... batons... water cannons. And prison equipment... shackles... pepper sprays... Tasers... all those nasty things your companies export for the suppression of the masses.

Do not worry... we will provide you with a list of forthcoming arms deals which must be immediately cancelled...

Make sure we have all the facts first, and then DC will need to work up a statement to be approved by us. GH

Britain must also announce that it will be cooperating with international efforts at the UN to regulate the arms trade... including providing complete information on its production and trade of weapons over the past twenty years.

I presume we have not received any list yet? I wonder why...

Hopefully, they've forgotten about it, although that seems unlikely. It will be highly embarrassing to publicise some of these deals, as I'm sure you're aware. GH

M: [inaudible]

P: —No, no... listen to me... the British government
       must announce a full public inquiry into British
       involvement in torture... and provide lawyers and
       human rights groups with any and all information
       relevant to the prosecution of those American agents
       who have engaged in torture over the past ten years...
       Britain will also need to announce that it will limit its
       cooperation with American intelligence because of its
       long and well-known involvement in torture...

       Michael, this is important... non-negotiable, in fact.
       Your government must immediately announce the
       payment of compensation to Iraqi and Afghan civilians
       killed by British forces and make a public apology
       for its role in the war on terror. In addition, it must...
       must... erect a memorial to stand in London to the
       victims of British violence in Iraq and Afghanistan...

       Do you need me to go on, Michael? Are you starting to
       get the idea?

M: Yes, Professor, I hear what you're saying... although
       there is simply no way the British government will
       accede to any of your demands while you are holding
       one of its people hostage. They don't take kindly to
       things like that. [...] As you well know, no government
       can be seen to give in to the demands of terrorists.
       We never gave any concession in exchange for
       hostages in Iraq, and we won't do it on home soil...

And I am also bound to say that this is probably not the best time to be engaging in a terrorist campaign. Everyone is preoccupied with other things... like the recession—

P: —No, no, no! You are wrong about this. You are forgetting how the media responds to anything related to terrorism. They are obsessed with it. An al-Qaeda operative sneezes and they give it wall-to-wall coverage for a week... experts are wheeled out... COBRA is convened... the president of America calls your prime minister. [...] No, no, no... You will see, my friend... our actions will shake the whole world... even if there is a recession. The whole world loves a good terrorism story—

M: —Be that as it may, Professor, what I don't understand is why you didn't do this a few years ago when public dissatisfaction with foreign military adventures was much higher... in 2005... or 2006? When there was real talk of ending Britain's involvement in the war on terror?

P: *Enta 'abeet ya akh Mikel?*[36] Can you not see how the world is changing... what a historical moment this is? Think of all the protests... the, the... the occupations...

---

[36] Trans. 'Are you simple-minded, brother Michael?' Note: Egyptian colloquial Arabic.

the, the... the ferment taking place all over the world. This is not a, a, a 'Spring'... it is a tidal wave! But these countries... these mass movements... will require real independence to succeed. They will need to be free from foreign domination... and pressure... all that continual interference. I think the next few years will be crucial... they will change everything. We want to ensure that the promise of this new era will be realised this time... that it will not be stillborn like so many before. But for this, a revolution will have to occur in both those societies that are struggling to be free, and in the other states like Britain which are so influential. The truth is... I do not think there has ever been a better time than now for changing history. You know it is true, Michael. You cannot deny it...

M: Actually, that's another thing, Professor. Why are you not back in Tahrir Square, fighting for democracy in your own country? Why are you attacking us when you could be helping your own countrymen?

P: No, well... yes, you are right. I suppose I could be in Egypt, fighting for the revolution. [...] The reason I am not is because I do not need to be... the people have already risen up. They are fighting for their freedom... their dignity. They do not need me.

I am here because no one is fighting you right here... in the heart of the beast. [...] Your own people are too,

too... too passive... brainwashed... to fight you.
They sit and drink their beer while you burn the world.
[...] They need a catalyst... a spark. [...] So this is
where I am needed. Besides, I have already explained
to you... you are one of the main, ah... participants in
the revolution in Egypt... Libya... Bahrain... all those
other places where dictators use the weapons you
gave them to crush the people. This is why I need to be
here... now...

[1.8]

Michael, there is a really important question I have
to ask... Do you know how I came to take the name
Samir Hamoodi... why I chose this name as my new
revolutionary name? Do you remember who he was?
No? [...] I can see that you do not...

Samir Hamoodi was a little boy in Al-Basra... eleven
years old. He was shot by a British soldier... in 2003.
I watched it happen. I was a witness to his death.
Afterwards, I took his name as a, a... a memorial to his
too-short life... a, a... a tribute, you might say. I believe
he was a martyr. I wanted to fight in his name... I
wanted to fight for all the children like him who died...
and continue to die... in all the forgotten places... killed
in your name. The fact is that I knew he would never
be remembered by those who had killed him. There
would be no commemoration of his life... no plaque with

his name engraved for all to see. His name would never
be read aloud on Memorial Day...

I knew the man who killed him did not know his
name.

[3.8]

You look a little surprised. You have nothing to say?
[...] I will tell you what I saw that day. A squad of
British soldiers was walking on patrol when a small
bomb... an IED, as you call them, well, it exploded
beside the path where they were. It was hidden
in a clump of dried grass. One man... Private Carl
████████████was his name, I believe... he was injured
in the explosion... the only one—

M: —How the fuck—

P: —small pieces of metal pierced his body. He lay on the
ground. I saw the medic examine him... the others
formed a defensive circle... they called the helicopter
to evacuate him. I could see through my binoculars
he was very badly injured. He could not breathe
properly... his face was all white and shiny... I heard
on the BBC world news the next day he had died
from internal wounds... You knew this man, did you
not, Michael?

M: Oh my God! You were there? <u>You</u>... yes... yes, he was
      a good friend... best man at my wedding, actually...
      I was best man at his... We'd been friends since our
      university days. We went through basic training
      together... I can't [inaudible]... sake!

P: I am very sorry. I too lost many close friends in that
      war... blown up... shot by your soldiers. One of them...
      Hafez... was captured... he disappeared. I never saw
      his face again. I heard a rumour he died in custody...
      beaten to death by his American interrogators. We
      never had a body we could bury... At least your friend
      had a funeral. <u>You</u> could say goodbye... But it was war...
      a war you started, not me. I was just there to defend
      the people from your aggression. Drive out the invader.
      If your friend had not been killed by one of my group's
      bombs, he might have gone on to kill many Iraqis... or,
      he might have died in one of the other operations we
      mounted—

[loud banging]

M: ARGH... [inaudible]... YOU MURDERING BASTARD!
      IT WAS YOU! [...] FUCK! [...] FUCK!

[2.9]

P: There is no point in trying that again, because you
      will not be able to break those handcuffs... or the

bolt in that desk... in a thousand years! We built it to
withstand the strength of any man... including you.
We could not take any chances...

I wish we had some progress on finding P's associates to report.
The failure to capture them could increase panic in the wake of the Shrivenham
incident. At the very least, it does not look good! Can we step up the investigation?
I am willing to authorise all necessary resources (there's no austerity here!).
On the former, we should probably say that with the evidence we have,
  we don't believe the two incidents are linked. What do you think? GH

M: [inaudible]

P: Anyway... that day in Al-Basra... after your friend
      had been airlifted away... more soldiers came. You
      and your comrades continued the patrol. You started
      moving through the streets... very fast... helmets on.
      It was clear... I could see it... your body language... it
      was obvious that you were really angry. Maybe you
      thought the people should have warned you about
      the bomb. You were going to punish them for this. No
      friendly smiles... no leisurely conversations with the
      market sellers... no sweets for the kids... no, no, no...
      not this day.

      I could not see everything, but from where I was...
      after a while... I heard the sound of shots... just two.
      'Pop, pop'... then a lot of shouting... a woman crying...
      wailing, actually. Soldiers were running this way and
      that. I saw you being dragged by your comrades. You

ran down the hill to the main road. After that... I could
not see you any more...

I decided to go and take a look for myself. I knew the
British did not know what I looked like... there was
only a small risk. When I came to the front of the
crowd, I saw a little boy lying in the alley. He was so
small... His eyes were wide... looking all around. He was
breathing really hard... like he had been running fast...
you know? You could see the ribs in his chest. There
were two small puncture wounds... a tiny trickle of
blood oozing out. He just lay there... like he had fallen
over.

All this time, his mother was wailing and crying...
'Sa'edouh, Sa'edouh, min shan Allah, la totrokny
yomma.'[37] The crowd was growing all the time... people
shouting... shaking their fists... Their faces twisted.
I looked all around but I could not see any British
soldiers... not a single one. You had gone... disappeared.
I stepped forward and tried to help. I called my men
and we took him to the hospital... but he died before
we got there. One minute he was breathing like a
marathon runner in the back seat... 'Heh, heh, heh,
heh'... like that. The next, he closed his eyes and was
gone. I tried to revive him, but when I pushed down on

---

[37] Trans. 'Help him, Help him, for God's sake, don't leave your mother.'
    Note: Iraqi Arabic.

his chest, blood came out of his mouth and nose... all frothy and bright red... There was nothing I could do...

Later, when we took his body back, I spoke to his mother. I asked about her son. His name was Samir Hamoodi... he was eleven years old. He had been playing with home-made firecrackers in the alley... you know those ones where you scrape the heads off matchsticks and then have a nail and wire that you smack together? It makes a cracking sound? No? It is not something British children have to do, I expect... I made one once myself... as a child... pyrotechnics for the poor.

Anyway... I told her to go to the, ah, ah... military base and tell the commanding officer the soldiers had killed her son. She should demand justice. I promised her we would avenge her son... he was a martyr and one day the people who killed him would know his name... they would pay the price for murdering him so casually in their arrogant, imperialistic war. I told her he would never be forgotten and in the future, the whole world would know his name...

Is there a record of this? Do we know who the woman is?
In other words, will some persistent journalist be able to track down this story? Further on there is mention of her making an official report, but was it ever officially filed? We must be prepared in case they put the woman on TV or ambush the former camp CO outside his house.
Hopefully, there's no remaining record and the woman has disappeared. However, just in case, we will need an explanation for why no action was taken.
I suggest you liaise with military PR. GH

That's it. That is how I got my new name... my
reborn name... like when a person converts to Islam
and takes a new name. And that is when I started
seriously looking for <u>you</u>, Michael. I knew that one
day I was going to find you and make you pay for that
little boy's death... and here you are... in the flesh...
Captain Michael ███████████, ███████ Battalion,
████████... Iraq veteran... child-killer.

[banging]

*Of course, if the video ever surfaces in public, these redactions
– and all the recording interruptions we've made – won't
amount to anything whatsoever. This is what haunts me.
Seeing M and P on the six o'clock news one day. GH*

[10.7]

P: Michael, I am sorry for the handcuffs... for chaining
you to the table. It is not personal, you understand.
It is just for security. I am sure you understand. You
are a really big guy... we could not risk you breaking
free and maybe breaking my soft little academic neck!
[laughter]

I would let you loose for a moment to stretch, but the
keys are with the others... a security measure, as I
said. Do you need something to drink? Here, have a
bottle of water.

M: No, thank you. I'm fine.

P: Are you sure? Please don't be angry... you must
be very thirsty by now. I know I am... What about

Do we know if they really were nearby at the time – or was this a bluff? How did the field agents miss this, and how can we not know where they went after the blast? We look like complete idiots. GH

something to eat? I could ask my men to bring us something. They are watching all of this on the video feed... preparing for the netcast. They could come over in a few minutes with food and water, anything you like? [...] No? OK... have it your way.

You should know... I understand what you have been doing these past hours... asking me a lot of open-ended questions... trying to build rapport, as they say in your training manuals. [...] This is a very good interrogation technique. It makes it much more likely that I will let something slip... provide a few details... mention my plans... a contact. And you can see who I am... what my weaknesses are... my character... my beliefs. I can tell you are very good at your job. Of course, the problem is that I am not your prisoner... you are mine. So what do you think you are up to, my friend... asking me all these questions... as if it is you in charge of me? Do you know something?

[2.9]

OK... never mind. So... let us start to discuss the real business of the night. I will ask you a few questions... and I need you to be completely honest. OK? I have been completely honest with you... I have told you all my reasons for what I am doing... my personal stories... my thoughts. Now you need to be honest with me. Do you understand?

[1.8]

[banging]

Do you understand me, Michael? This is important!

M: Yes, Professor. Calm down! For God's sake! Yes, I understand. I'll try and answer your questions as honestly as I can. Jesus.

P: Right... so... first question. When you were in military intelligence in Iraq... following the death of the martyr Samir... and they redeployed you so you would not be out on patrol again... were you involved in any way with training or assisting those death squads? I mean... I know that they did not come directly out of any British-led training programmes, but I thought you might have had something to do with them... or met some of the Americans who were involved. And by them, I mean those gangs who would turn up at a hospital... or the university... or when a line of police recruits was waiting somewhere... and take a dozen people away in their SUVs... only for them to be found dead on the side of the road a few days later, usually after they had been horribly tortured for days. Those guys were from the Ministry of the Interior, everyone knows... They were trained by the Americans... equipped by the Americans... funded by the Americans, and yet... strangely... the Americans had no idea, so

they claim, of what these guys were doing all over
Baghdad and elsewhere. What I mean is... huh? How is
this possible?

*Bugger! I thought this story had died a natural death.
At least we had no documented involvement. I suggest we maintain that we have
no knowledge or involvement and we refuse to make any statement
— unless you can suggest another approach? GH*

M: We did not—

P: —No, no... wait. Is it not a, a... a coincidence that John
Negroponte... this is the same man who also happened
to be an ambassador in Latin America when death
squads were so common then — all trained at the
School of the Americas — was also appointed as US
Ambassador to Iraq at this time? I mean... what are
the chances of that? Is he just unlucky, or what? Death
squads seem to follow him like... like... ah... fairy dust!
A bad smell!

Michael, it is very important to me. [...] Did you have
anything to do with these groups? Did you meet
anyone who was involved?

M: No, Professor, I was never involved in anything like
that. Mine was purely a desk job... as it seems you
already know. I collated intelligence on insurgent
groups operating in our zone. Reports would come in
from the field units, contacts... informers... I would
analyse them and then send on a report to those above

me... ████████████████████████████
████████████████████████████████ Actually,
that's when I first heard about you and became aware
that you were behind a great many attacks on our
troops. [...] But no, I didn't have anything to do with
any training of any military or intelligence forces...
clandestine or otherwise. I was never involved in
anything like that, nor was anyone in my office... as far
as I know.

P: But what about when you went to Baghdad for those
       briefings with the Americans? Did you hear anything
       while you were there, any rumours?

*It's rather shocking how much real intelligence the insurgents had.
Our counter-measures clearly failed. Luckily, this story never really reached the
light of day. Are we prepared for public scrutiny of our record in Iraq?
And are there any lessons here for counter-intelligence in Afghanistan?
Your thoughts would be welcome, as always. GH*

M: I do remember talking about it with a few American
       officers, when we were having lunch in the cafeteria.
       Just passing comments... nothing serious—

P: —And what was the tone of what they were saying? Did
       they talk about any operational details?

M: Well they didn't state that the death squads were their
       idea or that they were actually running them, if that's
       what you're after!

P: No, no, no. That is not what I mean. What I mean is...
      did they, ah... discuss how the death squads operated...
      how they, ah... chose their victims... that sort of thing?
      Were the death squads there for eliminating particular
      people as it were... or was it more to spread a random
      terror among certain groups... to stop them from
      supporting the insurgents? Were they just picking
      people up randomly... this is what I am trying to ask.

M: Oh, well, that's a level of detail that never got discussed
      in my presence. Mostly, it was just like, 'Did you hear
      the latest story, how they drove right up to the hospital
      and took ten doctors? Can you believe the balls of
      those guys!' Comments like that. They never went into
      detail... ████████████████████████████████████
      ██ But
      it was like they weren't really surprised... like they
      were tapping the side of their nose as they spoke. I
      remember it gave me a bad feeling. I really didn't want
      to know, frankly.

P: Did you tell the Americans about me?

M: What do you mean, precisely?

P: Did you inform them about an Egyptian... a former
      economics professor... who had recently arrived and
      started to operate in the area?

M: Of course, I did. That's why I'd go to Baghdad... to
       coordinate with American military intelligence. We'd
       share information on which groups were operating in
       our respective areas... who we knew was involved...
       where the supply routes were... patterns of attacks...
       which groups were cooperating... which were
       feuding. ███████████████████████████████████

       ██

       ██████████████████████████████████████ I told
       them all about you, and certain inquiries were made.
       I suppose because of their involvement in Egypt, they
       soon found out who you were and traced you ████████

       ██

[3.8] *As mentioned – is it in the public interest to detail a possible UK
       connection to Iraqi death squads? This has the potential to become
       quite embarrassing. Suggest a brief recording interruption. GH*

       Oh, I see what you mean...

P: My cousins were taken by a death squad... Ghassan...
       he was a lab technician. And his son... Stephan. He was
       just a boy... sixteen years old... still had pimples.

M: I'm truly sorry to hear that.

P: Yes... it happened a couple of months after I stayed
       with them. I feel so terrible. I suppose I knew they
       were targeted because of me... and now you have

confirmed it... Those evil bastards found out who I had stayed with... [inaudible] because of me...

My wife is Iraqi... as you know. Her family fled after the first Gulf War. We met when I was at university in London. Later... after we married... we moved together to Cairo. But she still had relatives in Baghdad... cousins... uncles... you know...

Anyway, when I decided I had to go to Iraq... it was the last thing she did to help me. She gave me the contact of one of her cousins who still worked at the central hospital. She said that they would take me in. They would do it because of family obligation.

So... after I got there from Jordan I went and found them. They were such nice people. They embraced me like their own son... gave me a place to stay. They said I could stay as long as I liked. I think they guessed why I was there suddenly in the middle of a war... but they never asked me a single question about anything... what I was there to do... who I was going to meet. And I never told them. I did not want to endanger them. I thought they would be safer if they did not know...

You know... they were not political at all. They lived very simply... working hard... trying not to offend anyone. They never talked about politics once the whole time I was there... not in my presence anyway. They cooperated with the Ba'ath Party when Saddam was in power... and they cooperated with the Americans when Saddam fell. They just worked hard and tried to enjoy the small things in life... like eating together with a long-lost relative from Egypt... joking... laughing... having a good time...

And then someone picked them up and cut their heads off... [inaudible] Some MOTHERFUCKER trained by the fucking Americans bound their hands with wire... burned them with cigarettes all over their bodies... and then hacked off their genitals! Stuffed them in their mouths... Stephan had his foot chopped off... with an axe! CAN YOU FUCKING BELIEVE THAT? A PIMPLY-FACED KID! [...] It was probably in front of his father too... And then they dumped their bodies by the side of the road... like so much garbage.

What kind of monsters, *Ya safala, ya wlad el wiskha...* *dah eblees nafsoh Hat 'annokom wati*[38]...

Even I have to admit, this is pretty appalling.
  Is there any concrete information on these killings?
   Do we know who carried them out?
 More importantly, will a journalist be able to reconstruct the story?
 I suggest we have something prepared in case we're asked for comment. Ideas? GH

---

[38] Trans. 'You (pl.) loathsomes, you (pl.) sons of a filthy woman, Satan himself can learn from you (pl.).' Note: Arabic Egyptian colloquialism.

[banging]

[3.8]

> *Erhamna ya Allah be'azeem rahmatek*[39]... it is just so,
> so, so... I am beyond language... beyond tolerance. [...]
> It cannot be done by sane human beings towards other
> human beings.

[1.8]

> It took more than a week for his wife to find them...
> identify their bodies. [...] And you know? Their names
> will also never be remembered. Like Samir, no one
> in America... or Britain... will ever even know they
> existed. There will never be a memorial to them... even
> though they were just as innocent as the victims of
> 9/11 and 7/7. Just like little Samir... who you shot and
> left to die... they will be the nameless victims of your
> war of aggression.

M: That really bothers you, doesn't it, Professor... that
      they won't be remembered?

P: It bothers me immensely, Michael... because it is
      symbolic of a much more widespread attitude... and

---

[39] Trans. 'God, engulf us with your great mercy.' Note: Classical Arabic with
Egyptian accent.

a, a... a moral hierarchy in which some people's lives are worth so little compared to others'. Really, it is symbolic of the complete lack of concern about all the people you hurt with your violence... people with their own lives... their own hopes and dreams. [...] But who are snuffed out without acknowledgement... without even any dignity... without even the courtesy of being named!

And more than this, it is about erasure and forgetting. How you... collectively... and individually... erase the suffering of real people so that you can launch more wars... over and over, again and again. What I mean is... if you remembered all those innocent people you killed before... if you knew their names and their stories... if they were read out in your schools and in your churches... you might... might!... be more cautious about starting the next war.

But what you do instead is you erase them... blot them out... not even counting them as a number... not recording a single one of their names... never mentioning them when you remember the war... only remembering your own soldiers. Tell me... what kind of perverse morality is it that you would honour the people who kill others but not a single one of their victims? How is it that a soldier who shot women and children at roadblocks... or who killed a child in a filthy alley... would have his name inscribed on a memorial...

but all those innocent people who died at his hands would be unmentioned... forgotten... as if they never existed? So... yes... I am angry... fucking angry!... I am enraged... that you do not remember them!

M: What can I say—

P: —Say nothing, Michael... just say nothing. [...] It is true what they say... 'The struggle against power is the struggle of memory against forgetting.'

[4.1]

Michael, I have a very hard question for you. Are you ready for it? [...] Yes?

[2.9]

When you were in Iraq... and since then... when you joined the intelligence services as a counter-terrorism officer... were you ever involved in the torture of any suspects?

M: Absolutely no. British intelligence is not, and has never been, involved in the practice of torture...

Check with Legal about the following section. Does this constitute prima facie evidence of UK involvement in torture? If one of those human rights lawyers files a writ as a consequence, can we be sure the CPS won't open an investigation?
          Suggest a brief recording interruption to be on the safe side. GH

P: Michael, are you trying to lie to me? To me? I did
       not think you would be such an idiot! I know you
       are a very intelligent man... and I told you all the
       facts of your country's history. In so many places...
       for hundreds of years... British forces have used
       torture against their enemies. They may have called
       it something else, but you know it is true. It is a, a... a
       tradition, you might say. You used it against rebels in
       Aden... against the CTs in Malaya... in Kenya against
       the Mau Mau... Northern Ireland—

M: —That was never proved. Technically... the, ah,
       European Court of Justice said it wasn't torture. There
       was some brutal treatment, yes... but it wasn't torture.

P: You should tell that to the men I met in Belfast... oh,
       you did not know I went there? Yes... well... I suppose
       it is OK to tell you. I went there to ███████████
       ███████████████████████████████████
       ██████████ our campaign. Some of the men I met
       there still suffer greatly from the <u>non</u>-torture your
       colleagues gave them. You should try telling them that
       they were not tortured... by being hooded... beaten...
       burned with cigarettes... kept awake for days... forced
       to stand for hours until they collapsed... subjected to
       mock executions. Some of them told me they confessed
       to crimes they did not commit after being <u>interrogated</u>
       by your colleagues. These days, they live with severe
       mental and emotional problems... the same problems

you can see in victims of torture the world over. Any
doctor can tell you the symptoms of a torture victim.

Anyway, it is no longer in doubt... all the confessions by
former interrogators and all the documented cases...
as well as all the victims who have come forward...
remove any doubt. British intelligence engaged in a lot
of torture in Northern Ireland. And it was still going on
in the 1990s...

M: That was a long time ago—

P: —The 1990s is not that long ago, my friend.

M: Be that as it may, Professor, the service has moved on
since those days. We don't do work like that any more.

P: Why should I believe you? I mean... with a record like
that, should anyone believe that you have suddenly
cleaned up your act?

M: Yes. Why not?

P: Because that is not how people are, Michael! That
is not how governments are... or organisations. Are
you so naive to believe that after decades... maybe
hundreds of years of behaving in a certain way... an
organisation is just going to suddenly clean up its act...
become all nice and shiny... morally pure? That is like

believing that, ah... soldiers... after millennia of taking trophies from the enemy dead... will suddenly stop doing it. Ohhf... that has not happened, has it, Michael? We hear stories about British and American soldiers chopping off the fingers of insurgents for trophies... pulling out teeth. In Vietnam, American soldiers cut off ears and scrotums...

Did you take any trophies, Michael? Did you cut off any body parts to bring back as a little trophy to take out and look at when you wanted to feel the excitement again... or perhaps to impress your friends with tales from the war zone... feel just a little bit more alive?

M: That's offensive, Professor. If you know so much about me, then you know I'd never be involved in such disgusting behaviour—

P: But your fellow soldiers probably did, do you not think? I mean... we know for a fact it happened all the time... more than most people realise. Did you personally know anyone who took a trophy?

[3.8]

M: I, ah... I saw one lad who had taken a tooth, █████████████████ I reported him to the camp commander.

For God's sake! I presume there's a nasty little paper trail on this.
We're going to have to get the military brass to quietly look into this to make sure
there's not a bigger story to be uncovered – you know the sort of thing:
'The secret souvenirs of soldiers' or something worse.
That's something The Independent would love to publish!
Your suggestions for how we might prepare for such an eventuality
would be greatly welcomed. GH

P: And what happened to him? Was he disciplined... sent
      to prison... returned home? What?

M: I never heard.

P: You mean... you were not told about his punishment or
      you never knew if he was punished?

M: I don't know if he was punished, but I saw him later. He
      was still there. He didn't get sent home.

P: We both know what goes on in war. This is not a
      surprise to me... or you, I expect...

      I still want to know about your involvement in the
      torture that took place. Anyone who can read a
      newspaper knows that British soldiers tortured a
      number of people to death in Iraq... and that British
      intelligence officers were present at the torture of
      certain British nationals at Guantanamo and other
      places too.

███████████████████████████ There are cases in the courts right now about these things.

Everyone also knows that Britain was one of the fuelling stops for those rendition flights by the CIA which disappeared people to places where they could be tortured. And everyone also knows... thanks to the newspapers... that your own government secretly agreed that intelligence gained by torture from certain... ah... shall we call them, <u>allies</u>... could be used by the intelligence services, if they felt it was necessary... ███████████████████████████

I think we can probably ride this one easily enough – that was the Blair government, not us.
Do you agree?
GH

What I am saying is... you and your service are up to your neck in torture and everyone knows it. You cannot just repeat the, the... ah... public relations line that Britain does not torture when everyone knows that is a big lie.

[2.3]

So, I ask you again, Michael... what has been your involvement in this practice?

M: I... umm... I, no... all I can say is... <u>I</u> have never used torture in any interrogation I myself undertook. Honestly. The fact is, I simply don't believe in it, like most of the interrogators I know... especially the older ones. It's a very poor tool of investigation. People being tortured will say virtually anything to stop the further infliction of pain. If you torture someone long enough, you can make them say whatever you want them to say. They'll admit that Osama bin Laden lived down the estate with their own mother!

The fact is, after a while, a tortured man will try very hard to say what he thinks the interrogator wants to hear, which, as you can imagine, can really screw up an investigation. I prefer to try and work with the facts and build a level of confidence with the suspect—

P: —just like you are doing with me now!

M: Mmm, OK, I suppose so... anyway, I always found that building rapport usually gets more reliable evidence than violating their trust by abusing them. Besides, it's my personal opinion that if terrorism is wrong for targeting people who can't fight back, then using violence against an unarmed prisoner is no better, don't you think?

P: Very admirable, Michael... but you still have not really answered my question. Even if you never personally participated in waterboarding someone... or, or, or stripping them naked and leaving them to freeze in a chilled cell all night... did you work with people who did? Were you ever in Abu Ghraib... or Camp

Cropper... Baghram... Guantanamo... ████████
████████████████ one of those black sites the
Americans like so much? Did you ever get information
from one of those countries where they do not have
such an enlightened attitude to the use of torture
which you knew was obtained by... ah, shall we say...
brutal methods?

M: Yes... I... ah... have been present when prisoners were...
      rigorously interrogated.

P: Where?

M: In Iraq, there were some occasions where we worked
      with Iraqi state security people. That was quite nasty.
      [...] It makes me sick to the stomach when I think
      about it, actually... I also had to accompany some of
      my American counterparts at a few of their holding
      centres in Iraq... the ones that didn't make the news.

P: Anywhere else?

M: Guantanamo... once.

P: And?

*Bloody hell! We're never going to be rid of this story,
are we? This is why I think it might be best to have a
recording interruption and avoid dragging it all up again. GH*

M: [inaudible] Morocco. Egypt. Turkey.
       Uzbekistan... a place in Romania. Diego Garcia
       ████████████████████████████████ Is that
       enough for you? You want more? Yes? ████
       ████████████████████████████████████
       ████████████████████████████████████
       ████████████████████████████████████
       ██It was also part of my brief to evaluate
       information that came through from some of those
       same countries. We knew it was obtained under duress,
       but we simply couldn't ignore it. I always believed it
       was unreliable, but the bigwigs didn't want to take
       the risk that it might, on this particular occasion,
       give us much-needed forewarning. They didn't want
       to be the ones to ignore something which might later
       come back to bite them on the arse. The reality is, if
       they ignored it and then a bomb went off in Piccadilly,
       there'd be political hell to pay, wouldn't you say? The
       whole world'd be asking why didn't we act if we had
       the information?

P: Thank you, Michael. You have not told me anything I
       did not already know... *bas*[40] it is important that you
       admitted it... for the peace of your own conscience...
       although it does raise an interesting question.

M: What's that?

---

[40] Trans. 'But.' Note: Arabic Egyptian colloquialism.

P: Who is the real terrorist in this room?

M: What're you saying?

P:

M:

P: Well... some might say that your involvement in torture... not to mention all your activities in Iraq... means that you are a terrorist... a <u>state</u> terrorist, as it were.

M: States can't be terrorists, Professor. They have a right to use any means to protect their national interests and the security of their citizens, including force... violence, as you call it. [...] And how exactly is the use of torture equivalent to planting a bomb in a pub or on a street? It's private groups that commit acts of terrorism. States can go to war, or perhaps engage in repression. But not terrorism.

P: Oh, OK then... what you are saying then is that if a
       Mossad agent... or a member of the CIA... detonates a
       car bomb on a Beirut street... which happened, by the
       way, Michael, as I am sure you know... this is <u>not</u> a case
       of terrorism? Hey... but we all know that if al-Qaeda or
       the IRA detonates a car bomb on a street... well, that
       <u>is</u> terrorism! How, in any universe, is that logical? By
       what perversion of reason is one car bomb <u>terrorism</u>
       and another car bomb is not?

M: Mmm, it's the intention, and who actually does—

P: —And what about the Lockerbie bombing? Would you
       consider this an act of terrorism?

M: Of course it was! It was clearly a terrorist act... a
       horrendous one. I remember that time really well—

P: —And yet... according to your own government... that
       bomb was planted by the agents of a state... Libya...
       and not some group like al-Qaeda. Therefore, it must
       follow that states can also commit acts of terrorism...
       is that not the case? Otherwise, we have to stop calling
       it an act of terrorism. Lockerbie was an act of, of... of
       repression... war... a crime? What was it?

       No, no! Do not shake your head again! I can give you
       so many other examples where governments and
       their agents did the exact same things as those they

condemned as terrorists. The, ah, ah, ah... the Italian
government organised for fascists to bomb the Bologna
train station... the Israelis sent agents to bomb cafes in
Cairo. Have you heard about this? Actually, the Israelis
are today assassinating nuclear scientists in Iran
with car bombs on public roads. This is terrorism...
by anyone's definition. And what about Belfast? Did
members of the RUC... representatives of the British
state... not ███████████████████████████████████
███
███████████████████████████████████████ and pass
on the names of Catholics to the loyalist paramilitaries
so they could have them killed? And the Russians...
bombing their own apartment blocks and then blaming
it on Chechens so they could invade and take control of
the oil?

> He certainly airs some dirty laundry. We will need some very
> clever statements about what HMG believes about the Iranian
> bombings, as well as our unfortunate record in Northern Ireland.

[1.2]

> GH

The fact is... terrorism... according to your own laws
is the use of violence... or the threat of violence... to
get some kind of political gain. It involves threatening
people or violating people to send a message to a
wider audience... intimidating a larger group. If we
understand terrorism in this way... then surely the
bombing of Hiroshima and Nagasaki were acts of
terrorism? It was the mass killing of a randomly

chosen group of people in order to send a message to the leaders and people of Japan... 'surrender or we will kill all of you'.

M: That's a minority view, as you well know, Professor—

P: —And what about the widespread use of repression... and torture... disappearances... the use of death squads to torture and murder people in order to intimidate whole communities... burning people with cigarettes... cutting off their feet and heads... and then leaving their bodies somewhere where they can be seen by all... as a way of seeding terror among whole groups of people? This is simply the use of violence against certain people in order to terrify and intimidate a wider group of people. It is terrorism! [banging] Or bombing people from the air... like the mustard gas dropped on Iraqi tribesmen by Winston Churchill in the 1930s... an attempt to instil terror in a whole country. The fact is... your government has been using terrorism for hundreds of years against millions of people all over the world.

You are shaking your head again. [...] What I am simply pointing out... you and your government were involved in a massive campaign of violence against Iraq... shock and awe, the Americans called it... they were trying to shock the people... stun them into a state of terrified awe... by demonstrating unbelievable levels of violence... in order to intimidate the leaders and people of Iraq into submitting to your demands. And the same with torture... you torture someone... they come out of your prisons with physical or psychological scars, and then they are like a walking message... their suffering acts as a warning to others. 'Do not become an insurgent or this might happen to you.' It is the same as a bomb... it is using violence to send a message—

M: —I don't see it that way, Professor. I doubt anyone does. I don't think it's the same—

P: —*EZAY YA'ENY?*[41] You just do <u>not</u> want to see it... you do not <u>want</u> to believe it. [...] And it means that out of the two of us... with all your actions in Iraq... and your admitted participation in torture around the world... you are the <u>real</u> terrorist in this room... I am an amateur compared to you...

M: [inaudible]... be fucking ridiculous! You should check the law some time. You're talking out your—

P: —But who makes the law, Michael? States do... governments do... and it is no surprise that when they do, they make it so that they cannot be condemned as terrorists under their own law. They make laws which

---

[41] Trans. 'HOW COME?' Note: Arabic Egyptian colloquialism.

say... 'whatever <u>you</u> do is terrorism... but if <u>I</u> do it, it is not.' Ha! It is so brilliant!

[laughter]

M: Oh, for fuck's sake. [mumbled]

[scraping sounds]

[8.8]

P: I expect you remember that it will be my birthday in a couple of hours.

M: Do you want me to wish you a happy birthday, Professor? Is that it? We're meant to be friends now?

P: Not at all... I just remembered it... that is all. [...] In the excitement of the events today it had slipped my mind.

[1.2]

Oh, no need to look sad, Michael! I have had much worse birthdays than this. [...] *Bas heya kedah.*[42] [...] Once... I, I, I... ah, spent my birthday hiding inside a communal latrine while coalition patrols ransacked

---

[42] Trans. 'But this is how it is.' Note: Arabic Egyptian colloquialism, meaning: 'But that's life.'

the houses all around. It took about a week to get the stench out of my hair and skin, I can tell you. It clung to me like a second skin... and I could not hold down any food for days. I still feel queasy just thinking about it. [...] Another time... in Afghanistan... I spent my birthday burying the bodies of my comrades... or, should I say... the pieces of my comrades. That is what an American daisy-cutter will do. All we had to bury were just little burnt hunks of meat... like a piece of *Boftek*.[43] [...] That was a day I would prefer to forget, I can tell you...

M: Actually, I was thinking that I hadn't realised that tomorrow, in addition to being your birthday, was also the anniversary of the invasion of Iraq. I see now why you chose this particular date for your, ah... operation.

P: Finally, you are learning to read events in a deeper way, Michael... although it is a little late for you personally. I just hope your government will have the requisite intelligence to decipher the message we will send them in the next few hours.

My God! Why didn't anyone act? How many clues were they waiting for?

M: What message, Professor?

---

[43] Trans. 'Veal escalope.' Note: Typical Egyptian cuisine.

P: Oh, yes... you will see. I will not say anything more.

[6.4]

P: If I might be so blunt, Michael... how exactly did you
        come to be killing children in Iraq? How does a man
        like yourself... an intelligent, disciplined man... a man
        so clearly in control of himself... shoot a child playing
        in the street? I know it was an accident. But really,
        how can this happen? By what confluence of events
        does it take place?

Check with legal. Is this prima facie evidence of a war crime?
See previous comment above regarding the torture issues. In any case, is it really in the
public interest – or relevant to the inquiry, I might add – to reveal British involvement
in the killing of a civilian? It's also rather undignified to hear M telling his grovelling
story, and it's certainly going to raise questions about why we're giving him a medal
now. Suggest recording interruption. GH

[4.7]

M: That boy... Samar... that's his name, isn't it?

P: No. It is Samir... Samir.

M: Samir. Yes. [...] he's the only person I ever killed.
        Extraordinary, isn't it? In my entire army career I was
        never involved in a lethal incident. Except for him...
        Actually, it was the first... and only... time I ever fired
        my weapon in Iraq. Don't get me wrong... I'd come

under fire before that. Out on patrol a few times... but
you couldn't really see who was firing at you, and it
soon stopped. Just potshots really. I never got a chance
to fire back.

Crazy, don't you think? Train for years. Go to Iraq. And
the only time you actually fire your weapon at a target,
you accidentally shoot a little, unarmed boy—

P: —and then run away—

M: —and then run away, as you say. Ha! [choking sound]
[...] After Carl was airlifted out... I, ah... I could see he
was really bad... He wasn't breathing right... The skin
on his face was all tight... He kept squirming like there
was something inside him trying to get out. Clenching
and unclenching his fists... his veins bulging.

The strangest thing was that he didn't look too bad at
all. He certainly didn't look like he'd been stood right
next to an IED. There was no blood... no holes in his kit
that I could see. Just a lot of dust down one side of him.
After the smoke cleared, he tried to get up... stumbled
to his feet. But then he started to sway and grimace...
his face was really shiny. He just sort of crumpled
back down. 'I think I must be hit. Am I hit? Did it get
me? No, it couldn't have got me.' He was talking a
hundred miles an hour. But then he suddenly went
really quiet... and really pale, which is when I started

to really panic. I shouted that we needed to get him out of there. Straight away. 'Call for evac! Get it here! Now!' ███████████████████████ ████████████ All the while, I'm kneeling down next to him. I'm saying, 'Carl, Carl, talk to me! You're going to be OK. The medics are coming. You'll be flirting with the nurses in Germany in no time, you lucky sod!' And he's squirming... straining... I don't know if he's conscious or not...

It was the longest twenty minutes of my life... felt like it went on forever... I started to feel really hot. I was literally panting for breath, even though I was just standing still. [...] And when they bundled him on to that chopper and took off, I knew he was gone. I just knew it. [...] My last words to him, I called him a sod.

[2.3]

After the chopper was gone, it went really quiet... or at least, it seemed that way. Like all the sound had just been sucked out of the atmosphere. We all looked at each other. It was like we knew what each other was thinking... we didn't even have to say it. 'Right. Let's go find the bastards that did that to Carl.' So off we went... all of us spoiling for a fight. I felt really hot... flushed... like I had been running hard for an hour. I was pumped... alive... angry. Really angry! It was all I could do to stop myself screaming and emptying

my magazine into the air. I really wanted to hurt
somebody... preferably the <u>fuckers</u> who had done that.

P: Like when you went to beat that drug dealer in your
youth?

M: Yes... I suppose so. I hadn't thought of that. Don't get
me wrong. I'm not trying to excuse myself. I'm just
saying that it was in this state of mind that we started
moving out... along <u>our</u> streets. We came through that
area a lot. It was part of regular British patrol. Usually,
you know, we'd go through with a relaxed attitude...
soft hats... smiles... sweets for the kids. All that. [...]
But that day? No, no, no. That day, we were pissed off!
We weren't going to take any shit. We were going to
find those motherfuckers who'd put that bomb there.
Yes, sir, we were going to even up the score... if it was
at all possible.

So... with my rifle cocked... finger on the trigger...
my thoughts all churned up about how someone was
going to have to pay... I run up to the entry to this
alley. I do a quick glance... you know, real quick, to
look down the alley... trying not to present a target.
Half of it is in sunlight, the other half in shadow.
Halfway into the shadow, I see someone... a figure.
He's carrying something. I don't know what it is, but
it's long and straight. It could be a gun. I'm thinking,
maybe this is it? Maybe this is where they plan to

ambush us? [...] Maybe this is one of the guys who
planted the bomb?

P;   Why did you not call your comrades to help you? Why
not wait for backup?

M: I, ah, don't know... I just don't know! [...] For fuck's
sake, what do you want from me? [...] I was hot. It
was hard to breathe... I was finding it hard to think
straight. I just knew I was going to jump into that alley
and blow those fuckers away. So I rush into the alley...
ducking down into a firing position on the other side...
up against the wall... my rifle aimed towards where I
saw the figure.

[2.3]

It was... I, ah... [...] What happened next is etched
in my memory forever. I can see it as clear as if it'd
happened a minute ago. You know what I mean?

P: Oh yes, I do, my friend. [...] Sadly, I know exactly what
you mean...

M: Just as I was going into my firing crouch, that little
boy, Samar, whipped his stick down—

P: —Samir—

M: —I remember seeing it flash through the air as it went from the shadow to the light. It hit the ground and there was a loud crack. From what you said about these firecrackers... he must have put a whole box of matches into that one, don't you think?

Anyway, I just reacted... training, I guess. Fuck! I did it! I fired two quick shots in succession. He fell. I waited a second or two to see that he stayed down and then I moved down the alley, sweeping from side to side, looking for other targets... and that's when it all went quiet... not a sound. The only thing I could hear was the blood pounding in my ears. The sound of my own breath. Then... gradually... the noises started to creep back in... louder and louder. I heard shouting. A woman was screaming. People started running into the alley... jostling me... I lowered my weapon and stepped towards the body. As I got closer, I could see that it was a little boy. He looked so <u>small</u>. You could see his chest heaving... his ribs moving up and down, trying to breathe. I remember he was gulping, like a fish when it's out of the water... its mouth opening and closing. Then he looked up at me with big scared eyes. I'll never forget that look... It was... just... I... 'Afwaka ya Rab.[44]

As above, this seems prurient to me, all these grisly details.
    Do we really need to leave this in? Does it help the inquiry in any way?
And think of his wife, family – having all this in the public domain. Suggestions? GH

---

[44] Trans. 'Your amnesty, oh Lord.' Note: Classical Arabic.

[5.3]

Well... you know the rest. You already told the whole
sordid story...

P: Yes, I, ah—

M: —You may not believe me, Professor, but I wanted
to stay and help. I really did. I knew right away
what I'd done... how he needed urgent help. I really
wanted them to call in the medics and get the boy
evacuated... get him some proper medical attention...
but the other squaddies dragged me away. ████████
████████████████████ We ran. They kept pushing
me. My legs were like jelly. When we got a short
distance away from the crowd, we started firing shots
into the ground... up in the air... so they... you know...
could say we'd been ambushed and had to fire back.
The ammunition... it's counted...

Once we were far enough away, we called it in to
HQ. Got them to come and pick us up... take us
back to base. It was then I started to feel really
nauseous. I vomited twice on the ride back. I had to
go straight to sick bay. I couldn't stop thinking... I
really wanted to go straight back to that alley and
help the little boy... to try and make it right, you
know? But what was so weird was that... in reality... I
couldn't speak... I just couldn't make myself say

any words out loud. [...] Not a single one... it was like
my mouth was paralysed or something. I would make
to speak, my mouth opening and shutting, but then no
sound would come out. [...] So I just lay there on the
bed. My stomach cramped... hot... tossing and turning.
I didn't say anything when they spoke to me. I would
just turn away... I was suddenly in hell, a hell made
even worse when they told me Carl had died in the
chopper...

Two weeks I lay there... vomiting, cold sweats,
hallucinations... the works. I couldn't keep anything
down. They had to put me on a drip... I even missed
Carl's funeral. I heard later that the guys had reported
to ██████████████████████ that after the IED
attack we had come under fire from unknown enemy
forces, and we'd been forced to withdraw. It was
an ambush. We'd returned fire, but there were no
confirmed reports of enemy casualties. When they
asked me what happened, I just nodded... I couldn't
bring myself to tell the real story.

I felt so ashamed, but I just couldn't get the story out
of my mouth. Even when the boy's mother came to the
camp the next day, everybody denied it happened that
way. They said the boy must have been shot by the
terrorists. ██████████████ made her fill in a form
and said he would investigate. I expect he put the form
in the bin the minute she left. In any case, it was never

mentioned again. Not a single mention of a little boy shot in an alley.

This seems like another legal minefield we probably want to avoid.
Imagine if it goes public that British commanders didn't investigate civilian killings in Iraq – there'll be a tidal wave of writs. And as I mentioned earlier, this could also blow up in our faces if there is a surviving official record of the event.

I suggest another brief recording interruption. GH

[5.3]

P: Well, at least you did not stab the boy with a bayonet because he asked you for chocolate.

M: What in hell are you talking about?

P: You did not know this story? It happened in Nad-e Ali district. I am sure you know it. He was a Grenadier Guardsman... out on patrol... he was still drunk from the night before... vodka, I think. He stabbed the boy in the kidney... ten years old... his name was Ghulam Nabi. This is what I heard.

[2.3]

Sorry, I digress... please continue.

M: I wanted to resign my commission there and then. I was ready to pack it all in and go home. I didn't think I could face walking out into those streets again... seeing those same people... knowing they'd be looking at me... seeing me... a child killer... knowing what I'd done. I went straight to see ███████████ and told him I couldn't do it... go back out there. I couldn't carry a gun again...

I suppose I was lucky he was such a decent bloke. I think he could see what I was going through. He could have made me see the shrink... or recommended discharge. I think he thought it was because of Carl... so he put me on desk duties, ████████████████████████████████████ Told me to let things settle and think about it before rushing into a decision...

It was a kind of natural progression from there. I started to work on reports from the active units... preparing briefings and whatnot. And hey presto! I get a call from Military Intelligence. Do I want to work for them? I'm feeling a little better by now. I don't actually want to go home. It would be too much of a failure... a dereliction of duty. [...] Also, I would've had to face Carl's wife and kids... I wasn't ready for that. This seemed like a way I could continue to be useful. So I served out my term in MI.

P: But you resigned your commission when you returned home?

M: Yes. When we withdrew from Iraq, I went home and put in my papers two weeks later. I didn't want to do it any more...

P: And then?

[1.2]

M: And then I was, ah, approached by MI5... as you no doubt bloody well know. [...] It made sense, I suppose. It allowed me to continue serving my country. And as it turns out, I'm pretty good at it. [...] And so here I am.

P: So this story you told me about applying for MI5 after you left university, it was a lie?

M: You always knew it was, Professor. [muttered]

P: What? Yes, yes, I did. [...] Do you still think about that boy... Samir?

[2.3]

M: I think about him every single day...

P: And what do you think about?

M: Ah, umm... I, ah... you know... obviously I still feel very bad he had to die... that I killed him. [...] But now I also, ah, think he might still be alive if people like you weren't going around planting bombs... ambushing people who are only there to help. Only doing their job! I think if I could do a better job of stopping <u>The Professors</u> of this world, there would be far less incidents of that nature, and other children wouldn't have to die!

P: Oh, so now you blame me for Samir's murder?

M: Yes, in a way, I suppose I do. Why not? You can't completely exonerate yourself from responsibility, Professor. You were attacking us in a public, civilian area. You planted that bomb... You can't do things like that and expect that no one will get hurt, can you?

P: But if you had not been in Iraq at all, in your illegal war, we would not have been attacking you in the first place... and that little boy would still be alive today.

M: Bullshit! If he hadn't died in that alley, there's a damn good chance Saddam would've had one of his goons kill him or his family—

P: —Or maybe he would be one of those demonstrators like you see now in Tahrir Square... Tunisia... Bahrain. Or, he might have been a freedom fighter... like the ones in Libya your government is so eager to support. The point is... he could have made his own choice.

He could have tried to win his own freedom from Saddam... without your army coming in and killing hundreds of thousands of his compatriots... installing your own puppet regime... giving preferential treatment to Western oil companies... stealing the country's oil wealth... committing abuses and then going home—

M: —Off he goes again! Professor, I'm afraid we'll just have to disagree... [inaudible]

[2.9]

P: I know you still suffer from the war, Michael. PTSD... is this not what it is called? You have visited a counsellor... once a week. And you took some time off work a few months ago... after you started weeping—

M: —Jesus! How the fuck do you know about—

P: — Oh, don't act so surprised, Michael. We know everything... what you did in Iraq... your recruitment to the Service when you returned... your family... your routine... your little fishing trips... your anti-depression medication... your visits to the doctor... ██████████ ████████████████████████ ... even the coffee you always buy when you get off the Tube. The truth is... we have watched you for many years. We had to know everything so we could plan properly.

Can you tell me how in God's name an agent with mental health problems gets put into the middle of an active operation? And more importantly, how do we explain it to the House? I know that he had direct previous experience of P in Iraq, but that's not going to cut it. We also need to have an answer for how a senior CT officer was the subject of a surveillance operation by the terrorists he was meant to be following. In my view, another little recording interruption here would circumvent some serious potential fallout. GH

M: [inaudible] am I meant to... [inaudible]

[4.1]

P: Ohhf... I am feeling so tired now. It has been a long
     night... my back is sore... it has been like this ever since
     Iraq. I need to walk again. [scraping sounds] [...]

     Michael, do you sometimes wonder what would
     happen if people... the public... really knew what the
     experience of war did to those who fought it? What
     I mean is, if people really knew... if they saw the
     statistics of how many former soldiers attempted
     suicide... or drank themselves to death... abused their
     families. [...] Did you see that soldier in America who
     came back from Iraq and poured gasoline over his
     wife, then lit her on fire? Ohhf ... [inaudible]... so many
     soldiers sink into depression... end up on the streets...
     homeless... Do you think that if they actually watched
     someone disintegrate in front of their eyes, would they
     still consider them <u>heroes</u>? Would they gladly send

their children... husbands... fathers... to war? [...] War completely, ah, ah... well, it fucks you up, does it not?

I read somewhere that something like eighteen Iraq vets try to commit suicide every week in the United States. About a, a... a million... can you believe it? A million! [...] Vietnam vets killed themselves in the decades after they came back from the war... not to mention all those who became homeless. And so many who have committed murder-suicide... killing their wives and children and then themselves...

[1.8]

Have you ever considered... you know... ending it all? Did you ever think of just going to sleep one day and never waking up? I have, I can tell you... how nice it would be... how I would finally be at rest.

I sometimes think about those young men who died from my hands... the lives they might have had... their children... wives and parents... friends... parties... careers. [...] It makes me feel sick to my stomach. I feel completely hollow... inhuman. I would do anything to escape it. I want to forget those faces... the young men from England and America who pass across my mind when I am lying alone in the dark. My personal theory is... I do not believe it is that people are trying to kill you in war that haunts your mind. That is not so unusual and it is easy to get used to... in my experience. No... it is thinking that you have killed another person that haunts you... the knowledge that you have taken away the life of another human being... who was probably just like you... you have taken away their future... their hope...

M: I hear you, Professor. As you said, I sometimes think I'll never get past what happened over there. Some days I can't even concentrate on my work... or anything for that matter... for going over and over and over it, again and again and again. I see that little boy... Samar, Samir... I see his cheeky little face. It reminds me of my own son... he's the same age. Then I see the shadow on the wall. I see myself, but it's like from a distance, pulling the trigger, firing, moving through the alley, swinging my gun all over the place. I see his body broken in the dirt... his little chest heaving... his mouth gulping for air.

[3.9]

Sometimes, I feel so depressed that I can hardly get out of bed. It's like a heavy blackness in my mind... a weight pushing down on my eyelids. I can't face anything... or anyone. I just want to close my eyes and sleep dreamlessly. I can't even look at my wife... my children. Can you imagine that? That one tiny moment... a few seconds of your life in a faraway land...

has spoiled my relationship with my children. I can
hardly look at them... or talk to them... without seeing
little Samir and feeling my guts tighten. It's pretty
shit, I can tell you... I can't sleep either. I lie awake...
sometimes for days at a time. And when I do sleep,
it's broken... full of awful dreams. And don't say 'What
about medication?' I've tried everything, believe me.
Nothing works.

P: I know, I know, Michael. [...] It is a very heavy price we
pay to be men of action. Each act of violence destroys
another small part of your, ah... humanity... your <u>soul</u>
for want of a better word... every time...

[2.3]

M: I have a recurrent dream too, just like you... except
mine is about, ah... Samir... I'm out fly-fishing. It's a
beautiful lake. The sky is perfectly clear. The sun is
starting to beat down. The insects are buzzing about,
hatching in the water. I can see fish rising all around...
and I'm completely alone. It's perfect... just the kind of
day I love... the kind of day I <u>used</u> to love...

I rig up with a dry fly and start to cast along the
shallows. The line loops perfectly... out and back, out
and back. It's a kind of poetry... a ballet on the water.
I cast at a rise a few metres away. I touch the fly down
gently in the fish's feeding zone. I give it a little twitch.

From where I am, it looks exactly like a little black
gnat struggling on the surface of the lake. If the fish is
still within a few metres, it should notice it and come
over. I tense, waiting for the strike...

That moment is so pure. It's timeless... and elegant.
When a fish comes out of the water with its mouth
open and takes the fly you have presented, it's... it's...
you know, perfection... and adrenalin... and thrill... all
rolled up in one...

Anyway, in my dream, nothing happens. No take...
the fly just sits there. The trout must have moved off.
I cast again, moving a little further along the bank.
Same result... nothing. This goes on for ages. Me,
casting at rising fish and they ignoring it. In my dream,
I try all different flies... different casting... different
places. I try every trick I know. Still... nothing. It's so
frustrating. Then, just as I am about to despair... on
my last cast... I hook a fish. I never even saw it. There
was no moment of joy when it took. I just have a fish on
my line. It's small and it takes no time and no skill at
all to get it in. It's a baby brown trout... hardly worth
keeping. It flops on the stony bank.... [cough]... I go to
grab it so I can take the hook out and release it, but
suddenly it's not a fish at all. It's Samir. He's lying half
in the water, he's got no shirt on... his chest is bare.
I can see two small bullet holes in his chest... oozing
blood. But the worst thing is, he's gulping like a fish...

his little mouth opening and closing. He's trying to breath but he can't...

I start to weep... like really deeply... the sobs rising up from within and wracking my whole body. I stumble backwards to get away as fast as my legs will carry me. I trip, and then, as I'm about to land on my arse in the water, I wake up with a jolt...

[3.8]

As you can well imagine, fishing has been completely spoiled for me. It used to be a real passion... a pure joy... It was a way I, I... I could escape... relax. But it gives me no more joy now. I've been out several times since I came back, but it depresses me. Argh... [inaudible]...

[4.7]

P: I can see you have paid a high price for your, ah... calling, Michael... like me... like all men of violence, I suppose... we pay the price sometimes in our bodies, but always in our minds.

I believe that committing an act of violence is a lot like the first time you see your father really diminished in some way... by shame or weakness. [inaudible]... that moment of revelation that your father is not

the infallible person you thought he was, and your
assumptions about the world are wrong... like the
day I saw my father slapped by one of Mubarak's
CFS thugs. I was fourteen years old. We were at one
of those neighbourhood political rallies they would
always have for some high-level party official. This...
boy... he could not have been much older than me, for
God's sake! [...] Anyway, he was watching us and he
thought that my father was not, ah, applauding and
cheering with enough enthusiasm. He started shouting
at him, insulting him, telling him to cheer louder... and
then he slapped him... right in the face! It was like a
thunderclap. I was so shocked by the sudden attack by
this, this, this... child... and by the look on my father's
face. He was so, so... humiliated. He looked utterly
ashamed... broken. He could not speak... and he would
not look at me... the crowd had to drag him away,
before he got arrested. That could have been much
worse...

Anyway, I, ah... I can hardly say what I felt at that
moment. My own father... my strong, proud father...
humiliated, beaten down... reduced to a naughty child.
I had never believed I could feel sorry for my own
father, as if he was a victim... you know, because he
had always been a rock, a real hero... ah... I felt my
world had changed. I would never look at my father in
the same way again.

[1.8]

What I am trying to say is that once you have killed someone... or caused them real physical damage... torn their flesh... it is like stepping through a door which you can never go back through to a time before... you can never recapture your innocence... just like you cannot take out from your mind the image... the feelings that welled up inside you... when you saw your father shamed... humiliated. What I mean is... you are changed... forever. There is no path to go back. You will always know what it is to destroy another human being... to cause them real pain... to end their existence... all the possibilities of their future...

This is a heavy burden. It takes a little piece of your humanity, your inner peace. I truly believe you kill a small piece of yourself whenever you kill another living thing... especially when it is a person like yourself—

M: —and you can't ever talk about it with anyone you know, unless they've been there too... and then they usually don't want to talk about it at all!

P: You are not wrong... from your lips to God's ears, Michael. It is not something that anyone... anyone... can understand... unless they have experienced it themselves. Unless they have had to do it too... which means you have to keep it to yourself. You have to hold it all deep down in your soul.

But of course, society cannot accept it. It cannot acknowledge the cost of maintaining the violent professions. It can never be honest about what happens to people when they join the military... the police... that they will inevitably suffer mental torment and personal trauma... that they will likely become depressed... maybe even kill themselves... or worse, their spouses. Imagine if army recruiters told the truth? 'Hey you! Come and join the army. Kill people... and then later kill yourself when you come home!'

[4.1]

Michael, do you believe we... [inaudible]... humans... can ever escape the consequences of our choices? Can we ever go back to a time of innocence... or are we trapped in this cycle of violence and destruction forever?

M: I couldn't say, Professor. I just know that I can never go back to a time before Iraq... before Samir. I just know that I have to keep going. I've got to keep trying to do the right thing... make amends somehow... I've got to continue trying to stop the cycle of violence...

P: [inaudible]... tell you something, Michael. I sometimes think that everything good inside me is dead... destroyed by this, this... this war... this struggle I have been forced to fight. I will never see my child again... or my wife. I will never see ███████ grow up, see her become a woman... marry... have children of her own. I will never bounce my grandchildren on my knee. I will never stroke my wife's beautiful raven hair again... or hear her whisper love in my ear in the early morning light... I will never watch her when she does not know I am looking at her. [...]

Do you know that my wife is a musician? Piano... so beautiful, her playing. Anyway, sometimes, when we would hold hands, her fingers would gently flutter and twitch on the back of my hand. It was completely unconscious... she did not even know she was doing it, unless I mentioned it, and then she would become self-conscious and laugh. [...] It was the music inside, notes flowing through her fingers, played across my skin. [...] Sometimes, I think I can still feel her delicate fingers walking across the back of my hand...

[1.8]

The tragedy is that I had to leave them completely behind... renounce them, as it were... for their own safety. I knew they would never be safe if I stayed. [...] And I will never experience the joys of teaching a class of eager students again or debating issues of great importance with my colleagues over a glass of sweet tea... I really miss that Kenyan black chai we drank, you know? I have not tasted it for so long! [...] My whole life was sacrificed on the altar of resistance. Now, I cannot even enjoy the simple things... like going out to watch a film... going to a restaurant by the Nile... watching a musical concert with friends... enjoying a conversation with the sellers in the market. The truth is that food tastes like ashes in my mouth. Music... literature... fine wine... none of it means anything to me any more.

M: So you regret your decision to fight? What I mean is... if you could go back, would you make a different choice... decide not to pursue the life you did... I mean, knowing what you know now?

[2.9]

P: *Abadan*,[45] no... I have never regretted it because sacrificing yourself for justice is the right thing to do. It is the small price we pay... the sacrifice we make... to achieve our aims. I was not ignorant of what would happen. I knew it would be a real... sacrifice... that I would become a, a... a murderer... a pariah. I knew it would be painful... that I would lose everything...

---

[45] Trans. 'Never.' Note: Classical Arabic.

including my own sense of self, my morality. But I
made that choice consciously... willingly. I believed it
was a price worth paying... for the sake of trying to
help my people.

What about you, Michael? Would you make a different
choice? If you knew then what you would do... what
would happen to you... would you still go to fight
militants in Iraq?

[5.1]

M: I don't know... seriously... I know it's cost me a lot... but
       I also believe I've done a lot of good.

P: Me too.

M: If I could change what happened that day, I would... I
       really would. I'd do almost anything. [...] But I don't
       think I could ever regret joining the army... or even
       going to Iraq. The intelligence work I did over there
       saved a lot of lives, I know... or the work I do now—

P: —How did you come to join the British Army, exactly?
       What led you to join such a violent gang of thugs?
       [laughter]

M: [inaudible]... don't be...

P: [laughter]... Seriously, by what path did you come to be fighting in Iraq?

M: Mmm... I suppose it was something of a family tradition for me. My father, grandfather, his father before him were all military men. And there were cousins, uncles, great-uncles. I came from a real, proper military family. Then there were all my parents' military friends.

Growing up, I suppose I heard all the stories... and we were always around military events... military culture, as it were. At school, I joined the cadets. It was just expected... there was never a question. In our family church, █████████████████████████, there were... are... plaques to our relatives, many who had served around the world. I actually have a great-uncle who died in Iraq in 1931. Can you believe that? His grave is still there. I visited it once. [...] You would see those inscriptions every Sunday, and it made you feel a part of something. I suppose I took pride in being associated with all that... history... duty... service. You know.

When I reached my teens, it seemed to be more just an expectation that I would follow in my father's footsteps. I never questioned it. I just followed the path laid down for me. It was my duty to serve... to follow the tradition... to do what I could for my country. And for me, the army is my identity... which is why I could never regret my decision to enlist. It's about who I am. About being British to my very core.

It might not be that obvious, but I take enormous pride in being a British soldier. I consider it a genuine, proper honour. I don't think I could be anyone else... or do anything else. It's been my whole life. Even my wife comes second, if I'm honest—

P: —Except that you resigned after Iraq. You are not in the British Army any more...

M: That's true... but you never really leave the army, do you? You're an army man for life, even if you leave. I still <u>feel</u> like I'm in the army... and in a way, I feel like I'm still working to protect and defend my Queen and my country... my people.

P: So you do not regret working for British intelligence, despite what you have been involved in... despite the torture and all the other undoubtedly dishonourable things you have had to do... despite ████████

████████████████████████████████████

[1.2]

Despite being here... in this room tonight?

M: No, not for one moment. I don't regret it at all. Of
      course, it's sad that violence is sometimes necessary.
      I regret that sometimes people get hurt. [...] But
      circumstances make it necessary. The actions of others
      make it necessary. Very bad people who want to do us
      harm... people like you, Professor... people who can't be
      stopped any other way, well, they sometimes make it
      necessary to use force—

P: —I could not agree more, Michael. I too had no other
      option than armed struggle—

M: —I know I'm doing the right thing... protecting people
      from... ah... bad people. Making people feel safer...
      saving my wife and kids... my neighbours... the old
      people living down the road... the children at the local
      primary school. [...] It's the right thing to do. The
      world is full of threats, and there are a lot of very bad
      people out there determined to do Britain harm...
      determined to cause mayhem and death. Someone has
      to try and stop them. That's my job... it's my duty.

[2.3]

      I don't know if you know this... if your surveillance
      of me, your investigations... would show it, but I was
      really influenced by certain political events. The
      first was the Omagh bombing in Northern Ireland. I
      mean... the regiment had been in Northern Ireland.

We had our dead comrades. Our stories of what had happened... and in a way, you could understand it. When they ambushed our boys on patrol or shot up an army post. That was soldiers up against soldiers... or at least, people who had made a choice to take up arms, to fight. But planting a bomb and killing all those civilians? When I saw those pictures on TV... ah, I mean... it made me so angry. How could they do that? What kind of animals would do such a thing? Especially when there were moves on to end the conflict... to find a solution? I knew then I was doing the right thing being part of the fight against that kind of... barbarity... that kind of evil—

P: —And of course, later you were influenced by 9/11, correct?

M: Yes, I was. How could anyone not be so deeply affected by that day? Seeing those planes exploding into flames? People jumping from the hundredth floor rather than face the flames? It was so shocking... so visceral.

Like everyone else, I spent the entire day... and many days afterwards... just watching those images of the planes smashing into the towers... seeing them crumble... that massive cloud of white ash like a bomb going off. Knowing that there were thousands of people inside. [...] It was actually quite hard to take in, the kind of <u>evil</u> capable of that. I mean... thinking about the kind of hatred it would take to fly a plane straight into a building full of people... in a plane full of people! Realising just how many were murdered on that day, when they had no idea that they would go to work and get incinerated... blown up... well, it made me realise that evil truly existed... that there were people out there who could not be reasoned with... or deterred... or made to realise the error of their ways. People who would not stop for any reason... certainly not because what they were doing was inhuman. They just had to be stopped. And it was my job to try and stop them...

Later, of course, 7/7 just confirmed that I was right. There <u>were</u> people who wanted to kill as many Britons as they could. People who for their own twisted reasons, felt that killing innocent civilians had some higher moral purpose. It's these kinds of events... the 7/7s, 9/11s, Madrid, Bali, Iraq, Afghanistan, and on and on... which confirms my choice... which makes it imperative that I do my job effectively.

P: So... in the end... you are trying to do the right thing... rid the world of evil... protect the innocent? [...] You want to save your fellow citizens from those who would seek to do them harm?

M: Yes, absolutely.

P: And you are doing it because you believe it is the only
       way... it is the best thing for your country... for your
       people?

M: Precisely.

[1.9]

       But I do sometimes wish that there could be another
       way... that it wasn't necessary to do some of the things
       I've had to do. That maybe there might be some means
       of protecting people... protecting the country... without
       recourse to the use of force. I really do wish we could
       create the kind of world you've been talking about...
       without all the violence and the domination, as you call
       it. But that'll never happen. Not unless you can change
       human nature. People are sometimes just... evil. You'll
       never be able to change that.

P: That is a very pessimistic view of human nature,
       Michael.

M: I'm surprised to hear you say that, Professor. You've
       been in war. You must've seen what people are capable
       of... what sheer depravity they can sink to... the pure
       savagery.

P: True, true... but I have also seen great heroism and
       selflessness... sacrifice in war. I have had comrades
       who gave themselves, sacrificed their freedom to save
       their friends... even when they knew they would face
       torture at Abu Ghraib... even if they knew they would
       be killed. I saw ordinary, heroic people run through
       a, a... a hail of gunfire to try and save an old lady who
       was trapped. [...] I sometimes think war brings out the
       best... and the worst... in people. It forces people into
       the extremes of behaviour. [...] But that is because
       of the nature of war, not the nature of humans. So...
       mmm, if we can change the conditions of war... the
       oppression and violence... hey, maybe we will no longer
       see these extremes...

M: Well, after what I saw in Bosnia, I just can't, ah...
       I mean, there is a core of evil to some people that
       nothing could ever cure. Evil exists, in some people,
       and all you can do is kill it. Eradicate it from the
       world. Not the ones you talk about. I've also seen
       some amazing acts of heroism, selflessness in war...
       but there are others who will sink to the very deepest
       depths of savagery. And not only that, they'll enjoy it!
       They'll be proud!

       No, when you've seen a woman who's been gang-
       raped, and then had her face literally cut off by her
       attackers... who then tried to set her on fire with
       lighter fluid, well, fucking hell, you have to think that

human beings are... I don't know... shit, basically...
pure fucking evil. [...] I once saw a man taking a shit by
the side of the road while he gripped the head of what I
can only imagine was his little boy... I tell you, that's an
image which never leaves you... along with the smell of
burning bodies—

P: —[inaudible] right, Michael. *Asharro fe-nnass la yafna
wa in qobero*[46]...

M: I couldn't agree more, Professor. There's no way to fix
human evil. You can't reform people who act like that.
I believe all you can do is try to stem the tide... keep it
away, outside the gates. [...] That's why you'll never get
rid of war, violence.

[2.3]

P: So would you ever consider... perhaps... quitting your
current job and working for the same ends... the safety
and security of your country... but by other means?
You know... like, like... ah, working for an NGO... one of
those international agencies you saw in Bosnia? Surely
it would be an alternative to what you do now? You do
not have to keep working for the government.

---

[46] Trans. 'Evil in humans cannot be made extinct even if they are in their
graves.' Note: Classical Arabic, from a poem called 'Mawakeb' by Jibran
Khalil Jibran.

M: I really don't think so. I chose my path already. I
       don't believe I can just stop now. I'm committed right
       through to the end... I'm on this train until the last
       stop...

       What about you? Would you give up your campaign
       and use other means to pursue your goals?

P: Ohhf... like you... I, ah... I believe it is too late now...
       even if I thought it would work. I too made my choices
       long ago. I have got to live with them. See things
       through to the end, you might say. [inaudible]... we
       are both trapped. We cannot escape our destiny,
       Michael...

[1.2]

       You know what I find most interesting, Michael?
       It is how similar we are. In fact, when I look into your
       face, I do not see my enemy. Instead, it is as if I am
       looking into a mirror. This is the tragedy... we are the
       same... brothers in war... Cain and Abel, perhaps. We
       are both fighting for the same things... family... our
       people... for the values we believe in. We both want a
       better world for our children... to protect those we love.
       And we—

M: —With respect, Professor, you and I are nothing ali—

P: —But then what confuses me about your motives is all the things we have been talking about... the lies of your government... the bombing... the torture... the constant intervention in other countries. By working for the British government, are you not supporting an inherently evil system... acting in support of imperialism... domination... oppression? [...] Are you not doing to others exactly what you claim to be trying to stop others from doing to you?

M: Apart from the fact that we're completely different... I just don't see it that way. Sure, democracy may be flawed in the way you've suggested, and governments are definitely flawed... are they ever! They make bad decisions... quite often, in fact. But surely what we have is the best of all possibilities? You don't think that if China... or Russia... or Brazil... whoever... ruled the world instead of America, and Britain, and Europe... it would be a more just, a more peaceful, world? Those countries have way worse human rights records than we do. And they make even less of an effort to act decently. Look at Chechnya, or Tibet, for God's sake! They make our actions in Iraq look like child's play. Surely, the world would be much worse off if they were running things instead of us?

P: Ha! So your argument is basically that it is better to have a small tyrant than a big one... that it is better to be a slave to a decent owner rather than a really brutal one? You are saying that because there <u>has</u> to be a world bully, it is better to have a nice, fair-play kind of bully like Britain—

M: —No, Professor! That's not what I'm—

P: —[inaudible]... Well, that is just [inaudible]... stupid, Michael. Do you know what is the difference between us? Huh? [...] It is that I do not limit myself to such, such... such ridiculously fatalistic choices. I do not see the world in your pessimistic... and simplistic... terms. <u>I</u> think we can actually make a world where people are free, rather than enslaved to someone... even if that someone is nicer than the other slave owners. I think we can fight for a world where no country... not even the nice ones... bomb and terrify and dominate others.

Besides, if we did live in a world where China or Russia or whoever was doing what you are doing but even worse, I would be fighting them too... the same way I am fighting you. I do not discriminate. Ha! Just because you claim to support human rights and democracy and value human life, it does not mean it is actually true, as I think we have established!

M: Oh, for fuck's sake... [inaudible] [mumbled]

[3.8]

[scraping sounds]

P: Oh my God... I am so tired. It has been such a long day...
       especially for an old man like me! Not like you, you are
       still a young man in his prime. [...] Actually, I confess,
       it has been a long life... a long struggle... I am really
       exhausted. My bones are tired. My mind is tired. This
       is definitely my last mission, I can tell you. I cannot
       live on the run as a murderer any more...

M: {inaudible]... do you mean?

P: [inaudible]... I know I am a murderer. 'This thing
       of darkness, I acknowledge mine.' [...] The difference
       is that the West... even you and your comrades...
       believe you are innocent... that you have not done
       anything wrong. [...] You cannot confess your crimes,
       even when you are faced with the plain evidence...
       even when your accusers haunt your very dreams!
       [inaudible] worry... [inaudible] soon be [inaudible]
       at daybreak.

[1.2]

       One thing puzzles me, Michael, if you will indulge me...
       how could the Iraq war happen... or, or... or how did
       Britain get involved when it was so obvious that your

politicians were lying... when it was so <u>clear</u> that it
would be a complete and utter disaster? How could
your politicians choose to join the Americans when so
many people... so many millions... all over the world...
were against it?

And what does this say about your country... about
the condition of your democracy... the <u>values</u> of
your country? You were saying just now that you
worked for the government because you wanted to
protect your country's safety... that you believed in
its values. But does not the Iraq war show how hollow
these values are... how really, your society is rooted
in militarism and the glorification of violence? You
might <u>think</u> you work for a liberal, democratic, secular,
advanced country... but that is not how it appears to all
of us on the outside.

What we... the world... sees, is a country where
militarism and military values completely dominate
your culture and your public life... even if they are
completely, ah, ah... <u>sublimated</u> in your own minds.
We see a country where the military are honoured on
every street corner with a monument... where films
glorifying military campaigns and heroic battles are
shown on television every day... and where children
play with guns or violent video games... where public
holidays celebrate military victories and heroic
sacrifice several times a year... where schoolchildren

join military organisations... where the military has recruiting stands at every university... where parades and tattoos and marches entertain the Queen and her adoring public throughout the year... I saw all these things when I studied here. Where every November, tens of millions of citizens put on a red poppy to venerate the military, and politicians recite the names of the dead soldiers in Parliament... and history in school consists of tales of generals and kings fighting great battles... where the military are honoured in every church with flags and inscriptions and special services, as you yourself told me... and where chaplains and padres go into battle with the soldiers.

[1.9]

What I mean is... in this context, it does not surprise me at all that your country has gone to war half a dozen times in the last decade... and that it went to war against a country that posed no threat and had no connection at all to terrorism. With the greatest respect, do you not think you might have been brainwashed, Michael? No wonder you joined a violent military organisation... no wonder you wanted to grow up to be a soldier. Your society is one big military indoctrination machine...

[recording interruption]

[2.1]

M: Professor, I've been completely honest with you, even though I had no reason to—

P: —Apart from those lies about how you joined MI5. [...] Besides, it is part of your training. You are taught that in a situation such as the one we have here that you should always cooperate... try to build a personal relationship with your captors... try to get them to relate to you as a, a... a real human being, not a, a... a victim. This will... so your theory goes... make it more difficult for them to physically harm you—

M: —Wait... no, it's not like that... you don't need to... I mean, OK, I suppose in a way, you're right. We are trained to listen carefully, you know, really try and, ah, understand the, um... you don't think I could have some water now, do you? I'm feeling a bit—

P: —Of course, of course. Here you are... drink.

[scraping sounds. Sounds of drinking water].

M: Thanks. I didn't realise how parched I was...

P: You are welcome. [...]

[1.9]

M: Are you going to kill me now, Professor? Is this it?
      Have we reached the end?

[2.3]

P: Mmm... if I did not know better, I would think you
      know something I do not. [...] You are up to something,
      my friend. I can see it in your eyes... the way you keep
      looking at the door.

[6.9]

M: [inaudible] like you, I'm totally knackered. It's been
      such a long day... and my arse feels like a sack of
      concrete. These chairs are bloody uncomfortable,
      aren't they? Couldn't you have found somewhere
      better than this, Professor?

P: I wish, Michael. But our options were very limited. It is
      all we could afford.

M: Come on, Professor! What are we waiting for? Don't
      you think it's cruel to keep someone waiting like, you
      know, to, ah...?

[2.3]

P: Have some patience, Michael. What will be will be, in
      its own time. [...] Why don't you tell me about your

family. What is your son like, little ███████████?
What does he like to do? Is he a happy boy?

M: Wait! Are you threatening my family again? Promise
       me... swear it, they're not a part of this, are they?

P: No, no, no, they are perfectly safe, Michael. I was just
       interested to hear about your boy.

M: OK, OK... yes, sorry, I'm just nervous. My boy, I think
       he's fairly happy... despite his dickhead of a dad! [...]
       He likes fishing—

P: —Like his father!

M: Yes, just like his father. I remember one time... when
       he was just a small lad... I took him fishing. We were
       just on the wharf trying to catch little herrings or
       whatever. I wanted to let him catch some small fish to
       try and get him really interested in it. There's nothing
       like the excitement of actually catching a fish to get
       someone hooked. Ha! Just a small pun there... oh God,
       I'm so tired. Anyway, that's how I became a fishing
       enthusiast. My grandfather ███████████ took me
       fishing at ███████████, and we always caught lots
       of fish. It was so exciting. There was so much to learn
       about it. I found myself eager to get better and do it
       again, and again...

So we went fishing off a wharf just near ███████
███████, and I accidentally hooked a really large
herring. It must have been about two, three pounds...
probably this long—

P: —That is very impressive!

M: Yeah, I know... I say accidentally, because I really
didn't mean to catch a properly big fish. We were just
trying to catch the little ones that shoal around the
wharf...

So... I had hooked it on a really small rod and line... I
had to play it for ages. All the time, ███████████
was so excited. He couldn't wait for me to bring it in. I
was just worried that I'd lose it. It would snap the line
and be gone. I didn't want to see the disappointment
on his face if that happened, so I was super careful and
kept playing it, and playing it, and playing it...

After what seemed an age, I eventually managed
to get it close to the edge. I had to climb down some
wet, really slippery steps to grab it. I took it up
and you know ███████████████ was literally
dancing around with excitement. I knew then he'd
be a fisherman for life. It was quite hilarious. Once
it was dead and had stopped flapping about, he
marched up and down the wharf shouting at the top
of his voice, 'Ladies and gentlemen, the biggest

fish in the world.' Everyone laughed... It was really something...

[2.3]

It's one of my best memories of him, actually. I remind him about it a lot... although I think it embarrasses him a little now he's nearly a teenager... I do hope he'll keep fishing...

P: That is a nice story, Michael. Thank you for telling me—

M: —The other day we went to a Japanese restaurant. You'll appreciate this one—

P: —Oh, yes?

M: Anyway, they had *gyutan* on the menu and I mentioned it to my wife. He asked me what it was, so I told him it was beef tongue. He screwed up his face, [laughter], and he said, 'Yuck, tongue! I can't imagine eating something that comes out of an animal's mouth! That's disgusting!' Then, [laughter], you'll love this [laughter], he said, 'Do they have any eggs, dad? I love eggs.'

[laughter 5.1 seconds]

M: The thing was [laughter] he couldn't understand what we were all laughing about. He was just looking from one to the other... a baffled look on his face. I had to explain it [laughter]... oh, God! I'm so tired...

P: That is very funny... eggs. Ha!

[1.8]

P: Will your son join the military... like you?

M: I used to hope so. Now I'm not so sure. It's not the same these days. I mean, it's not like we fight normal, ordinary wars any more... where you know who the enemy is and what you have to do to win. Now it's either irregular war on the streets of Baghdad... or, or... special ops on the streets of Bradford! I suppose the main thing I hope for is that he can choose his own life... that he won't <u>have</u> to join the military just because he feels he has to... or because there's some big new war...

P: That would be very nice, would it not... if there was no need for Britain to go to war again?

M: [inaudible]

[6.3]   *Is it really in the public interest to reveal operational tradecraft like the following? It could put other agents at risk in future if terrorists know where the microphones are. If there's any place for another recording interruption in the name of national security, it's here.*

Don't you agree? GH

M: Wait a minute. Wait a minute. What are you doing,
        Youssef? Youssef! [...] No! Please put that away. I'm
        not ready. Please, please! Don't do anything rash! We
        can talk about it. Professor... we can talk, no, no? Wait!
        You know this whole thing... right from the start...
        has been a set-up, don't you? A charade? ███████████

███ You
don't think I've been so calm up to now because I'm,
ah... brave? Ha! That's not me. No, no, if I thought you
were really going to execute me, I would be absolutely
shitting myself. Do you know what I mean? I'd be
screaming and begging and crying. I certainly wouldn't
be calmly talking about my wife... my fucking dreams...
about bloody fly-fishing! The fact is... everything we've
said here tonight... all this... has been monitored and
recorded by colleagues of mine who are somewhere
very close by... just outside the door. Look. Look. See
these cufflinks? Concealed microphones. And here in
my shirt collar... another one. My shoes too... just in
case. The truth is, we knew that you and your friends
were coming. We planned everything. Right down to
my outfit for the day... ███████████████████████████

████████████████████████ Why'd you think it was so easy for
you and your boys to grab me and get me in the van?
Weren't you surprised how empty the street was...
or how little I resisted? I thought that would give the
game away, frankly. I thought you'd smell a very large

rat and call it off. I told them you were way too smart
to fall for such an obvious set-up... But I guess you
must be losing your edge, Professor.

Anyway, I'm glad to see you're sitting down again...
you scared me for a moment. [...] The whole place in
████████████████ was staked out and a full tactical
team followed us here. There's a tracking device in my
shoe heels... in my belt. I'm sure you can understand
that it was too good an opportunity to pass up. The
Professor... here in the UK... part of a gang plotting to
kidnap and execute a former soldier... releasing the
video on the Internet. At least, that's what we hoped...
that it really was you. And we were clearly right, as
here you are. Once we figured it out, we took a strategic
decision to let the game play out... to flush you out
into the open. Those other two... they'll be picked up
later. It wouldn't surprise me if they've been arrested
by now. You haven't heard from them for a while now,
have you?

We must prepare a statement about how the investigation is ongoing and we are
getting close to catching these other two. It could be embarrassing to have this
passage thrown in HMG's face in the House. How did they escape, anyway? GH

What I'm trying to tell you, there are lots of heavily
armed and very well-trained men just outside these
walls, very close. I'm sure you know what they're
capable of. They don't mess about. Not these lads.
They can be inside this room and firing in a matter of

seconds... you won't actually have time to get around
the table. Trust me, Professor... at least put the knife
away again... you don't need that...

[2.3]

Why are you shaking your head, Professor? What's
that smile about? Please, please don't do anything
rash. There's no point in dying in some futile gesture
just to make a point. Despite the kind of world we both
live in... and the things we've both done... the deaths
we've caused... I think we can choose to act differently.
Neither of us has to die needlessly in this shitty room.
I can assure you that I have understood what you've
been saying. I have heard you, Professor! And we can
talk again... many times. You can explain everything
you've told me here tonight in a court of law to the
whole world. You can explain your theories... your
reasons... to the world's media... to anyone who'll
listen. We'll give you a real voice. [...] That's what you
want, isn't it? A platform... an audience?

I think that in time, you'll see there could be a new
life for you... maybe even a chance to go back to your
scholarly work. If you cooperate just a little... give us a
few bits of information... ██████████████████████
██████████████████████████████ We could
certainly arrange for you to see your daughter again...
and your wife... look after them... make sure they don't

get any undue attention from the Egyptian authorities. And your comrades... I'm sure we can do something for them. After all, Professor, you haven't done anything really serious yet—

P: —except kidnap a ranking intelligence officer and undertake to execute him live on the Internet. What kind of sentence does that bring, would you say, Michael? How many years in prison exactly would I need to serve? Would I ever get out at all... or would you then deport me back to Egypt to enjoy the attentions of the secret police there... to get a little bit of enhanced interrogation, as they say? Or maybe you will hand me to the Americans and I will disappear into one of their secret black sites... ████████████████████ never to be seen again.

M: OK... yes... there is that... But I could pull some strings... offer you a deal. You haven't actually done anything yet, Professor. In fact, you've treated me quite decently. And... if you were to cooperate... demonstrate your genuine remorse... maybe help us with a little backgrou—

Good try, M. We don't make deals like that these days, but I suppose it was worth a shot. We may need an official statement on our recruitment of former terrorists, in case some nosy journo asks us whether we are running agents in today's terrorist groups – like we did in Northern Ireland.
                                    Can I leave that with you? GH

P: —What was the name of your operation?

M: What?

P: This operation... the one to get me here... now?

M: Oh... Operation Moriarty.

P: Moriarty... ha! That is very nice... the evil professor in your Sherlock Holmes stories. But you give me too much credit, I think. Moriarty was very clever... and very bad! Ha! I suppose you are Sherlock in this story. No?[...]

       Do you know what our operation was called, Michael?

M: No, we never had that intel.

P: We called it Operation Red Sea.

M: Red Sea... Mmm... I don't really understand. [...] Is this because you're Egyptian?

P: No, not really... although now that you mention it, I suppose it relates in some way to my Coptic identity. Later, I am sure your religiously minded colleagues will understand the meaning...

M: Oh, [inaudible].

[6.9]

P: Michael, please, have more water. I can see you are
      very tired.

M: OK, yes, please.

P: Let me help you... yes, that's it. [...] drink...

[scraping sounds. Sounds of drinking].

M: Thank you. [...] Professor, did you really plan to go
      through with it? Would you have killed me, in cold
      blood... right here... now?

[2.3]

P: Oh, Michael... do not look so sad. It is not personal—

M: —Killing someone in cold blood is not personal?—

P: —I told you already... there is simply no way out
      for you and me. We have to see out this drama...
      this little piece of political theatre... right through
      to the end. The fact is... we are trapped in this world
      of our own making... this room of wills. You are not
      going to back down... at least not any time soon... and
      neither am I. So we have to keep going... until one of
      us bends. It is the only way. You and your government

will either bend me to your will, or me and my group...
the oppressed of the world... will bend you to ours.
That is the nature of war and it is the only possible
outcome. [...] And, no, it is not personal. We both know
that, I am sure. We are soldiers... warriors. We are
doing our duty.

I believe, in a strange way... we are already there...
in God's waiting room... that special place reserved
for people like you and me. All this... this is not really
an old factory storeroom. No, no, no... this is our own
private hell, the place where we are condemned to
go round and round and round in our special cycle of
violence and recrimination...

The truth is... I am ready to die, Michael. It does not
frighten me any more. Your soldiers... the Americans...
the Iraqi security forces... they tried to kill me so many
times already. I have faced death a hundred times.
Besides, there are worse things than dying.

M: Like what? What could be worse than death,
Professor?

P: Like living as a slave... as a dog who is kicked every
day... or living with the shame of daily humiliation...
dishonour... or maybe living with the burden of guilt is
worse than dying. What do you think, Michael?

[2.3]

P: Anyway, after what I have seen... [inaudible]... I have
        reconciled myself to death...

M: How does one reconcile themselves to their own death,
        exactly? I'd bloody like to know, I can tell you...

P: By just accepting that you are already dead... a
        dead man walking, as they say in America. In Iraq,
        I considered myself lucky every day I was not blown
        up by a bomb in my bed while I slept... or shot by a
        helicopter when I stepped out of the door. I considered
        myself blessed if at the end of the day I did not meet
        God...

        But now I am so tired... it is not the sleepless
        nights... the bad food... the relentless tension... the
        people trying to kill you... the constant fear... all
        the physical hardships. I can endure this... I have
        endured this, for years. No... it is the endless struggle
        that drains you... the magnitude of the fight... the
        way it takes over your entire life... every inch of it.
        And the way it slowly changes you. I have been fighting
        for so many years now, I do not know if I am anything
        else but the struggle... nothing but a killer. [...] This
        was not the person I wanted to be, Michael... when I
        was young...

I believe it is time to pass on the baton... to leave an example for others to follow. I want to end it before I completely lose every last shred of my humanity. This is my free choice, Michael—

M: —I can't agree, Professor, there's always—

P: —No, no, I am sorry, Michael. It has to end now. I hope your colleagues are coming through the door [inaudible]... so we can bring this performance to a suitable finale... [inaudible] *Esma'ena, ya Allah, ya mokhalesana, ya raga' aqtar al ardh kollaha. Wa anta ya rab taHfazna wa tonagena min haza al geel wa ela al abad. Ameen.*[47] [muttered]—

[loud banging]

M: PROFESSOR! YOUSSEF! WAIT! NO, STOP! GET OFF ME, YOU FUCKING [inaudible]... ██████████ HOLMES! HOLMES! ████████ —

Do we really need to include this?
  It's a bit prurient, don't you think?
  We could redact in the name of protecting M's family.
              What do you think? GH

---

[47] Trans. 'Hear us, O God, our Saviour, the hope of the regions of the whole earth. And You, O Lord, keep us and deliver us, from this generation and forever. Amen.' Note: Traditional Coptic prayer said in Arabic.

P: —Captain Michael ███████████, you have been
        found guilty of waging illegal war, oppression, state
        terrorism, imperialism, torture, and the murder of the
        Iraqi child Samir Hamoodi! You are hereby condemned
        to death! Who so sheddeth man's blood, by man shall
        his blood be—

[loud banging]

M: ██

[multiple unknown voices shouting, 2.3 seconds]

V1:   ARMED POLICE! ARMED POLICE!

P: —[inaudible] death will serve as a—

V2:   ARMED POLICE! DROP THE WEAPON!

V3:   STEP BACK NOW! SHOW YOUR HANDS!

P: —[inaudible] ready to meet—

V1:   ON THE FLOOR! ON THE FLOOR!

V2:   I REPEAT, ARMED POL...

[sound of explosion]

[end of audio file]

End of transcription.

I don't know if you've listened to the original recording – I've had to on several occasions. A transcript can't communicate the sheer terror in M's voice.

And then the explosion which killed all those good lads. I swear I could actually hear them dying. Anyway, I think if we give the transcript one more flush along the lines I've suggested, we can at least limit the potential fallout to HMG – stop some of the shit from actually sticking. I presume you've heard that the PM is going to announce a whole raft of new anti-terrorism measures, including extended pre-trial detention, expanded surveillance powers, a programme to stamp out extremism in the universities, shoot-to-kill powers for the police, etc?

It's about time, I say. Anyway, the main point is that we can always hope that this document will only cause a minor ripple in the media and then be forgotten by the weekend. I suggest we release it late on a Friday before a big Premier League match. But if it does cause a media storm, we must be prepared. GH

PS: Don't forget to deal with this document properly.
We can't take the risk of it ever surfacing now, can we?
And I hope we'll see you and the girls at our little soiree on Sunday.
Diane is dying to see you and Linda again.

further reading

In writing this fictional account of a terrorist, I drew heavily upon the large academic literature on the nature, origins, causes and responses to terrorism. For readers who want to follow up on some of the key issues raised in the novel I have listed a few useful works below.

For an informative general introduction to the topic of terrorism, please consult the following books.

- Barker, J. 2002. *The no-nonsense guide to terrorism*. London: Verso.
- Goodin, R. 2006. *What's wrong with terrorism?* Cambridge: Polity Press.
- Jackson, R., Jarvis, L., Gunning, J., and Breen Smyth, M. 2011. *Terrorism: a critical introduction*. Basingstoke: Palgrave Macmillan.
- Townshend, C. 2002. *Terrorism: a short introduction*. Oxford: Oxford University Press.
- Zulaika, J. and Douglass, W. 1996. *Terror and taboo: the follies, fables, and faces of terrorism*. London: Routledge.

The following books provide important information and analysis on key questions relating to the subject of state terrorism.

- Blakeley, R. 2009. *State terrorism and neoliberalism: the North in the South.* London: Routledge.
- Campbell, B. and Brenner, A., eds. 2000. *Death squads in global perspective: murder with deniability.* New York: St Martin's Press.
- Chomsky, N. and Herman, E. 1979. *The political economy of human rights, volume I: The Washington connection and Third World fascism.* Nottingham: Spokesman.
- Gareau, F. 2004. *State terrorism and the United States: from counterinsurgency to the war on terrorism.* London: Zed Books.
- George, A., ed. 1991. *Western state terrorism.* Cambridge: Polity Press.
- Grey, S. 2006. *Ghost plane: the inside story of the CIA's secret rendition programme.* London: Hurst/St Martin's Press.
- Grosscup, B. 2006. *Strategic terror: the politics and ethics of aerial bombardment.* London: Zed Books.
- Herman, E. 1982. *The real terror network: terrorism in fact and propaganda.* Cambridge: South End Press.
- Jackson, R., Poynting, S., and Murphy, E., eds. 2010. *Contemporary state terrorism: theory and cases.* Abingdon: Routledge.
- Johnson, C. 2004. *Blowback: the costs and consequences of the American empire,* 2nd edition. New York: Holt.
- Sluka, J., ed. 1999. *Death squad: the anthropology of state terror.* Philadelphia: University of Pennsylvania Press.
- Stohl, M. and Lopez, G., eds. 1984. *The state as terrorist: the dynamics of governmental violence and repression.* Westport: Greenwood Press.
- Stohl, M. and Lopez, G., eds. 1986. *Government violence and repression: an agenda for research.* Westport: Greenwood Press.

- Walter, E. 1969: *Terror and resistance*. New York: Oxford University Press.
- Wright, T. 2006. *State terrorism in Latin America: Chile, Argentina, and international human rights*. Lanham: Rowman & Littlefield.

The following books discuss the extensive spread of torture as a core tactic in the 'war on terror' and some of the main ethical and practical arguments against it.

- Brecher, R. 2007. *Torture and the ticking bomb*. London: Wiley-Blackwell.
- Danner, M. 2004. *Torture and truth: America, Abu Ghraib, and the war on terror*. New York: New York Review of Books.
- Ginbar, Y. 2008. *Why not torture terrorists?* Oxford: Oxford University Press.
- Greenberg, K., ed. 2006. *The torture debate in America*. Cambridge: Cambridge University Press.
- Levinson, S., ed. 2006. *Torture: a collection*. Oxford: Oxford University Press.
- Rejali, D. 2007. *Torture and democracy*. Princeton: Princeton University Press.

The following books, which include academic studies, journalistic accounts and autobiographies by militants, are all very useful for gaining a deeper understanding of 'terrorist' motivations.

- Atran, S. 2010. *Talking to the enemy: faith, brotherhood, and the (un)making of terrorists*. New York: HarperCollins.

- Baumann, B. 1977. *How it all began: the personal account of a West German urban guerrilla.* Vancouver: Pulp Press.
- Burke, B. 2003. *Al-Qaeda: the true story of radical Islam.* London: Penguin.
- Della Porta, D. 1995. *Social movements, political violence, and the state: a comparative analysis of Italy and Germany.* Cambridge: Cambridge University Press.
- Devji, F. 2005. *Landscapes of the jihad: militancy, morality, modernity.* Ithaca: Cornell University Press.
- Gambetta, D., ed. 2005. *Making sense of suicide missions.* Oxford: Oxford University Press.
- Gerges, F. 2001. *The far enemy: why jihad went global.* Cambridge: Cambridge University Press.
- Gunning, J. 2007. *Hamas in politics: democracy, religion, violence.* London: Hurst.
- Hafez, M. 2003. *Why Muslims rebel? Repression and resistance in the Islamic world.* Boulder: Lynne Rienner.
- Hafez, M. 2006. *Manufacturing human bombs: the making of Palestinian suicide bombers.* Washington, DC: United States Institute of Peace Press.
- Hellmich, H. 2011. *Al-Qaeda: from global network to local franchise.* London: Zed Books.
- Horgan, J. 2005. *The psychology of terrorism.* London: Frank Cass.
- Kepel, G. and Milelli, J., eds. 2008. *Al Qaeda in its own words.* Cambridge: The Belknap Press of Harvard University.
- Khaled, L. 1973. *My people shall live: the autobiography of a revolutionary.* London: Hodder and Stoughton.
- Krueger, A. 2007. *What makes a terrorist: economics and the roots of terrorism.* Princeton: Princeton University Press.
- Lawrence, B., ed. 2005. *Messages to the world: the statements of Osama Bin Laden,* trans. J. Howarth. London: Verso.

- Mahmood, C. 1996. *Fighting for faith and nation: dialogues with Sikh militants.* Philadelphia: University of Pennsylvania Press.
- Ness, C., ed. 2008. *Female terrorism and militancy: agency, utility and organisation.* London: Routledge.
- Pape, R. 2005. *Dying to win: the strategic logic of suicide terrorism.* New York: Random House.
- Rajan, V. 2011. *Female suicide bombers: narratives of violence.* Abingdon: Routledge.
- Sjoberg, L. and Gentry, C. 2007. *Mothers, monsters, whores: women's violence in global politics.* London: Zed Books.
- Taylor, P. 2011. *Talking to terrorists: a personal journey from the IRA to al Qaeda.* London: HarperPress.
- Zulaika, J. 1988. *Basque violence: metaphor and sacrament.* Reno: University of Nevada Press.

The following books provide excellent analyses of some of the key issues relating to responding to terrorism in effective and ethical ways.

- Crelinsten, R. 2009. *Counterterrorism.* Cambridge: Polity Press.
- English, R. 2009. *Terrorism: how to respond.* Oxford: Oxford University Press.

acknowledgements

Writing fiction is a very different challenge to academic writing, and one for which I still feel ill-equipped. There is simply no way that I could have written this novel without so many generous friends and colleagues who provided large doses of helpful advice, constructive criticism and real encouragement during my journey. I cannot mention every single person who helped me along the way, and I apologise for any obvious omissions. However, I have to start by thanking my delightful colleagues and students at the National Centre for Peace and Conflict Studies, the University of Otago, New Zealand. They have been nothing but encouraging, and I feel they are my greatest supporters in this new venture.

Richard Maggraf Turley, Professor of Engagement with the Public Imagination at Aberystwyth University, encouraged me at the earliest stage of the project, providing expert advice and wise counsel on structure and approach, and encouraging me to persist. I never would have made it off the starting blocks without his professional guidance and honest reassurance. Charlotte Heath-Kelly, Martin Taylor and Maari McCluskey also read early drafts and offered formative and incredibly helpful observations and suggestions for improving the manuscript.

Elizabeth Dauphinee inspired me by sharing her own wonderful book, *The Politics of Exile* (Routledge, 2013), and then she encouraged me to keep going during a period of genuine existential despair. I would have given up but for her incredibly supportive and graceful words. For this, I am eternally grateful, as the novel probably would not exist without her.

Rula Abu-Safieh Talahma, my wonderful doctoral student and colleague at the Centre, read the manuscript carefully; her advice about the Professor's Arabic outbursts and his Egyptian background and culture were invaluable, and made the Professor really come alive in a more fully human way. I will always be grateful for this precious gift. Of course, all remaining mistakes and errors in the text are my own.

Ken Barlow at Zed Books also read drafts and offered expert and inspired counsel which improved the text immeasurably. More importantly, he believed in the novel, and then worked hard to get it published, taking a real chance in the process. It is my great fortune to have worked with him and his expert team at Zed.

My generous and talented brother, Steve Wells, provided the amazing photograph on the cover of this book. To see more examples of his fantastic photography, I recommend a visit to his website (www.stevewells-photo.com). I am extremely grateful for the donation of this image and very proud to have it on my book.

Finally, I could not have done any of this without the support, encouragement, plot and character suggestions and expert editing of Michelle Jackson, my long-suffering wife and soulmate. I would not even have attempted to write this, or kept going, without her constancy, love, encouragement and insightful suggestions. This book belongs to her.

Richard Jackson
October 2013